SACCHI GREEN

To Desiree,
I hope you enjoy
the ride!
Sacchi Green

WILD

RIDES

AND OTHER
LESBIAN EROTIC
ADVENTURES

Table of Contents

Introduction

I love editing anthologies. In the last fourteen years, I've published sixteen of them filled with stories by scores of fine writers who've trusted me with their work, and who have my deepest gratitude. But my first and enduring love has always been writing short stories of my own, beginning in the science fiction and fantasy genres, and becoming gradually seduced by the erotic side of the force. A chance to assemble a collection of my own work has a very special appeal. Most of the stories here have been previously published, some long enough ago that many readers have never come across them, some appearing in excellent books that never found as much readership as they deserve, and a few with characters that I wanted to revisit, even though numerous readers may already have met them.

My first collection, seven years ago, was *A Ride to Remember & Other Erotic Tales* from Lethe Press. Even then, I had plenty of other stories that couldn't fit in that one, and I've written many since, so the urge to do another collection has been getting hard to resist. I was amazed and grateful when Dirt Road Books agreed to publish this new one, *Wild Rides: And Other Lesbian Erotic Adventures*. Each story, with or without a literal ride involved, has its own kind of impact, and even though each has a degree of eroticism, the story as a whole is what counts most.

In anthologies, I try to choose a wide variety of themes, characters, settings, etc. For this collection, I didn't have to try. My muse just works that way. From the Old West to Vermont to Paris; from pirates in the Pacific in WWII to WACs in Vietnam to veterans of the war in the Mideast; from a vampire to a fashion model to kickass women in prison. If not all readers find every story appealing, I hope they'll all find something to enjoy, and something to think about as well.

I've certainly been having a good time. I hope it's good for you, too.

Sacchi Green
Amherst, MA

Bull Rider

Amsterdam.

Am-ster-god-fucking-*damn*!

Sin City of the '70s, still sizzling in the '80s. Cheap pot you could smoke in the coffeehouses, but that's not what lit my fire. Sex shows and leather toy shops? Coming a whole lot closer—but what really ignited a slow burn low in my Levi's were stories of the working girls displaying their wares behind lace-curtained windows. Something about the dissonance between elegance and raunch struck a chord. "Fine old buildings," ice-maiden Anneke had told some of the Australian riders, with her slight, Mona Lisa smile and a sidelong glance at me. "Many visitors tour the Red Light district just to view the...architecture."

I should have tried harder to figure Anneke out. A damned fine rider, in total control of herself and her mount, she was all blond and pink and white with cool, butter-wouldn't-melt-in-her-mouth self-possession. But a certain preppy princess with a long chestnut ponytail and a cute round ass—and delusions of being a world-class equestri-enne—had been using up too much of my energy at the time.

That was all over now. With a vengeance. A fair share

of it mine, true; but I still needed to drown my sorrows in whatever fleshpots I could find. I was not going to leave Europe without at least a taste of decadence.

You don't get to taste much, though, without a few guilders clinking in the pockets of your jeans. Which I didn't have. Damn near didn't even have the jeans. First French-tourist jerk-off to point at my ass and say, "'Ow much?" came close to losing his business hand. "Chienne! Pour les Levi's!" he hissed, rubbing his numbed wrist.

"More than you've got!" I stepped away, and he scurried in front of me with a fistful of bills. "No way," I said, lengthening my stride until he dropped back. Before I made it across Centraal Station plaza I'd had two more offers, Spanish and Japanese, and damn sure would have taken one if I'd had any alternate covering for my BVDs. But, after that fiasco at the Equestrian Tournament, I'd left behind everything except my hat, buckskin pants, and fringed jacket. And I'd pawned the leathers to raise plane fare home. Too damn cheaply, if even torn jeans reeking of horses and stable muck were in this much demand.

Maybe the stable muck was the selling point. Authenticity. I could've made a fortune if I'd known enough to dirty more jeans! The question now was, could I parlay all that authenticity into getting laid? I had 24 hours before my flight to find out. And a conniving little preppy to purge from my system.

Oh, hell, there it went again, like a movie in my head. My jaw and fists clenched—and my clit, too—as I sat on a bench at the edge of the square and spread a map across my knees. I lowered my head as though the names of streets, canals, and landmarks were all I saw.

She'd planned it from the start. All those weeks spent coaching her to signal the horse with her knees—and to wrap her thighs, naked and moist, around my neck; to lift her tight little butt in rhythm with the horse's gait—and to tilt her hips to the thrust of my demanding hand, and all along she'd known that moment would come.

Her moment was all the better since she'd been about to come herself. I saw it in her eyes as they went from deep and velvety to glittering and triumphant. She focused on something over my shoulder. My fingers slowed, and she switched all her attention back to me. "Eat me, Toby! Eat me!" she commanded, pushing my head toward her pussy. The musk of sex and the rich aromas of hay and horses blended into a powerful aphrodisiac. I delayed a bit, in-clined to make her beg. Then she flicked her little pink tongue over her lips like a kitten licking drops of cream, and I forgot everything but getting my own mouth into her cream, and my own tongue deeply into where it would do the most good.

She'd never wriggled with more abandon, never let her gasps and moans and ultimate shrieks rip so freely. No faking it, either. Her internal spasms surged right through her pussy into my mouth and hands and rocked me to my toes, but it was no tribute to my skill. When I came up for air I saw her eyes fixed again on someone behind me, and a look on her face like the proverbial cat who had deep-throated the canary.

Some instinct made me roll away just before his fist could connect. It's a wrench to shift from surging lust to fight-or-flight, but I made it fast enough to have ten feet and the business end of a hayfork between us before he could swing again. I recognized him from the picture she'd shown me. Charles, the fiancé. I almost felt sorry for him.

"You Goddamn fucking dyke!" he sputtered at me, as much pain as rage in his voice.

"Oh, Chub, do you always have to state the obvious?" Miss Pony-tail languorously brushed hay out of her chest-nut hair. "Afraid you can't do as well as a stable hand?"

Stable hand. I swung the hayfork toward her, then back toward Chub's more physical threat.

I'd worked my way through the same elite Eastern women's college she was lounging through. Stable hand, stable manager, eventually assistant riding coach. What she called me didn't matter as much as the contempt in her tone.

"So, Chub," I said. "Let me know if you need any more pointers." I hurled the fork just barely over his head into the bales of hay behind him, and got out of there fast before he could pick himself up off the floor.

Any sympathy evaporated late that night when he caught me alone in the barn and came at me with rage in his eyes and a serious bulge in his pants. Poor dumb bastard. I left him hurting so bad he wasn't going to have the means to please Miss Preppy any time soon.

If I'd left it at that, I might still have been able to fly back to the States on the chartered plane with the rest of the equestrian team. If I hadn't charged into the Bitch Princess's room, shoved her face into the pillow, immobilized her with my knee between her shoulder blades, and taken my knife to that long chestnut hair until no fancy hairdresser was going to be able to conceal all the ragged gaps without cropping it even shorter than mine, the police and the International Equestrian Organization officials wouldn't have been called into it. But I did, and they were, and I barely got away ahead of arrest with my passport and leather duds and the clothes I'd been wearing to load the horses into the vans for the transport plane.

So here I was in Amsterdam. I'd fed the chestnut hair strand by strand to the wind from the back of some Hungarian biker dude's motorcycle when he'd picked me up hitching on the outskirts of The Hague. The breeze here in the city was pretty light, smelling of canals and the ocean, but I folded my map and stood and ran my fingers through my hair and tried to imagine the hot scent of her expensive perfume and greedy pussy being blown away over the North Sea.

Then I headed for the Walletjes Red Light District in search of replacement memories.

Okay, decadence is a subjective concept. Packaged, Health-Department-Inspected sex doesn't do that much for me, and the cruising scene seemed to be, no surprise, mainly the boy-meets-boy variety. There had to at least be a women's bookstore somewhere. I can handle that scene, as long as I can steer the conversation to the better bits of Colette, just as I can coach show riding and could compete myself if I could afford a show-class horse, even though at heart I'm Western all the way. But literary foreplay, especially with language barriers, wasn't what I had in mind.

The ladies of the night weren't disappointing, exactly. The tall, elegant windows glowed with discreetly red-tinted light, and the flesh casually displayed was enticing enough. One blonde, dressed only in a long white men's shirt, saw my interest and treated me to a knowing smile over her shoulder as she straddled a chair and did a slow grind on its plumply upholstered seat. Then a paying customer caught the vibes and knocked on her door. After a close look, he invited me to come in, too. I declined. The window shade came down. I moved on.

The neighborhood provided plenty of rosy-fleshed occasions for fantasy, but none of the others quite did it for me. I began to have a sneaking suspicion that one particular pink-and-white-and-blond vision had been making my subconscious simmer. I sure as hell wasn't going to find her here, but I might know where I could. For all the good it would do me.

Anneke had always been civil, but reserved. Once, when I'd helped her with an emergency repair in the tack room, she'd said, "Toby, you should be riding that fine horse, not her," with a nod of her head toward Miss Preppy.

"Could never afford it." I wrestled with multiple interpretations. Riding the horse instead of riding the girl?

"No, nor could I." Her trace of accent was tantalizing. "The brewing firm that employs me keeps a show stable for...what is it in English? Public relations?"

"That's it," I said. "You work for them? I thought you must be family."

"Oh, no, I work summers in their Amsterdam clubs, as bookkeeper and assistant manager. The newest is a country-western bar on Warmoesstraat. All the rage, like that movie *Urban Cowboy*. They would go crazy for you there, Toby."

Then she was gone, and like an idiot, I didn't follow up. Now it hit me hard just who I wanted to go crazy for me, just what smooth, white skin I wanted to raise a flush on, what cool, half-smiling lips I wanted to suck and bite until they were red and swollen and begging for more. And whose butter I wanted to melt in my mouth.

How hard could it be to find a country-and-western bar in Amsterdam? I even remembered the name of the street. Had she meant me to? Anneke had always been so collected, so focused on her riding. Maybe I'd been afraid to try anything, afraid it might matter too much.

The neon outline of a rodeo bull rider told me I'd found the right place. I hesitated in the doorway, well aware that I didn't have the means to buy a lady a beer, and even if I did, this might be the kind of place where a move like that could get me thrown out. Then again, the way the people inside were rigged out in wannabe Western gear, where could I get more mileage out of my battered hat and authentically work-worn (and pungent) denim vest and jeans?

It was early, but crowds were building. Behind the bar a large woman with a generous display of pillowy breasts scanned the room as she wiped the countertop. When her gaze crossed mine, it moved on, stopped for a beat, then swung back.

Without looking away, she pulled a phone from under the counter and spoke briefly into it. *Oh shit*, I thought, *are the police here looking for me?* My "victims" couldn't have wanted that much publicity. Then a grin lit her round-cheeked face as she replaced the phone and beckoned to me. I might've resisted the good-humored gleam in her eyes, but the foaming stein of beer she offered was something else again. I hadn't had anything to eat in almost twenty-four hours, and nothing to drink but water from public fountains.

"On the house, honey." Her nametag said "Margaretha," but her accent said New York. "You look like you might liven this place up. Ever ride one of those?"

I followed the jerk of her head. Through a wide archway I saw, rising above the sawdust on the floor like some futuristic mushroom, a mechanical bull just like the one Travolta and Winger rode in *Urban Cowboy*.

I wiped beer foam from my mouth. "You mean, does my ass live up to the advertising of my Levi's? Lady, you have no idea."

"Don't bet on it, darlin'." Her assessing look assured me

that one way or another, a good time could definitely be had. Much as I appreciate older women—hell, one saved me from fratricide—my hopes for something else grew. If it wasn't the police she'd called, who on this continent but Anneke would have described me to her?

"Yeah," I said, "I've ridden those, and the snorting, stomping, shitting versions, too. For another beer and some of those hefty pretzels, I'd be glad to demonstrate."

"Wait a while." She refilled my stein and slid me a bowl of pretzels and cheese-flavored breadsticks, and I did my best not to stuff myself. Some things are better on a less-than-full stomach. Bull riding is only one of them.

"So, where are you from, Toby?" she asked, chatting me up while keeping a close eye on the door.

"Montana." I definitely hadn't told her my name.

"They let women ride bulls in rodeos there?"

"Not yet. Not officially. Except at small local shindigs where anything goes." I paid close attention to my beer and pretzels, not wanting to talk much about it. But there was no way I could keep from remembering the surge of wild triumph when I had outridden them all, even my brother Ted. The way my blood had pounded—the pressure building until I had to explode or die—and the revelation that, to achieve explosion, I needed to wrap myself around my old friend Cindy's full, smooth curves.

Back when we'd been twelve, Cindy hadn't minded a little mutual exploration. She'd just got back from being away for a few years, though, and this time, as I tried to pull her close, she twisted loose and ran around the grandstand to throw herself on Ted. Another revelation, that life was a bitch, seared me. No matter how much I could work like a man, even beat the men at their own games, their rewards were officially off-limits to me.

I was young and naive, and the shock filled me with rage. I leapt for my brother, and only the intervention of Miss Violet Montez, sultry lead singer for the intermission entertainment act, kept me from killing him.

"Hey, *tigrina*, come with me." She pressed herself against me as Ted struggled to get up. "I have what you need. And what you don't even know you need." And she surely did, or close enough.

When I rode back to the ranch at daybreak, too drained to sort out the remnants of pleasure and pain and smoldering resentment, Daddy was waiting in the barn. He couldn't quite meet my eyes. "Looks like maybe you'd better go East to school the way your Mama always wanted."

"Looks like," I agreed. And that was that. Someday I'll find the words to tell him that it wasn't his fault. I'd never have survived being raised any other way. And how could he, after letting me know all my life I could do anything a man could do, tell me that the one thing I couldn't have was a woman of my own?

Besides, he'd have been wrong. Going to a women's college didn't make a lady of me, but I sure learned a lot about women.

Not that there wasn't always more to learn.

Anneke came through the door and stood for a minute, cool as ever, with just a hint of defiance.

"I'll be damned!" Margaretha muttered from behind the bar. "I knew you'd made an impression, but jeez!" From the dropped jaws and arrested strides of several waiters I got the feeling that they weren't used to seeing Anneke in tight, scant denim cutoffs and a gingham blouse molded to all the delectable curves below those peeking out over her plunging neckline.

Body by Daisy Mae, face by Princess Grace. A divine dissonance, but what the hell was I supposed to do with it in a public place and a culture I didn't wholly understand?

I sure had to do something, though, with the surge of energy pounding through my body. "Maybe it's time for a ride," I growled, and jerked my head toward the room with the bull.

"Good idea." Margaretha shoved some coins at me across the bar. "Go for it." As I turned away, she grabbed my shoulder and swung me back. "Take it a little easy. She may not admit it, but she's new to this." I didn't think she meant the bull.

I set the controls on "extreme" and vaulted aboard the broad wooden back, my hat held high in the traditional free-arm gesture. It was a damn good thing the bull was mechanical; my body could handle all the twists and lurches without involving my brain. Matching wits with a live, wily, determined bull would've taken concentration I couldn't spare, with Anneke on my mind.

I was vaguely aware that a crowd had gathered. The music was "The Devil Went Down to Georgia," and Anneke was leaning against a nearby post watching with her Mona Lisa smile. Less vaguely, I realized I was going to be sore tomorrow—though nowhere near as sore as I'd like to be, unless some vital moves were made. When my wooden mount slowed to a stop and the room held still, I tossed my hat toward Anneke, who caught it deftly and allowed her smile to widen. Then I shifted my ass backward to make room and held out a hand to her. With no hesitation she let me pull her up to straddle the bull.

Someone, maybe Margaretha, put more money in the machine and set it on "easy." The music changed to "Looking for Love in All the Wrong Places," and I was in the kind of trouble worth dreaming about.

Riding without stirrups can be an erotic experience all by itself. Riding with Anneke's ass pressed into me, kneading my crotch with every heave of the bull, was sublime torture. Her slim back against my breasts made them demand a whole lot more of my attention than they usually get, while her own luscious breasts... I nuzzled my face against her neck and gazed over her shoulder at the rounded flesh gently bouncing and threatening to surge out of the low neckline. From my vantage point, glimpses of tender pink nipple came and went. Much as I wanted more, I didn't necessarily want to share.

"Your décolletage is slipping," I whispered into her ear. Instead of adjusting it, she turned her head so her smooth cheek curved against my lips.

"Help me, Toby," she murmured. "Hold me." And I was lost.

I cupped her breasts, gently at first, as the motion of the bull made them rise and fall and thrust against their thin gingham covering. Then I felt her back arch slightly, and her flesh press more demandingly into my hands. There was no way I could help moving my fingers across her firming nipples. I felt her soft gasp all the way down to my toes.

Her ass began to move against me, independent of the bull's motion. My clit felt like it was trying to scorch a passage through my jeans. My grip on her breasts tightened, and her nipples hardened and pulsed against my fingers as she leaned her head against my shoulder. "Toby," she breathed, "You are making me so sore!"

"Want me to stop?" I teased her tender earlobe with my teeth.

"No...don't stop...make me sorer still, please, Toby..."

How could I refuse? I unbuttoned her blouse at the waist and slid my hands across her silky belly before filling them with the even silkier flesh of her breasts. Then I drove her to as much sweet, sore engorgement as hands alone could provide. My hungry mouth made do with the soft hollows and curves of her neck and shoulders, feeling the nearly soundless moans she couldn't suppress. Her pale hair was coming loose from its intricate chignon, so I pulled out the fastenings with my teeth and let the golden curtain fall across the marks my mouth left on her skin. Her hair gave off a faint, clean scent of herbs and roses.

I hadn't forgotten our audience, but I was beyond caring. During my first wild ride there'd been whoops and cheering, but when Anneke joined me the sounds had dwindled to a low hum, an almost communal moan. Somebody put more coins in the machine, and "Looking for Love In All the Wrong Places" played on.

My problem was the accelerating need to get right down to it in ways even permissive Amsterdam couldn't handle. Or, if it could, I couldn't. "We have to get out of here," I growled against Anneke's cheek. She gave a slight nod.

"Soon," she said, with a shuddering sigh. "Help me turn." I admired her flair for showmanship as she swung one leg over the pommel, poised briefly in sidesaddle position, twisted so that her hands could brace against my shoulders, and pushed herself up and over until she was facing me astride.

Okay. A little more for the paying customers. Just a little. My hat, now upside down on the floor, had become a target for a fair number of coins and bills.

I urged Anneke's legs up over my thighs and got a firm grip on her waist. She leaned her head back as I savagely pressed my mouth into the hollow of her throat and let anger flicker through desire. New to this, was she? New to what? Performing with a woman? What had she done here with men?

My mouth moved down and Anneke leaned farther back, both of us as balanced as if our moves had been choreographed and rehearsed a hundred times. I tore at her shirt with my teeth until the buttons let go and I could get at her arched belly. A collective sigh rose from the audience as the fabric slid aside to leave her round breasts and jutting, rose-pink nipples naked. I knew what they wanted, but there was only just so much I could share.

She lay so far back now that her legs were around my hips and only my grip kept her upper body from sliding off the gently heaving bull. I probed my tongue into the ivory rosebud whorl of her navel as her thighs tightened and jerked.

My clit jerked, too. I ran my mouth down to the waistband of her shorts and then over the zipper, biting down gently just where the seam pressed against her clit. The fabric was wet and getting wetter. Our musk rose like a tangible cloud, mixed with the scent of roses and the earthy reek of the stables.

I bit down harder, tugged at the thick seam, pressed it into her, and knew by the spasmodic thrusts of her hips I could make her come right now, right here. And knew I wasn't going to.

I may have a streak of exhibitionism wide as the Montana sky, but some desires are too deep, too intense, too close to the limits of self-control for any but private performance. I pulled Anneke upright and kissed her long and hard, letting her feel the sharpness of my teeth. "There's an old show-biz saying," I said against her mouth, my voice harsher than intended. "Always leave 'em wanting more."

I swung us both to the floor and stood, still holding her in my arms, until the ground stopped heaving under my feet. Her legs tightened around my waist, and so did her arms around my neck, reminding me, for all the enticing tenderness of her flesh, that she was a world-class athlete. The dazed look in her blue eyes retreated slightly. "But, Toby, what if *I* want more?"

"You'd damned well better want more. You're going to get it. But not here." I started toward the door, not knowing where I was going. Hands reached out as we passed, some just stroking us, some stuffing money into my jeans.

Margaretha called out. Anneke turned, laughed, and caught the big old-fashioned key spinning toward her through the air. She shouted something in Dutch, and thrust the cold iron down inside the waistband of my BVDs. It slid, of course, much lower, producing new and interesting sensations as we ran hand-in-hand through the Amsterdam night.

The little houseboat rose and fell gently on the moonlit canal. Anneke went down the steps to the deck, turned, caught me by the hips, and burrowed her face into the crotch of my jeans. My legs nearly failed me.

"Mmm," she said, inhaling deeply. "I never thought to breathe anything as sweet as the smell of a horse. But mixed with the scent of a woman..." All her cool reserve had melted. She looked up at me with eyes darkened by night and arousal, and just a trace of laughter on lips still swollen from my kiss. "I never thought to touch a woman, either, until I had such dreams of you, I thought I must go mad."

I came down the last few steps and pressed her against the low door to the living quarters, trying desperately to feel in control of a dangerously reeling world. When I kissed her as gently as I could, her tongue came tentatively to meet mine and my clit lurched as though it, too, had been touched.

"But, Toby," she whispered, turning her mouth away just enough to speak, "I must get the key. I must...is it all right?" She touched my crotch lightly, then drew her hand up along my zipper to my belt.

"Yes..." I managed to gasp. It wouldn't have been all right for anyone else. Even now, I couldn't let her slide her hand down into my pants before I had mine deeply in hers. It was too late for control—I knew I was going to lose it any second, going to come at the touch of her fingers on my throbbing, aching clit—but I'd be damned if I was going to come alone.

Experience counts for something. And Anneke wasn't wearing a belt. I had my whole hand curved around her pussy before she'd gotten farther than the waistband of my briefs. She gasped and paused, as I worked my fingers between her folds, not penetrating yet—the night was still young—just gently massaging the increasing wetness and circling her clit with my thumb tip. She arched her hips forward, but her hand slid down over my mound, and in desperation to distract her, and myself, I lowered my mouth to one breast and licked at her pink nipple until it was hard and straining. Then I sucked her, hard and harder, biting a little, and she pressed herself deeper into my mouth. Her gasping breaths turned into deep moans, but her hand still moved down and her fingers curved in imitation of mine.

I pressed my fingers deeper, moved my thumb faster, harder, more demanding against her clit, and her fingers moved too, tentatively, but more than enough to push me to the edge. The iron key, shoved back now between my ass cheeks, only intensified the sensations.

I had to cheat. I gripped her wrist with my free hand and raised my head. "Wait," I said against her lips. "Just feel, feel it all." Then I covered her mouth with mine and sucked and bit and probed and worked my whole hand back and forth in her slippery depths, spreading her juices up over her straining clit, stroking faster and faster until she spasmed against me and sobbed into my hungry mouth. Finally, I let her pull away enough to breathe.

"Toby," she gasped, "please, let me, I have to...let me touch you." She struggled to move her hand against my grip.

I had to let her. And had to bury my face in her soft neck in a vain attempt to muffle the raw cries tearing through me on waves of explosive release.

She withdrew her hand, and the dripping key, slowly and sensuously. "Oh, yes," she said with a sigh, "much, much better than the dreams. And there is more?"

"More," I assured her, still breathing hard. "All you can handle. This was just a taste."

She smiled wickedly and touched her tongue to the key. "A fine taste." Then she turned, used the key, and the door swung open.

In the snug interior, lit by a hanging lantern, I opened her to pleasures she hadn't yet dreamed of. I took it a little easy, since she was, after all, new to this. Then, as her demand grew, she drove me to extremes. And invented new ones. Being with someone whose strength matched mine, who, like me, had as great a hunger to touch as to be touched, was a new and disconcerting experience.

By morning, when Margaretha dropped off some coffee and hot rolls and my hat filled with cash, we were both sore and exhausted. And as high as if we'd just won the gold.

"Take all this." I dumped the money on the bed between Anneke's splayed legs. "If my half is enough, could you get my leathers out of hock and send them to me? I'll find the pawn ticket...in a minute...if I ever manage to move..."

"Maybe I shall find a way to deliver them in person." Anneke rolled over to straddle my thigh. "You won't mind, Toby, if I wear those snug leather trousers a bit, maybe ride in them? And think of you, and get them very, very wet?"

"We could send them back and forth," I said, "until they're seasoned enough to travel on their own. But in person would be a damn sight better." I found the energy to flip her over. Maybe the coffee was kicking in. I nuzzled my face into the pale-gold fur adorning her finely seasoned pussy. "Just how wet did you have in mind?"

Exhaustion forgotten, I was ready to ride again, caught up in the wild joy of the moment, without a thought for just how far and often those buckskin pants of mine might ride in the years to come.

Lipstick on Her Collar

The DC-7 burst from clouds over the South China Sea at an angle so steep, Viet Cong rockets had no chance at a target. My breath caught and my butt clenched. At the last possible instant the plane leveled off, touched down, and came to a jolting stop.

I'd seen the same thing too often to be seriously alarmed. But I wasn't on board. And I wasn't Miss Maureen O'Malley from the *Boston Globe*, getting her first taste of the adrenaline mill that was Vietnam in 1969. I wondered whether Miss Maureen's panties were still dry. And how long she'd last at this war correspondent game. If she couldn't handle the heat, the sooner she headed back to the Ladies' pages, the better.

She wasn't hard to spot on the tarmac. Miss Boston's dainty sandals, blue plaid skirt, and matching jacket were about what I'd expected. The fine legs beneath the short hem, however, exceeded expectations.

I wasn't the only one looking her over, but I was a lot more discreet about it than the guys. Any overt attraction to women could have landed me, if not in the brig, at least back Stateside with a dishonorable discharge.

She showed the strain of flying halfway around the world. Sweating in the sudden, brutal heat of Tan Son Nhut airfield, lipstick blurred and tendrils of dark hair curling damply on her cheeks, she seemed absurdly young. I'd have been all encouragement with a nurse or WAC just arriving in-country, but the orders to ride herd on a journalist were really chafing my chops.

"Miss O'Malley," I said firmly, seizing her attention, "I'm Sergeant Hodge, your driver. Let me get that bag." I bent to the heavy suitcase. Yes, very fine legs, and naked. No pantyhose. "C'mon in under cover while they unload the rest of your baggage."

She focused on me hazily. Probably hadn't slept for at least twenty hours. I felt just a smidge of sympathy.

"Oh...thanks...this is all there is."

Well, that was a point in her favor. "Okay, good, but I still have to pick up a few packages." I was about to offer to show her the rudimentary ladies' room when she blurted, "But...I was expecting a woman driver."

"And I was expecting Maureen O'Hara," I said, amused. Passing for a teenaged boy often comes in handy. "Southeast Asia needs more redheads." I shed my helmet and brushed back my russet forelock. My short hair didn't tip her off, but my grin did the trick. She surveyed the rest of me more closely.

"Oh! I'm sorry." Her face flushed from more than the heat. She gestured at the insignia on my shirt sleeve. "That means you're a WAC, doesn't it. I still have a lot to learn."

No kidding. I silently steered her into the terminal, aimed her toward the restroom, and left to retrieve the packages I'd promised to pick up. It wouldn't hurt to let her stew in a bit of embarrassment for a while.

Not for long, though. She emerged looking tidy and composed, makeup freshened. As she stepped up into my jeep, she caught me admiring the nice rear view, and her deliberate wriggle as she settled into the seat made me wonder with a touch of paranoia just what this reporter had come to 'Nam to cover. A juicy scandal about dyke WACs would put women in the military back decades, just when we were needed most.

Through the dust and traffic, I kept my attention on the road, weaving around troop transports and the occasional heavily laden water buffalo. I could feel her assessing gaze on me.

"Miss O'Malley," I said, when the traffic diminished, "my orders are to take you to WAC headquarters at Long Binh. The captain will sort out what happens next. Apparently, you have authorization to bunk in our compound, unless you'd rather check into a hotel in Saigon. Some of those places the French built are as ritzy as anything in Paris."

"I can't afford a hotel," she said frankly. "It was all I could do to get here. Three papers gave me accreditation, which just means they'll consider printing what I write. None of them are willing to pay my way until I prove myself. Which I will." Her face looked suddenly less cheerleader-pretty—and much more dangerous.

"I heard you wanted to write about the women serving over here," I said casually.

"Just for starters. I had to use that line to get anywhere. WACs, nurses, Red Cross workers, maybe some orphanage scenes."

"Look, Miss O'Malley," I said sharply, "You won't get far assuming the women here are just 'soft' news for the Sunday Supplement. Or the orphans, either."

She looked startled. "Sorry, I didn't... Well, thanks for reminding me to stay open-minded. I'll need all the help I can get to learn the ropes. But just call me Maureen, won't you? Should I call you Sergeant?"

"Not as long as you're a civilian," I said. "I'm Marjoe to just about everybody." I darted a quick glance at her. "Pleased to meet you, Maureen."

"Nice to meet you, too, Marjoe. And my apologies for not being Maureen O'Hara." Her teasing smile produced an all-too-charming dimple beside her mouth.

I looked her over. "Actually, you remind me more of Miss Connie Francis. That's just fine."

"Wasn't she here last year?"

"She was, and I have the autographed picture to prove it." A little casual conversation wouldn't hurt. "I wasn't a big fan before that. 'Who's Sorry Now' and 'Lipstick on Your Collar' aren't my style—I'm more of a "Born to Be Wild' and 'Light My Fire' kinda girl." I gave her a wide grin. Let her make what she wanted of that. "But Connie Francis sure got my respect. She went places Bob Hope wouldn't, hopping flights in Hueys and Chinooks to give the boys in the boonies a look at what they're fighting for." I wouldn't admit it to anyone, but I'd even sung along at Can Tho when Miss Francis led the crowd in "God Bless America."

Maureen sat up straighter. Her sweat-dampened blouse showed the distinct contours of her nipples. I managed not to stare.

"That's what I want to do. Get to see the real war, meet the guys and tell their true stories. I'm going to get out to the front, after a few weeks behind the lines learning my way around."

We were within the outskirts of the town by then. I jerked the wheel abruptly, pulling off into an alley. Miss See-All-Tell-All would have seen plenty of mortar craters already if she'd been paying any attention.

"You want to learn something?" Anger sharpened my voice. "Get out right here for a minute." *Don't let her get to you...keep your cool...* But I wasn't listening to myself. She was getting to me. In too many ways.

Maureen stared for few heartbeats, then stepped down onto the dusty ground. I kept my eyes strictly away from her enticing backside this time.

I grabbed a lug wrench from the rear of the jeep. Maureen looked me right in the eye as I approached, holding her ground, hands on her nicely curved hips.

"Behind the lines?" I asked. "Lady, there are no lines. See the chicken wire on the windows of that bus going by?" She nodded, but her gaze didn't leave my face. "That's to deflect grenades." I drew a groove in the dirt with the wrench halfway around her. "The only line in 'Nam is the one you pull around yourself to keep your shit together."

She seemed to grow taller. I suddenly knew what was meant by that old cliché "flashing eyes." How had I missed noticing how green hers were?

"Sergeant Hodge," she said icily, "if you ever call me 'lady' again in that tone of voice, I'll have those stripes off your sleeve, and the sleeve off as well!" She looked me up and down with disdain—until a hint of a smile made her dimple flicker. She dropped the briefly assumed British accent. "And quite possibly the whole shirt."

I closed my gaping mouth, then opened it to take a deep breath. "Wal now, Miss O'Hara," I drawled, regaining some control, "Yuh shore are purty when yer angry."

"Thank you, Mr. John Wayne," she said primly, and relaxed into a giggle. "Just never forget, I'm no lady, I'm a journalist."

"Thanks for the warning," I said. Some woman! It was going to be damned hard to think of her only as a reporter, but her mental tape recorder was probably spinning right now.

Back in the jeep, I kept up a running commentary on bombings and mortar attacks by VC infiltrators, usually targeting troop transports and the bars and restaurants favored by American servicemen. Maureen reached into her shoulder bag for a notebook and did, in fact, start jotting down notes.

"Was that during the Tet offensive last January?"

So, she had done some homework. Could be more to her than a pretty face, a knockout body, and a wicked sense of humor.

"It goes on all the time at some level, but, yeah, that was the worst of it. I was up north at Nha Trang back then. Never seen anything like it, and hope never to again."

"I hope you won't. Just the same... Don't get me wrong," Maureen said quickly, leaning toward me so that I couldn't help noticing her breasts pressing against her blouse, "but if a major offensive like that did come again, I wouldn't want to miss it."

"No chance it'll miss you." I didn't bother with trying to squelch her voyeuristic instincts. On some level, I understood them perfectly well. "It was bad here, bad everywhere. I was handling the nurse's motor pool, and every vehicle had to double as an ambulance, every driver as a corpsman, with or without medical training. Five straight days—never time to clean up the blood—they were handing out Benzedrine to keep us awake." I stared ahead for a minute or two, remembering things I'd rather forget. Maureen leaned close, so absorbed that she'd even stopped taking notes.

"Some of the things I saw there," I went on, "still keep me awake. Some of the things I had to do..." My knuckles clenched the steering wheel, white under their tan. "And that was nothing to what the nurses went through."

A current of empathy flowed from Maureen. *A tremor in my voice, a catch in my breath, and she'll reach out to touch me, comfort me, put that half-raised hand on my shoulder...my thigh...*

I turned abruptly with a half-smile. "But, yeah, if it had to happen, I wouldn't have missed it. And later, when we had our perimeters more or less under control, there were nights when we'd take a case of cold beer up on the roof of some old French villa and watch Puff the Magic Dragon blast away at VC island outposts in Cam Ranh Bay. Or we'd see our choppers hammering the hills with rockets and tracers. Better than any fireworks you ever saw, and we'd cheer for the good guys—until time to go try to put the broken ones back together. Or into body bags."

Maureen straightened and got her pen moving. "Um, Puff?" she asked, eyebrows raised.

"C-130 heavy cargo plane fitted out with heavy-duty artillery. Don't know who came up with the name, but it sure works up a storm of fire and smoke."

"Okay. Puff. Good one. I won't ask whether beer was all you had up there on the roof."

"If you can't manage a laugh once in a while, one way or another, you get so brittle, you crack," I said. "It's all about survival." Maureen nodded. I had the feeling again that she might reach out and touch me—and I knew for certain that my body's reaction would be far from anything resembling comfort. Disappointment battled with relief as I pulled into the WAC compound.

Our guard dog jumped up into the back as soon as I slowed. "Here's another fine dragon," I told Maureen, and ruffled his ears. "This is Spike."

"I see that this one's armed with heavy-duty teeth," she

said, extending a fearless palm to be sniffed. Spike, putty in female hands, leaned his big ugly head on her arm, nudged against her breast, and sighed.

I nearly sighed, too. It was no use pretending that she didn't set off a fizz under my fatigues. Good thing the ride was over, and Miss Maureen O'Malley/O'Hara would be somebody else's responsibility. My only hope of resisting temptation was to assign another driver from the motor pool to show her around if we were stuck with her for long.

The few girls off-duty clustered around the jeep, either to get a look at the newcomer or to collect the packages I'd picked up for them. Lila Tunney cradled her shipment from Tokyo with care. "I'd be happy to share some of this makeup with you, Marjoe," she said slyly. "One of these days the captain might start enforcing regulations and make even you wear lipstick."

"Not so long as she needs her wheels kept in running condition." This was no time for Lila's teasing. After brief introductions I herded Maureen toward the admin building, resisting the urge to put a more-than-friendly arm around her.

What was the deal with this sudden, dangerous attraction? Yeah, sure, the stresses of wartime and all that. But I'd managed so far to keep a purely sisterly attitude—well, mostly pure—toward the women I worked with. Was it because Maureen wasn't "family" that my subconscious was allowing lust to break on through?

"Captain Ramsey will be right with you." The unit's cute

little secretary surveyed Maureen with open curiosity. "Help yourselves to coffee."

"Thanks, Wilma." I was already at the hot plate in the corner. "What do you take, Maureen?"

"Black is fine." She accepted a cup. "What was all that about regulations?"

"Just a holdover from the fifties." If Wilma wanted to listen, she might as well get her money's worth. She always got a kick out of bringing out the worst in me. "Now and then the military gets a bee up its butt about women soldiers being models of femininity. In the States, some officers get tight-assed about it, but nobody enforces it in war zones."

"Sergeant Hodge!" The one voice that could make me jump sounded right behind me. I spun around so fast that hot coffee sloshed onto my shirt.

"I think it's time to make an exception in your case." Captain Ramsey's tone had taken on a don't-you-challenge-me edge. "I expect to see you wearing lipstick within the next week. Consider that an order."

Wilma snickered. The captain turned calmly to Maureen, who had just handed me a napkin. "Miss O'Malley, I hope Marjoe has been taking good care of you."

"Oh, yes," Maureen replied demurely, watching me dab at the wet splotch on my left breast. "Very helpful."

"I'm glad to hear it. Your Congressman has asked that we give you every possible aid and protection."

"I'd appreciate that," Maureen said sincerely. "Just while I get my bearings."

"This next week could be difficult," Captain Ramsey said. "The Tet holiday is coming around again. Our intelligence indicates stepped-up activity, though not on the scale of last year. While you're here, under our protection, I'm going to have to insist that you go nowhere beyond the base perimeters without Sergeant Hodge. She'll be your designated driver." She looked at me with an entire lecture condensed into one stern glance.

"But Captain, I'll be too busy... I thought I'd assign..."

"I'm delighted to hear that you've been thinking, Marjoe," she said drily, "but no one else has sharpshooter rating on both 45s and M16s. It's a matter of security."

"Women don't get sharpshooter ratings," I protested. "We're not even technically allowed to carry weapons."

Wilma had kept quiet about as long as she could manage. "Just the same, it's in your 201 file," she said. "From Basic at Fort Benning, but you'll never see a badge for it."

"So that's settled," the captain said with finality. "Wilma will handle any further details. Show our guest around, Marjoe, take her over to the mess hall, and then finish whatever motor pool maintenance is scheduled. Wilma can be my driver for the next week."

She held out her hand to Maureen. "It's been nice meeting you, Miss O'Malley. Don't hesitate to let me know of any problems. I suggest you have Marjoe drive you into Saigon tomorrow for some orientation."

"A sharpshooter?" Maureen asked with interest when the captain was gone. "How did you pick up that skill?"

Wilma was miming putting on lipstick, pursing her lips and working them together with gusto. I grabbed at Maureen's diversion. "Where I come from, in northern Wisconsin, the better you shoot, the better you eat. It's an old family tradition."

"So, what brought you all the way to Vietnam?"

I could sense that mental tape recorder flickering behind her green eyes. "Getting as far away from family tradition as possible," I said. "So, Wilma, where do I dump Miss O'Malley's gear?"

In her room, temporarily vacated by a lieutenant on leave, Maureen slumped onto the narrow cot. I retreated to the doorway.

"Jet lag hitting hard?" I asked. Her short skirt was hitched so high that I could tell what color panties she wore. Pale pink. "How about you get some rest, and I'll save a sandwich for you."

She yawned, and stretched. Both skirt and undies inched higher. For an instant, I could also tell, no surprise, that she was a real brunette. Then she sat up.

"No, they say the best way to reset your internal clock is to eat meals on the local schedule. Just let me change into something that hasn't been sweated in for twenty-four hours, okay?" In one sudden motion, she pulled her blouse off over her head. Her pale pink bra was very nicely filled indeed. She bent to rummage in her suitcase, breasts nearly spilling over, and I edged farther away.

"Marjoe?" Her voice was muffled by the knit shirt she

was pulling on. "How come I'm not bunking with you? For security?" Her eyes emerged, gleaming with mischief. Her skirt slid down to be replaced very, very slowly by a pair of sleek black slacks. Every wriggle was deliberate. She knew exactly what she was doing to me. What I hadn't figured out was just why she was doing it.

"I sleep with the jeeps. Alone, except for Spike." *And he wouldn't be any protection for you.* I gave thanks as never before for my lean-to hooch built against the side of the motor pool's Quonset hut. I'd be in desperate need of some alone time tonight—if I could wait until then. She was building enough tension to have me punching holes through plywood if I couldn't get relief soon.

The WAC division didn't have its own mess hall, so we ate at the 24th Evac hospital with the nurses and the ambulatory patients. I didn't try to prepare Maureen for what she'd see, but after one quick clutch at my arm, she handled herself like a real trooper. By the time I left, she was circulating among nurses and amputees and men trailing IV trolleys like the best of the Red Cross Donut Dollies (a term I use with the greatest respect).

I looked back once and saw her kneeling beside a wheelchair, listening intently to a kid who could barely speak through his bandages. Her hand rested on his arm. I wondered cynically, or maybe jealously, whether it was compassion or journalistic skill that drove her.

She was still at the hospital at six, pale and strained behind her bright lipstick, but managing to smile for the boys.

I tracked her down in a ward of patients who couldn't make it to the mess hall. After forcing her to come along for some dinner, I half-carried her back to the barracks. Jet lag and sudden immersion in the realities of war had pretty much knocked her out.

"Get some sleep before you forget how." I eased her onto the cot and tried to get away. She held tight, her arms around my hips.

"Stay with me, Marjoe. Please." Her face was pressed against my crotch. She had to know, by my aroma, by my pulse, how much I wanted to stay.

"I can't." I pulled away. My butt burned where her fingers had dug in. "Maureen, I have a job to do over here. I need to keep my hands clean." Hands that shook with the urge to reach out to her, stroke her dark hair, pull her face hard into the ache between my legs...

"Always?" she asked.

"Except for motor grease and mud. And blood," I added, before I could stop myself. So much for keeping it light.

"You've never touched a woman over here?"

"Who's asking? The reporter?" I asked nastily.

Those green eyes really were magnificent in anger. Relenting, I added, "I'm not absolutely sure. There was this head nurse—we both dived into the same bunker one night during a heavy bombing. She asked what I had in my canteen. When I told her it was water, she said, 'Good, mine's whiskey. We can mix and share.' Which we did. I can't remember clearly just how much mixing and sharing went on."

"Right," Maureen said sarcastically. "How much liquor does it take to get you in that state? And where can I buy it?"

"Forget it. The next time I touch a woman, I intend to remember it."

I stepped forward. She inhaled sharply, lips parting, breasts rising. I yanked the army blanket up to cover her. "Get some rest," I said. "You'll need it."

I shut the door behind me carefully. If those plywood walls hadn't been too flimsy to filter out even a whisper, Miss Bright-Eyes-and-Heaving-Bosom would've had more than jet lag and in-country shock to exhaust her.

Maureen seemed rested by morning, but I wasn't. Much more of this, and Spike would go looking for a quieter hoochmate. He sniffed my crotch with interest before I lit out for the showers extra early. I was reaching for my towel with dripping hands about the time Maureen stepped naked behind the canvas partition. I caught her checking out my ass. Fair enough. One brief glimpse had left her smooth curves printed indelibly on my memory.

The twenty miles to Saigon had their share of tension. I usually traveled with a Colt 45 tucked inconspicuously down beside the driver's seat, regulations be damned, and this time the captain had wangled an M16 rifle for me. I didn't ask how. No firepower would deflect a grenade or a mortar, but you did what you could and wore risk like an extra stripe on your uniform.

As we started out, Maureen said demurely, "My mother taught me never to distract the driver, so I'll try not to bother you."

"You'll distract me less once we get you outfitted to blend into the background," I told her. The tight black slacks and white tank top definitely stood out. The helmet I'd made her wear looked more jaunty than utilitarian. "Rumor says the North Vietnamese have offered $25,000 for an American woman, a 'round-eye.' I've never heard of anybody collecting, but there's no point offering one up gift-wrapped."

"Only $25,000?" She preened teasingly, hands running over chest and thighs.

"A journalist might bring in more." I reached out to give one breast a sharp pinch. No point now in letting her get away with much. "Especially one more generously upholstered than the typical Vietnamese girl. At least the NV value us more than the U.S. Army does, with the puny $10,000 life insurance policy we get."

I steered the subject into the universal griping-at-bureaucracy routine. Maureen was good company the rest of the way, asking intelligent questions, paying attention to the answers, and keeping teasing to a minimum.

In Saigon we drove down boulevards lined with elegant French Colonial architecture, crowded with trucks and old Renaults and the pedal-driven rickshaws called cyclos. I pointed out the Caravelle Hotel, where most war correspondents hung out.

"Writing 'front-line' dispatches at the bar behind a line of brandy-and-sodas," Maureen said dismissively. "Getting all their news from the Pentagon's 'five-o-clock follies.' No thanks."

I looked at her with new respect. Maybe she knew this reporter business better than I'd realized.

At the notorious Thieves' Market you could get anything that had ever passed through an American PX, and many items that never would. We got Maureen outfitted in tan and olive drab shirts and pants and the ubiquitous blue jeans.

"Wait a minute, we forgot something," Maureen said urgently over lunch at the California Bar and Grille on the liveliest strip of Dong Khoi Street. She waved toward the honey-skinned working girls replenishing their makeup, preparing for a later influx of horny GIs.

"You want one all to yourself," I asked, "or can we share?"

"Not my type," she shot back. "I'll stick with round-eyes. But shouldn't we pick out some lipstick for you? Captain's orders?" She made kissie-mouths at her compact's mirror while freshening her glossy lips. "How about my Burgundy Passion?"

I'd been working on forgetting that little incident. But the Captain wouldn't. "Lila offered to share. Just once will get me off the hook."

"Cocky, aren't you," she said, with a look that made me consider some blacker-than-black-market shopping, but we needed to beat the rush hour, Saigon's most dangerous time.

Not that danger couldn't strike any minute. Fifteen miles out, we hit a military roadblock. Smoke billowed from around a curve. I detoured onto a longer, narrower riverside track, making sure my guns were accessible.

Maureen kept quiet for a while, but finally blurted out, "Did you ever shoot anyone?"

"Maybe," I said shortly.

There was firing in the distance, either from the road ahead or the roughly parallel highway we'd left. The driver of a supply truck going the other way motioned us wildly to go back. I slowed, started to turn—and heard the unmistakable *whoosh* of a rocket launcher somewhere behind us. An explosion rocked the area where the supply truck, now out of sight, might have been.

"Hang on!" I veered off on a rutted cart track toward the river a hundred yards away. A fringe of trees would hide the jeep, I hoped, but just in case I made Maureen scramble out and lie with me farther along, behind a log where I could brace my M16. We waited, watching the road.

Maureen pressed against my side, her body shaking just slightly more than mine. "I don't know whether I've ever killed anybody," I said conversationally. "In Nha Trang they overwhelmed our perimeter, looking for medical supplies. It was dark, chaotic, but I think...well, I don't usually miss. And we beat them off."

I was wound tighter than Jim Morrison's guitar strings. Maureen stroked gently up my spine to the nape of my neck and massaged away some of the tightness, but tension of a different kind radiated from her touch, ripples of heat licking all the way down my body. Even my toes twitched inside my heavy boots. I couldn't keep my hips from shifting. Maureen slid her hand down my back to my butt.

"We do what we have to," she said, her breath warm on my ear. Her dark hair tickled my cheek. "You'd be out there leading a platoon if they'd let you." The pressure of her hand increased, her fingers digging in just slightly.

"Maybe," I said, steeling myself not to react visibly, however damp my khaki briefs were getting.

Maureen's fingers dug deeper, then moved between my butt cheeks. "Am I distracting the driver too much?"

"Hell, no! Good practice for capture and torture." Danger and lust pumped adrenaline through me, triggering a fight-or-fuck response. If I didn't fire a gun soon, something else was sure going to go off.

Maureen heard the approaching truck a fraction of a second before I did. I lifted my head, tightened my grip on the rifle—and she pulled me back down, cramming her helmet over my hair. "Don't wave your fucking red flag at them!"

"Thanks." I peered carefully over the log at an ancient flatbed farm truck. The grim-faced young Vietnamese riding on the back didn't look like they'd been laboring in the fields.

We didn't breathe. I could feel Maureen's heart pounding in time with my own. The truck passed out of sight, and still we lay immobile.

"Will there be more?" Maureen asked at last.

"Maybe. We'd better wait—"

My words were cut off by her mouth covering mine. I'd barely set the guns aside before we were in a rolling clinch, scrabbling to get through each other's clothes.

Maureen won. Her hands were inside my pants, one on my bare butt and the other working hard between my thighs, before I got through her shirt and clinging tank top. With my fingers finally inside her lacy bra, I hung on, pinching her swelling flesh. The feel of her nipples hardening to rigid engorgement intensified my clit's response to her demanding thrusts.

She worked me hard and fast, our mouths pressed furiously together with only a few moans and grunts escaping, until I had to get enough air for the noises she forced from me. With one wild glance to be sure the road was empty, I let go and shouted up into the quaking leaves of the trees.

By the time I could breathe, Maureen was naked with her shirt spread under her arching hips. I dove right in to her luscious tenderness, feeding her need with tongue and hands until her yells made the leaves quake, too. And then, after a short rest in each other's arms, we started all over again. Frequent checks of the road for traffic only added a spice of danger to our frenzy.

As sunset approached, I had to consider what to do next. We'd finally gotten dressed, and cleaned up at the edge of the muddy river, when we heard cars approaching slowly. Two jeeps. One driven by an MP, one by Wilma.

"Company," I murmured. Maureen barely managed to brace before a furry, joyful Spike rocketed into us.

"Easy, boy!" I grabbed his collar and went to meet the captain.

"You're both all right?" she asked sharply, then saw Maureen emerging from the trees with hair quickly combed and burgundy lipstick freshened. "It's a good thing we brought the pooch. He alerted us that you were in there."

"We took cover for a while, Captain." I looked her straight in the eye. "There were indications of enemy activity ahead and behind." Whatever she might suspect, I could defend my reasons for leaving the road.

"You were right," she said. "But the area is secured for now, so let's get moving."

By the time I retrieved my jeep, the MPs had gone and Wilma was chatting up Maureen. Her prattling ceased, and she began whistling a familiar tune. Everyone looked at my rumpled shirt. I'd scrubbed my face in river water, but...

"Marjoe has lipstick on her collar," Wilma said gleefully, in case anybody hadn't recognized the Connie Francis song. "That doesn't count, though. She's not off the hook yet, is she?"

Maureen stepped right up to the plate. "Of course it doesn't count. But this should." She put her arms around my neck and kissed me hard enough to weaken my knees. "Thank you, Sergeant," she said, pulling away, "for taking such good care of me."

The captain's face was impassive, except for a twitch at the corner of her mouth. She wiped a neatly folded handkerchief across my lips, gazed at the results thoughtfully, and said, simply, "That will do."

A week later, Maureen wangled a ride with a chopper pilot heading toward Pleiku in the highlands. Two months later she sent a clipping of her first published article. Others followed. I kept them deep in my duffle bag, along with several intimate items imbued with her scent, mementos of a few more rushed, intense encounters scraped out of the quagmire of war. I have them still, wrapped in a rumpled, burgundy-lipstick-stained shirt that will never be washed again.

Jessebel

"See there, Cap'n, ain't she somethin'? Jezebel, they calls 'er, but most likely she's just plain Mabel or Hildy underneath it all."

I looked through a blur of drifting cigar smoke and shifting bodies. Maybe three or four of those figures were recognizably female, for damned sure not counting my own well-concealed form, but there was no doubt as to which one had sparked the old stable hand's enthusiasm. I couldn't see much—her back was to the door, and a rancher's burly arms enveloped her in a most unchaste fashion as they danced, but even so, there seemed to be a glow about her that drew the eye. Chestnut curls tumbled across slender shoulders, and emerald silk clung to rounded, swaying hips that promised the uttermost in carnal delights without sacrificing the least degree of elegance.

"Sure is, Bill," I agreed, "but what's a fine piece like that doing in a place like this?"

"Plenty of business, that's what." Bill elbowed me in the ribs. I only just managed to pivot enough to keep my bound-up tender bits from taking the full impact. When I turned back the girl swung around so that for a moment, before her partner's bulk blocked the view, I saw her face, beautiful in spite of all its paint, not because of it.

The room swirled around me. The floor tilted. I clutched at the back of a chair, muttered an apology to the card player occupying it, and lurched back out through the swinging doors.

The last time I'd kissed that face it had been ashen, dirt-smeared, streaked with blood and my tears. The last time I'd held that dear body in my arms, life and warmth had seeped away.

The last time I'd seen her, she'd been dead.

Great gulps of cool autumn air revived me a bit. The dizziness subsided, and common sense got a foothold. I'd been mistaken, addled by smoke and old grief and going far too long without the pleasures of the flesh. Maybe the name, as well, far too close to the one I remembered. That painted, seductive, brazen whore looked nothing like Jessebel. Not my Jess. My Jess, who was gone forever. I knew that.

I was only too well acquainted with death. I knew it when I saw it, and all the savage ways war could rip the soul out of the body. War, and its aftermath. Jess and I had been together since Vicksburg, when I'd found her huddling in a farmer's root cellar, gray uniform in such tatters that it scarcely hid her private parts. She'd been running away not just from capture but from something else she could never bring herself to speak of. I'd scrounged her a blue uniform small enough to fit, and watched over her for the last two years of the War, only to lose her to a looter's bullet before we could start west to make a real life for ourselves.

"Cap'n?" Old Bill poked his head out. "You okay?"

"I'll be right fine in a minute or two. Town crowds take some getting used to when a fellow's been up in the mountains so long."

"I s'pose that's so," Bill said doubtfully, coming closer.

I fished out a coin from my pocket and sent it spinning. He forgot anything else in the catching of it. "You go on and order that drink," I said, "and if you've downed it before I get to the bar, I'll just be obliged to buy you another one to go with mine."

Bill knew well enough that I'd be good for three or four drinks anyway, but he hared right back inside to get an early start. The old fellow was my habitual bridge to human society on my twice yearly expeditions out of the mountains. In the spring I'd be bringing in the fruits of my traplines to the fur traders, and in the autumn I'd stock up on whatever winter needs my gun wouldn't supply.

Either way, my horse and mule would get put up at the livery stable where Bill worked, and Bill would fill me in on whatever versions of world and local news were being bandied about. It gave me a chance to get accustomed to another human voice without having to exercise my own too much all at once. He'd always taken me at face value, too, never questioning the shabby Union captain's uniform I'd ridden in with three years ago, and neither had anybody else.

The Union part was right enough, and I'd worn a uniform throughout the war, as had a fair number of other females I'd encountered or heard tell of, besides Jess, but the clothes I'd worn at the last had come from an officer who would never need them again. Leather and fur and two new flannel shirts a year suited me better now.

Bill's big news this time had been the new girl at the Hard Ride Saloon. The girl who... I got a firm grip on my wandering mind. She wasn't Jess. And she wasn't for me. The tawdry regulars at the Hard Ride were good enough old girls, but I'd never yet trusted one of them with my personal...eccentricities, and I wasn't about to start now with a flashy stranger who'd look more at home in New Orleans or San Francisco.

As I pushed through the saloon door I did, however, wish fleetingly that I'd bought my semiannual new shirt already, and gone to the trouble of visiting the local bath house out behind the barber shop.

At the bar, I ordered a whiskey, gestured for Bill's glass to be refilled, and only then turned, leaned back, and viewed the room as a whole. Or tried to, but somehow the scarlet woman in emerald green drew the eye, as if all the light shone particularly on her, or even from her. It wasn't just me, either. Seemed like every man in the house was watching and panting after her, and those card players whose chairs faced the wrong way were continually hitching themselves around to steal a look. If I could have looked away myself I'd have considered playing some poker just to take advantage of the general befuddlement and inattention to serious business.

Bill wiped his sleeve across his mouth, ready to take a short pause from knocking back his liquor. "See? Ain't she a corker, just like I said? I s'pose she'll move on soon's she's emptied the pockets 'round here, and wore out a few more big spenders."

"A few more?" The man with her was perspiring, but hardly looked worn out. More like pumped up fit to burst, which was entirely understandable. Her dress was so fancy and fine a fellow might be afraid to touch it, but the way her body moved roused a powerful urge to rip her clothing right off. I was in as bad a case as any, but in my own way, with damp heat throbbing between my thighs and a maddening pressure building in my bound breasts.

"Yes indeed, she's had more'n one stumblin' around like a winded horse after a night with her. Old Dunlap at the bank was so bad, his heart near stopped, and he ain't even been able to speak a word since. But he'd been sickly for quite a while, and should have known better, the old sot."

Maybe she felt our attention on her, maybe it was just by chance, but suddenly, as the piano player paused to mop his brow and the dance music stopped, her eyes looked right straight into mine. Great gray eyes with long lashes needing no artifice to darken them. Eyes that knew me.

The light in them flickered. Her practiced smile froze. This time I was stunned instead of dizzy, and before I could move she tugged her partner toward the staircase. In his eagerness he came near to carrying her up to the gallery above, while she clung to him and hid her face in his shoulder.

Rage, lust, and an eerie horror filled me, each so strong it didn't seem possible one heart and mind could hold any of them. I surged forward, staring upward. My breath caught when she looked down at me for a mere instant, and in that heartbeat I saw my Jess as I'd so often seen her—pale, hungry, brave in the face of danger, hair cropped like a boy's, lovely gray eyes aglow with love—and then there was only a glimpse of chestnut curls and emerald silk. And then she was gone.

"Cap'n!" Bill was clinging to my belt. I was halfway up the stairs, in such a daze I didn't recall getting there. Other, stronger hands tugged at me, the saloon owner's hired bully boys. I'd have taken them on one at a time, being as tall as the average man and about as hefty, but I had just enough sense left not to tackle a crowd, or be tackled by one.

"Hold your horses, chum," one of them said amiably enough. "Go sleep it off. Maybe you'll get lucky tomorrow, if you've got the cash. Her Highness don't take but one beau a night."

I subsided, and let myself be pushed out the door. Bill still hung close by, so I waved him off and said I needed time to clear my head, and would move along to my bed in the boarding house soon.

"I was sure enough right, wasn't I just!" he said in parting. "That fancy filly is really something! Something else!"

Oh, God, yes, I thought. *Something else, But what?*

I had to know. And whatever the explanation, or whatever…whatever she'd become, I had to see Jess again.

In the narrow alley behind the saloon I moved along stealthily, listening, trying to make out which upper room held Jess and her customer. A forced giggle through the first window was clearly from one of the other girls. On the far end, though, sounds so urgent and guttural they made my innards clench struck me like a brutal blow. They were hard at it. Jess's soft, high moans that I remembered so well could be heard in between the man's deep grunts of extremity. When those finally tapered off, I could still hear Jess, her cries oddly muted now, as if her mouth were pressed to him.

I was in such a state of heat that I could have rubbed myself off right there, but my need to get to Jess was even greater. The alley was so narrow here that the low shed in back was scarcely more than an arm's reach from the window, so I hoisted myself onto its roof and looked across.

The light of an oil lamp showed Jess's bowed head as she knelt beside the bed, and just a glimpse of the now-quiet man. By the tremor of her naked back and shoulders she seemed to be sobbing, whether in grief or pleasure, but at that moment I didn't care which. I just hungered to feel her touch on me, her mouth crushing down hard where my pounding need was so intense it burned, her fingers squeezing into flesh demanding to be unbound, her rounded buttocks filling my hands.

Then she raised her head, and I saw her wipe a trickle

of blood from the corner of her mouth. The brute had hit her! She saw me at just the same time, sprang up, and threw open the window. "Oh, God, Lou...help me!"

I was through and into the room so fast I had no time to think about it. The man on the bed didn't stir. What help did she need, whoever...whatever...she was now?

"Lou!" Jess's eyes had a strange, glazed look, and she scrabbled at the lacings of the tight corset she still wore. "Lou, please!"

I got right at the garment, tearing and peeling, looking for injuries, but her body beneath was unmarked by anything beyond the normal lines and creases such fashionable instruments of torture impart. Before I could halfway finish Jess kept interfering, grasping at my hands, trying to press them to her breasts, her belly, and the hot sweet cleft below.

"Touch me, damn it! Fuck me!" Her voice was rough with urgency. "He was so...so full...blood so hot, so wild..."

I tried to stop her talk with a kiss, but her head jerked sideways, so I dropped my own head to her breasts and sucked fiercely at one extended nipple and then the other. That did the trick, and I managed to finish stripping her, hard though it was with her demanding thrusts and whimpers and the swelling of her flesh against my tongue.

When I was finally free to get at her skin, she writhed and panted and seemed to demand everything at once, pulling my hands here and there and here again, grabbing at her own tender bits when I clutched at her elsewhere, until I tore off my shirt, yanked up the bindings of my breasts, and held her so tightly against me she could scarcely move.

"Hold still so's I can get at you!" I was in a frenzy of lust myself by then, with her wriggles against my own nipples coming near to undoing me, but I pushed her back against the wall, got my fingers between us and right into the wet heat of her center, and gave her what she needed with the sure, hard strokes that had always driven her to glory. She got there right away, riding the peak hard and long, gasping and crying out until she had no breath left, but still clenching me inside her fit to bruise. I began to fear she'd faint from it.

She slumped finally enough for me to reclaim my hand. Then she rested her head against my breast, which of course kept my flesh perked right up. I figured she was too wrung out to give me a turn yet, and wasn't sure how I could bear it. But after a moment she twisted out of my grip, dragged me toward the bed with a strength she'd never shown before, and heaved at the sheets until the man lying there tumbled to the floor on the other side. He still didn't stir. I didn't look close for fear of what I wasn't prepared to see, not while Jess was pulling at my belt and pushing me onto the mattress.

I got my turn, right enough, but in snatches between Jess's fits of renewed desire. She rubbed her body all over mine, took a goodly expanse of breast into her mouth, tweaked my imploring clit between her fingers, and then got distracted by the need to grind herself against my hip or belly or rump until she exploded again. And again. And again. I was streaked all over with her juices. She was insatiable, beyond thought or pleading. I was in such a fury of lust myself that it didn't take much to set me off, and when she rode my thigh with her knee pressed tight into my crotch, or when I could hold her right over me so that her writhings hit in just the necessary spot, I went off like firecrackers, too, more times than I'd ever done before.

Finally, Jess slowed enough that I could hold her face steady down where I needed it most, and once her tongue got a taste of my flow, she set to working me in steady strokes that got me riding a long, rolling wave of pleasure ending only when my breath and voice gave out.

She hitched herself up beside me at last and clung tight, her face hidden between my neck and shoulder. "Lou," she murmured, "I don't want to hurt you. Don't ever let me hurt you."

I stroked her long, tangled curls, new to me even though the texture and scent of her hair had been imprinted in my heart long ago. "I've never minded any hurt from you before."

"Things are different now. So different..." Her tears were hot against my throat.

"I know." Just as I knew that Jess had been dead, and was now alive. And that the man on the floor was dead, permanently. Back in Connecticut, when they talked of vampires, nothing like Jess came to mind, but there must be some ancient truth behind such stories. "You'd better tell me about it later. You need to get away from here before they find him on the floor. I'll be right along, but it's best they don't connect us. Too many here have a general notion of where I hole up in the winter."

So, I lowered Jess from the window, and she disappeared into the shadows, wrapped in a dingy blanket. Twelve hours later I was on my way, mule and horse loaded with sacks of cornmeal and bacon and ammunition and all such winter supplies. Three miles down the trail I paused to water my critters where a tangle of brush rimmed a small creek, and when we resumed our travel Jess was perched up in front of me. My old Jess, in boy's clothes stolen from some laundry yard and chestnut hair chopped short and ragged—yet not the old Jess.

"Back in town they're using that word," I told her, not quite wanting to say it myself. "The doctor says the fellow's blood was drained so low he couldn't live."

"Vampire, that's the word. Might as well call it that. The old woman that raised me did, said I had the taint, though there was no way to tell how it might turn out. That's all I know. Never knew any family. Never felt any difference, nor special powers, nor...nor needs, not until I was dead—and then I wasn't dead."

I held my arm tighter around her middle. "How does it work? Does it pass on to...to whoever?" For a moment I wondered whether Jess's blood would taste different now than when I'd kissed the streaks on her face as she'd died.

"Not that I've noticed yet. Not from just once, anyway. That fellow last night, well, I went too far. I didn't mean to. But I was distracted on account of seeing you, and wild to get filled up before you got to me so I wouldn't need to, well, hurt you."

I pondered that for a while. "How often do you...well, how often do you need it?"

"Depends on a lot of things. I can get by with animals, but it's not the same. Even with folks it's not always the same. After that old banker, I felt near as bad as he did, but that fellow last night, so pumped up with lechery, well, that was really something."

"Sure was." I savored the recollection. "Anything else I should know?"

"Plenty I should know myself but don't. I'm working my way west, hoping maybe in San Francisco there's some like me I can learn from."

"Time enough for that when winter's past. The mountain passes are already getting snow. We'll manage fine in my cabin."

Jess didn't object, just settled more comfortably against me. We'd manage, with the critters I shot for food. If it came to it, I knew where a she-bear denned for her winter's sleep, and if her blood made Jess sleepy too in the dead of winter, that might be just as well. Any time my own blood rose, I was pretty sure I could get Jess to indulge enough to get her going. The thought of her teeth sinking into my neck, or my breast, or my belly, got me shifting in the saddle already.

She wouldn't go on to San Francisco alone, either. If it

suited her to be Jessebel there, in fine silks and corsets, well, I could handle that, and even put on fine gent's togs to match. Didn't matter who, or what, she was to anybody else. Our bond held. She'd always be my Jess.

Although I did wonder just how long "always" might turn out to be.

Spirit Horse Ranch

Someone *was* behind her.

Emmaline, deep in the root cellar, hadn't heard Sigri's truck pull in or Chinook bark a welcome, but the sense of a presence was unmistakable. It had to be Sigri, or the dog would've sounded a warning. Sigri could sneak up on grazing elk, when the wind was right. Even if Emmaline hadn't been hammering at shelves for her preserves, she might have missed any sounds. She'd been humming, too, immersed in the joy of working among provisions of her own raising. Not that she wasn't always, on some level, listening for Sigri every bit as intently as the dog did.

Sigri would sometimes press up against Emmaline from the rear with no warning, nuzzle her neck, and reach around for further fondling. If she was in the mood, why not go along with it? The thought certainly put Emmaline in the mood. She lowered the hammer and moved back a step, as though surveying her handiwork. Her breasts and backside tingled in anticipation.

A touch on her hair made her jump. "You're back early," she said. "Didn't figure you'd get here from Bozeman so— Ouch!" Fingers tightened on her long, thick braid, and icy-cold knuckles dug into the nape of her neck. Somebody pulled, hard.

"Hey!" Emmaline tried to turn. The hidden tormentor jerked her head back viciously and yanked again. Tears burned her eyes and fear pounded in her veins.

It wasn't Sigri.

Sigri wouldn't do that. She knew enough about Emmaline's past, and the things that triggered memories. And no one else who knew would dare, or care enough, to search her out after twenty years—if he was even still alive.

Terror snapped into sudden rage. Emmaline wasn't fifteen and vulnerable anymore. She kicked back sharply at ankle-height, let out a yell worthy of an old-time Blackfeet war party, and swung the hammer at what should be a thigh—or, better yet, more vulnerable parts.

Her foot didn't connect with anything. Neither did the hammer. But her yell brought Chinook scrambling down the stairs from the kitchen in a frenzy of barks and growls. Could the cellar, crowded with sacks of winter-keeping vegetables and shelves of canning jars, hold Emmaline, the intruder, and an enraged German Shepherd all at the same time?

Emmaline wrenched sideways to free herself. Resistance ceased so abruptly that she spun right around, her russet braid flipping over one shoulder. A gust of cold air rushed past; she staggered, nearly fell, and grabbed at Chinook's shoulder for balance.

There was nobody there.

A bulb dangling from a cord hooked to the ceiling lit the space well enough. None of the sacks and crates looked disturbed. Nobody could have gotten out past the dog, even though her growls had subsided.

"C'mon, Chinook, upstairs." Emmaline couldn't keep her voice steady. The chill where her neck had been touched crawled all the way down her back. *What if he wasn't alive—but had come for her anyway?* No! She had to get out of there, get her thoughts under control.

She moved toward the steps, overwhelmed by a desperate need for Sigri—and just as glad Sigri wasn't there to witness her weakness.

"Chinook, come!"

The dog's tail wagged to show she'd heard, but she kept sniffing among the crates. Just doing her job, searching for whatever had made her mistress yell like a damn fool. But when she clambered onto a heap of potato sacks and starting nosing at the packed earth wall, it was too much.

"Drat you, Chinook, come on!" The dog kept poking at the wall. Small chunks of dirt had dribbled down, a few feet to the left of the new shelves. The hammering must have jarred them loose. A few bits of old sticks or roots showed in the roughened earth, but there wasn't a hole, so far as she could tell without going closer, which she wasn't about to do. Nothing big enough to let a mouse through, much less a rat. A rat?

She bolted upward, not looking to see if the dog followed. Her scalp still stung from the tugs. No rat could have been that strong!

Better that, though, than anything else occurring to her. She could deal with vermin. Still…a great filthy rat clinging to her head? She scrabbled at her braided hair until it hung loose around her shoulders, shaking it so hard her brains seemed to slosh like flapjack batter. Her heart pounded, anger mixing with fear. She tried hard to let the anger win out.

A bark and a high-pitched whine came up from the root cellar. Emmaline went to the top of the steps. "Get your furry butt up here," she yelled, beginning to lower the trap-door. Chinook, not wanting to be shut below, left off what-ever she was doing and bounded up into the kitchen.

"If you haven't caught 'em yet, you won't, not without tearing up my spuds and onions!" The scolding was mostly to keep her own voice steady. "Wait for Sigri to get home!"

At the sound of that name, the dog padded hopefully to the screen door and looked out at the empty, dusty road connecting the ranch to the rest of the world. For all her devotion to Emmaline, Chinook looked to Sigri as her one true goddess.

No argument there, Emmaline thought. To see Sigri riding against the backdrop of the mountains, lithe, strong, the herd of horses running with her for the pure joy of it, any passing stranger might think Montana was as close to heaven as earth could get. At night, in ways no passerby could imagine, Emmaline knew for sure she'd found her own personal paradise. The thought rekindled the anticipatory heat she'd felt when she thought it was Sigri behind her.

But what was she going to tell Sigri? That she'd freaked out in the root cellar, panicked about ghosts, when it might be just rats? Even in the familiar normalcy of the kitchen, she couldn't really believe that. Whatever she decided, it would go better after supper, and there wouldn't be any supper if she didn't get on with it.

Chicken and dumplings had been her plan, with leftovers from the hen she'd roasted Sunday. But she'd forgotten to bring carrots and onions up from the cellar. Forgotten? Well, not exactly, but nothing was going to get her down into that hole again just yet.

That hole? Now anger did win out. She'd been so proud of the root cellar, clearing out generations of trash, building shelves and bins, reinforcing the support posts and steps with Sigri's help. It was older than the ranch house itself, part of a pioneer dugout home carved into the hillside. Most of it had caved in well over a hundred years ago, but when Sigri's great-great-grandfather had built his house of red cedar logs the kitchen had overlapped what was left of the hole just enough for the trapdoor and stairs to connect with it. Back then, it had been used as a root cellar, but not in recent years, until now.

Emmaline had found things in the rubble that could have been there since before the cave-in. Once she'd dug out a flat tin box, barely protruding from the wall, and found inside two long, faded coils of hair, one blonde, one reddish. Maybe two pioneer girls sick with the fever had needed to have their hair cut when it got too tangled, as was common in the old days. In an odd way it had given her a sense of connection to those long-ago settlers. She might not belong here in any conventional way—she knew the townsfolk preferred to think of her as Sigri's house-keeper and business manager, nothing closer—but she did belong to the tradition of growing and harvesting and tending loved ones.

Which included making supper. Question was, could Emmaline let herself be scared out of her own root cellar by…well, once she knew for sure what it was, maybe she wouldn't be so scared.

For now, there was plenty left of the big kettle of chili Sigri cooked once a week. Emmaline could whip up a batch of cornbread and pull some greens from the autumn garden. Sigri wouldn't object, having pretty much lived on nothing else in the years she'd ranched here alone.

A tensing of the dog's back, a perking of ears, brought Emmaline to the screen door. Dust puffed in the distance, where the road was no more than a crease in grasslands tinted gold by the afternoon light. Beyond, blue mountains streaked with early snow rose in jagged ranges, the Absarokee and Beartooth to the south, the Crazies to the west. To Emmaline they were guardians, shielding her against where she'd come from, who she'd had to be. But even their grandeur dimmed behind the glint of sunlight on the approaching truck.

Chinook's whines rose to a frantic pitch. It didn't take the dog's quivering rump, ready to break out into a fit of wagging, to tell Emmaline that the truck was Sigri's. She knew, as surely as the dog, and she understood the impulse to race to meet the loved one, but Chinook, for all her size, was barely out of puppyhood and still needed her training reinforced. Her job, her sacred charge, was to stay close to Emmaline every minute.

Sigri had swapped the stud service of her Appaloosa stallion for the pick of a neighbor's litter of pups. "Folks around here are pretty much decent, mind-their-own-business types, whatever their beliefs," she'd said, "but punks can sprout up anywhere, even Montana. A good dog can make 'em think twice about trying to get at...well, at a woman out here alone."

No need to spell it out. It wasn't just being a woman alone. What had happened down in Laramie to that boy Matthew Shepard was on both their minds. Sigri, when she'd lived alone, hadn't worried—nearly everybody within fifty miles was related to her, or owned horses she'd trained. She was one of their own. Emmaline, for all her farm-girl background, wasn't.

The red truck was close enough now for her to make out the familiar lines. Where the road dipped down to ford the tree-lined creek, green-gold leaves hid it for a moment. This was when Emmaline would generally head out to open the gate in the stock fence. Right now, she wasn't sure her legs would take her that far without some wobbling Sigri was sure to notice.

"Stay!" She pressed her hand down hard on Chinook's

wriggling shoulders. Sigri reached the gate, got out to open it herself, looked searchingly up at the house, and got back in. Emmaline waited until the truck stopped between the barn and the house and then, finally, let Chinook out.

Sigri stood, stretched her rangy body after the bumpy ride, pushed back her Stetson until straw-pale cropped hair showed above her tanned forehead, and looked again toward the house. Glimpsing Emmaline inside the doorway, she flashed a boyish grin that would never grow old, no matter how many lines time and weather etched on her face.

The dog pranced around her legs in frantic welcome. Weanling fillies along the paddock fence whickered in greeting. Emmaline, aching to be there, too, watched as each animal got its moment of affection. When Sigri finally hauled sacks of groceries out of the truck and strode toward the house, Emmaline barely had time to tie on her apron, pour flour and corn meal into a bowl, and get enough on herself to look like she'd been in the middle of mixing.

The screen door swung open and shut. As soon as the bags and a banded bundle of mail were safely on the kitchen table, and the Stetson tossed onto its hook, Emmaline proceeded to wipe her hands on the blue-checked dishtowel and rush to grab a big hug.

Sigri'd noticed something, though. "You okay, babe?" She stroked the loose tangle of hair Emmaline had forgotten to tidy. Fear came surging back.

With her arms around Sigri's lean body and her head nestled against a firm shoulder, Emmaline managed to say,

"Sure, I'm okay. How'd it go in Bozeman?"

"Not too bad." Sigri tried to get a look at Emmaline's face. "I dropped off your baked goods at the café. Claire wrote a check for last week and this week, too, so we're all square there. And Rogers at the bank seemed pretty sure we can get an extension on the loan. He knows I'm owed enough by the horse trek outfitters to cover it."

Emmaline burrowed a little closer, then tilted her head back for a kiss. Chinook, firmly trained not to interrupt such proceedings, lay down with her head between her paws, and then, impatient, went to nose around the edges of the trapdoor.

Emmaline became vaguely aware of the rattle of some small object being pushed around the floor behind her. Sigri, looking past her shoulder, broke the clinch. "What's that dratted dog got? Chicken bone?"

"Not from my kitchen..." Emmaline stopped. Chinook was offering her prize to Sigri. Held tenderly, in jaws trained to pick up eggs without breaking them, was a four-inch sticklike object. Not, they both knew, a stick. Bone, or two bones hitched together, but not chicken bone. Chickens don't have fingers.

Sigri knelt. "Good girl," she said, ruffling the dog's ears. She took the bone and inspected it. "Not fresh, at least. Old. Real old, I'd say, but not prehistoric. Where'd you get that?" She looked up. "Where's she been?"

Emmaline managed to yank a chair out from the table and slump into it. "Just here, in the house, or right beside me outdoors. And...down in the root cellar. I was putting up some more shelves."

Sigri's long body straightened. She hauled out a chair, straddled it backwards, and surveyed Emmaline keenly. "Down in the dugout? Guess you must have been hammering up some storm to get yourself so bedraggled."

"Well, I was." Emmaline steadied herself with pure stubbornness. "I built a good strong set of shelves. And maybe shook a little dirt loose from the wall, but I swear there wasn't any crack big enough for...for a rat."

"What's a rat got to do with it?"

"Nothing!" Emmaline fastened her hair back tight with the rubber band from the bundle of mail. A couple of magazines unfurled to show covers she wouldn't have wanted the local postmistress to see, which, along with the occasional specialty mail order delivery, was why they kept a post office box in the university town of Bozeman.

"Then why'd you mention it? Come on, Em, tell me what's been going on."

Emmaline drew a deep breath, let it out, and tried again. "I don't know. Maybe one of those flashback things like they write about. But I was feeling so happy right then, safe, my preserves and vegetables all set for winter...and when I felt somebody behind me I figured it was you." She reached out a hand. In an instant Sigri's fingers were warm and firm on hers.

"But it wasn't you," Emmaline went on. "Somebody... something...yanked hard on my hair, pulled my head right back, just like that old bastard used to do. I yelled and swung the hammer and jerked around, and...nobody was there. Just Chinook, scrambling down the stairs, growling fit to scare a bear from its den."

Sigri looked a shade paler under her tan, but her voice held steady. "Good for her." She stood to pull Emmaline into another hug. "So, what's this about the rats?"

"Nothing, really. She just went poking and whining at the rough spot in the wall, and wouldn't come upstairs until I started to close the trapdoor. So, I thought of rats, and wondered if one could have jumped on me."

"Do you still reckon that was it?" Sigri was so close her breath warmed Emmaline's cheek. Emmaline wished her cheek could never be any farther away, although warming other bits of her anatomy would be just fine, too.

"I...well, I don't believe in ghosts any more than you do, so..." She stopped, feeling a slight tensing of Sigri's body. "But...you don't, do you?"

"Don't I? Can't say as I recall ever discussing that particular subject." Sigri didn't seem about to say any more.

Emmaline made a lame attempt at humor. "Well, generally you're so level-headed, snow could build up a foot deep and not slide off if I didn't tip you over from time to time."

It worked. Sigri chuckled. "If it's tipping you've got on your mind, girl..." She lifted Emmaline right off her feet and up until that warm mouth was pressed right between her breasts. The long, slow slide back down was so sweet and tantalizing it could almost make them both forget what else was on their minds. Almost.

The finger bone lay on the table, seeming to point right at them. Emmaline itched to knock it off, kick it out the door, and scrub both table and floor.

Sigri sighed, and set her down. "Guess I'd better check things out. My grandmother wouldn't go in that cellar on a bet, always had a strange feeling about it, but I never paid any heed." She hoisted up the trapdoor fast, as if in a hurry to get it over with before she changed her mind. "Looks like you left the light on down there."

"I guess I did." The hole was swallowing Sigri feet first as she went down the stairs. Emmaline hurried to the edge to keep sight of her.

"Hang onto the dog," Sigri called from below. "Danged mutt seems to have clawed out a fair bit more before you got her upstairs."

Emmaline, already gripping Chinook's collar, nearly asked, "A fair bit of what?" But she already had far too good a notion. "Bones?" she managed to croak.

"Yep, looks like two hands, most of an arm, and signs of more where those came from. Don't worry, though." Sigri glanced up over her shoulder and flashed a wan imitation of a grin. "I haven't been stashing the remains of my exes in the wall. These've been here for a mighty long time."

"They'll keep, then, till the sheriff or somebody can take them away," Emmaline said sharply. Fear was rising again, but not so much for herself. "Sigri, please, come on back up here." She moved down a step, still holding the dog back.

Chilly air gripped her ankles.

Sigri, bending over the jumble of dirt and bone fragments and rotted scraps of cloth, didn't answer. Emmaline took another step downward.

Sigri's head jerked sharply back. She let out a strangled yell, kicked wildly at thin air, and clawed at her own throat. Emmaline and Chinook took the stairs in three mad leaps. By the time they got to her, Sigri was flat on her back, writhing, cursing, flailing with arms and knees at an unseen attacker.

The dog snarled and whirled, not knowing what to lunge at. Emmaline, without any thought at all, flung herself right over Sigri and hung on as though she could ward off the attack with her own flesh. Maybe it worked. Something so cold it burned streaked along her back, and was gone.

Sigri's breath came in such tearing gasps that Emmaline raised up to a crouch so as not to smother her.

"It's okay," Emmaline soothed, hoping fervently that she was right. "We're okay, it's gone."

The dog was barking right at the wall now, as though some malevolent force had retreated back into the earth.

Sigri struggled to sit up. Emmaline backed off and stood up. Sigri took her hand, got to her feet, and shook herself like a dog who'd rolled in dirt. Or carrion.

"Em..." She tried again. "Whatever...whatever's going on, looks like we're in it together."

"You're damned right. But we can just as well be in it together upstairs." She tugged Sigri toward the steps, and

Chinook, foreseeing the closing of the trapdoor, followed them quickly.

"Get out of those clothes," Emmaline ordered, "and into the shower. Then we'll call the sheriff's office, and after that you'll tell me every last thing you've ever heard about the dugout."

It might not make sense, but somehow knowing that she wasn't alone in this steered her away from panic and into problem-solving mode.

"How about you get your clothes off, too," Sigri said, clearly beginning to recover, "and we'll talk about it in the shower together."

Emmaline hadn't realized until that moment that she too had been rolling in that unspeakable filth on the cellar floor, or at least crouching in it. "Great idea," she said.

But the supply of hot water was limited, as always, and the need to cling together in the warm, sheltering flow was intense, so not that much talking got done, although a great deal of feeling did. "Em, are there marks on my throat?" Sigri asked after a while.

Emmaline checked. "No bruises that I can see. A few scratches, likely from your own fingernails. What...what was it like?"

"Just...well, scrabbling at my hair, at first, and then choking, and then...knocking me down, poking, trying to touch places..." Sigri faltered.

"Places nobody but me gets to touch," Emmaline said grimly. "Could be he thought from your short hair you were a man, and then got the notion maybe you weren't and was set on finding out." She touched her lips to several of the areas in question, very gently at first until Sigri wasn't so tense, at least not in the same way, and then applied them to the hollow of her throat with such fervor that there soon would be some interesting marks. Sigri held her even tighter, but the water was cooling, and neither of them was in a state to tolerate chills.

When they'd dried off, dressed, and steeled themselves to get on with it, Emmaline handed the phone to Sigri.

They hadn't discussed what to say. Sigri kept to the bare facts as coolly as anybody could who'd found a body buried in their cellar. "Must have been somebody caught in that cave-in back in eighteen-whatever. Early seventies, I think. Before my people got here. Anyway, I figure that's your department, or the coroner's, or maybe some archaeologist's. Appreciate it if you'd come out and take a look." There was a pause. "Well, we sure do want it out of there, but I guess it's not likely to go anywhere before morning. See you then. And, Frank...say howdy to Shirley for me."

"Tomorrow," Emmaline said flatly. "Well, all right, then."

The sheriff and his wife were cousins of Sigri's to one degree or another, just like most everybody in the county. Two or three had come up to Emmaline on the street in town to say hello, and go on a bit about Sigri having somebody to feed her up and get her accounts in order. There'd been no mention of visits, but things could have been worse.

"Should I..." Sigri made as if to dial the phone again.

"No, you did right. The rest is purely our own business. But…how about we sleep in the barn tonight."

Chinook was nosing uneasily around the edges of the trapdoor. Sigri nodded. "Good idea. Talking of the barn, I've got chores to do before dark."

Emmaline gave up any thought of cooking, and went to help herd the weanlings inside and feed all the critters that needed feeding. Sigri got fed cold chicken and leftover biscuits.

The barn was warm with the breath and smell of horses, the sweet scent of hay. Warm and safe, as they snuggled together under wool blankets. They'd slept in the barn often enough before, in foaling season, when there was a chance a young mare might need help in the night. "Tell me about the old dugout now, and the cave-in," Emmaline said.

Sigri was still shaken, and not hiding it. The times when she opened up, let some vulnerability show, told Emmaline most surely what she herself meant to the tough rancher.

"I never listened a lot to old stories when I was a kid," Sigri said. "Always trailing after the men and the horses, learning from them, not putting much stock in women's talk. There was one thing, though…" She hesitated. "Well, you asked about believing in ghosts. They said it was a horse caved in that dugout, stomped on top of it, broke his legs and likely had to be shot. A big one, crossbred draft horse—my grandad's grandad hauled away the bones from on top of the rubble when he bought the land."

"Nobody dug to see if anybody'd been caught inside?"

"Not that I know of. That was some years after it happened. But folks seemed sure the people living there, two young brothers wintering over on the way to try their luck in Canada, got out okay and traveled on, though the horse they'd ridden here died trampling down the dugout in some kind of fit."

"So...where does the ghost part come in?"

Sigri drew in a deep, slow breath.

"Have you ever wondered why I call this place Spirit Horse Ranch? I've seen spirit horses, times when nobody else could. And I've seen that horse. On clear nights, under moonlight, down across the creek near the hollow where the bones got dumped. You could still see humps where the grass grew over them.   After the first time, I used to ride back now and then, and mostly he'd be there. He'd lift his head and look at me, and my horse would whicker a little, and then he'd just...fade away. Never any footprints in the daylight, when I went back to look, even if the ground was muddy. Haven't seen him in years, though, not since the creek flooded through that hollow and washed away everything, bones and all."

"So, maybe getting rid of the bones gets rid of the ghost." Emmaline was trying to puzzle things out.

"That'll be just fine with me." Sigri stretched, and yawned.

Emmaline couldn't rest quite yet. "Sigri, remember that old tin box I showed you, with the hanks of hair in it?"

"Sure, one of 'em towheaded and the other a redhead

like you." She nuzzled the loose russet hair on Emmaline's shoulder.

Thoughts swirled in Emmaline's mind, notions twisting themselves around a time or two and settling into a possible pattern. The ghost had grabbed her hair, and tried to grab Sigri's. Could be he was searching for somebody, somebody female.

But Sigri was nuzzling now with clear intent, and nothing could be better than to stop thinking for a while and turn to pure feeling, the kind that built until the body was arching and thrashing and wild with a need that was glory in itself, a need filled at last by a bolt of ecstasy piercing flesh and soul like lightning.

At last they lay panting and laughing and flicking bits of stray hay off of each other, and Sigri's breathing gradually evened out into sleep.

Emmaline stayed wakeful for a bit, but at peace. The barn had always been a place of life to her, of birth in foaling time, as far from long-ago death as any place could be. If the ghost had been watching their lovemaking—and she didn't believe he had been, with his bones far away in the root cellar—let him eat his rotted heart out.

The sheriff arrived just past morning chore time. With him were the coroner, two deputies in a pickup truck, and Shirley.

Emmaline had reclaimed her kitchen before sunrise. The parts about no footprints, no bruises on Sigri's throat, and her own hair not coming loose until she'd torn at it herself, all led to the near-conviction that ghosts couldn't do you real physical harm, unless your fear did it for them. Pain, yes, that came from the mind; they could make you feel like you were being attacked, but maybe nothing more. Still, the more his bones had been dug out, the worse the assaults had felt. Digging out the whole thing might be more than anybody should have to deal with.

So she lifted the trap door, and carried the open tin box down just a step or two. Nothing stirred except a cold breeze. "Look," she called down into the dark. "They got away, they're long gone." She raised each coil of hair to display. "We're not the ones you're looking for!"

Safely back in the kitchen with the trapdoor shut, she peered down into the box. There'd been a tiny clink when she'd replaced the hair. She lifted the coils again and saw two small, broken, tarnished rings. The last bits of the puzzle fell into place for her, whether anybody else would believe it or not.

Then she fixed up enough coffee and apple cake to feed whoever came. Hadn't counted on the sheriff's wife, but her kitchen was nothing to be ashamed of, if you didn't count a body buried under one corner of it.

Shirley was vigorous, fiftyish, a rancher in her own right on land passed down through her family. Emmaline braced herself for whatever might come, but she took the woman's offered hand and shook it firmly.

"Can I call you Emmaline? Well," as Emmaline nodded, "I'm ashamed you've been here near a year and I haven't managed to stop by to say howdy. I hope you don't mind my coming today, but with all this happening, it's bound to be hard for you, and I hoped maybe I could help."

Emmaline, still wary, said she was glad of the company, and after more introductions and much hearty appreciation of coffee and cake, the trapdoor was raised.

"Emmaline," Shirley said kindly, "maybe we could head down by the barn while they tramp around in here. You could show me the new crop of young 'uns. Nobody breeds horses as fine as Sigri's."

By the time they reached the paddock, Emmaline had made some hard decisions. "Shirley," she said, "I'm real glad to have this chance to meet you. And I hope you don't mind, but there's things I need to tell somebody. I know folks have questions about me."

"You're not obliged to satisfy anybody's curiosity," Shirley said.

"Well, I'll tell you as much as anybody needs to know, and I don't care who else hears it." Emmaline leaned on the fence, watching the horses. "I come from a little place all to hell and gone in Utah. Nobody's heard of it. I was married off when I was fifteen. Not legally, not with my consent. I got away when I was sixteen. The old bastard had plenty of wives left."

"I've heard of such things, even in this day and age," Shirley said. "Good for you for getting out."

"I got by on washing dishes in diners and cafés from Idaho to Oregon and back here to Montana. No fooling with men." Emmaline glanced sideways. Shirley, knowing just what she meant, nodded.

"Along the way, I picked up some education in cooking and baking, and moved up from dishwashing. Took night classes whenever I was in a college town—general education, woodworking, accounting, whatever might come in handy. Accounting class was where I met Sigri, in Bozeman."

Shirley chuckled. "I did hear the only thing Sigri got out of that class was you."

"Well, she'd already got a degree in animal science years ago. Anyway, what with needing somebody to handle the bookkeeping, and getting a taste for my cooking—" here Shirley let out a muffled snort of laughter— "she asked if I'd ever considered ranch life." Close enough. Sigri'd said something more along the lines of, "Think you could put up with being a rancher's woman?"

"So, I'm here. And I'm staying, as long as Sigri needs me."

Shirley put her arm right around Emmaline's shoulders. "My grandad used to say Sigri'd got no quit in her, which was why she'd make a rancher. Never was any use trying to change her mind. I reckon you'll be around as long as ever you want to."

Emmaline gave her a quick hug, and looked back toward the house. The sheriff and deputies had come out, and were dragging shovels and a big pine box out of their truck.

"Shirley, parts of what I told you gave me some ideas about what might have happened with that…body. I'd like to tell the sheriff now, before they get to digging."

Shirley nodded, and kept close beside her as they went.

Emmaline tapped the sheriff on the shoulder. "Sheriff—Frank—I might have some helpful information."

He turned, a hint of embarrassment crossing his face. "I'd sure appreciate anything you can tell me, miss. Uh, ma'am."

"Emmaline," his wife put in firmly.

"Oh. Right. Well, we're going to have a hell of a time figuring out who this guy was and what to do with him."

"First off, you might think of getting a Mormon preacher," Emmaline said. "If there's any bit of identification, wallet, initials, whatever, the genealogy experts in Salt Lake City might be able to help."

The sheriff raised an eyebrow. Even Sigri looked puzzled.

Emmaline went on quickly, "Back when I was clearing out the root cellar, there was this one tin box mostly buried in the wall, so I dug it out." She bent and picked up what she'd set under the front steps that morning, not sure whether she'd show it or not. She pried off the corroded lid. Everybody strained to get a look.

"Then, last night, Sigri told me that there were old stories about two young boys living in the dugout, one blond, one redheaded."

Now Sigri, who hadn't said any such thing, or not exactly, raised a quizzical brow.

"I'm thinking," Emmaline said, "those weren't boys at all. They'd run away and cut off their hair, but they were girls. Or women. And then there's these, that I hadn't seen until today." She lifted out the two thin silver rings, each cut through. "Wedding bands, maybe, that they'd cut off, as well."

Frank looked dubious. Emmaline hurried right along. "Now, I'll be the first to admit it's likely just my own background talking, but I think those were two wives of a Mormon patriarch, back when that was still legal. And that...thing...caught in the cave-in there," she jerked her head toward the house, "was either him, or somebody he'd sent to chase them down."

Sigri's arm was around her now. "Could be something to go on, Frank," she said. "Might even be that horse they tell of knew what he was doing caving in the dugout on that dirt-bag, but we'll never know. It'll be good to get all that out of here now, anyway. The sooner the better."

It was over by mid-afternoon. The sheriff took down statements, the deputies shot pictures, and Shirley helped clean the kitchen floor after all the tramping through it. Finally, Emmaline and Sigri were alone.

"How did it go in there?" Emmaline asked, when they'd sat quietly on the front steps for a little while.

"Nothing happened," Sigri said, "but everybody sure was jumpy. I didn't go all the way down till they'd dragged the bones out. Not enough room for all of us, anyway." She stared down at hands scrubbed so hard they were red. "Em, I did try to clean up your stuff down there, but there's three or four sacks of spuds you may not want to keep."

Emmaline didn't say anything. After a while Sigri turned

to face her. "I've been thinking maybe…well, how will you feel about living here, after all this?"

"You'll stay on," Emmaline said. "You won't leave your land."

Sigri's face, for the first time Emmaline could remember, showed every one of her thirty-seven years, and more. "I'd quit the land before I'd quit you, Em."

Emmaline reached her hand out. "I think it'll be all right, now that everything's been cleared away. And even if it isn't, those are my hard-raised provisions down there, and my home and heart right here." She pressed Sigri's fingers briefly to her lips. "Nothing's going to chase me away. Like your grandad said about you, I've got no quit in me, and don't you forget it!"

Her expression was fierce, but Sigri got so close, so fast, that expressions didn't matter a bit. What mattered was settled, once and for all, beyond the power of man or ghost to rend apart.

Carved in Stone

Brick walls crowned with razor wire closed in behind me. I'd envisioned stone walls, like a castle. Stone I understand. Granite, sandstone, marble. But brick has no character. At least the iron bars on the entrance gate provided a touch of grim atmosphere. Inside, a wide expanse of grass gave way to acres of pavement, then acres of brick buildings so featureless that even the few small barred windows did nothing to interrupt the blandness.

Fuck the stupid details. I gave up trying to distract myself from what lay ahead. Prison wasn't intended to appeal to me. That was the whole point.

The van pulled up to the front entrance. I got out, retreating into myself, forming a shell of detachment. At least the urge to throw up had receded.

Inside, I pushed my papers across the counter. "Alexandra McKenna."

The correctional officer had the heft and menace of a female movie cop and the trademark stony expression, although the twitch of one eyebrow hinted at curiosity. My salt-and-pepper androgyny doesn't attract much attention unless I want it to, but you don't work with blocks of granite and marble without developing some muscle, and my jeans and old white T-shirt didn't hide much. They'd be taken away soon enough. Everything I'd be allowed to keep was in one manila envelope.

Officer...I glanced at her name tag...Officer Gantry shuffled through the photos, a sketch pad, and the list of addresses in the envelope. "You know you'll be searched?"

"Yes." I do stony-faced pretty well myself.

At the next stop, I got patted down by another husky female cop. Strip, squat, and cough. Prison-issue baggy clothes followed, along with sheets, a blanket, and a stroll through a noisy dining hall. From the looks and smell of the food, throwing up might still be an option. From the change in tone of the general buzz, some idle speculation about me was spicing up the meal. I kept my eyes on my bundle of bedding and my guide's ample ass.

"Top bunk on the right," she said, unnecessarily, since the other three beds were made up already. "You can dump your stuff and maybe still get what's left of lunch."

A shell of detachment could only take me so far. "Thanks, but I'll pass. Just point me toward the lavatory, okay?" Getting there ahead of the crowd from the dining hall seemed like a good strategy, or as close to one as I could manage.

Or would've been a good strategy if it had worked.

"So-o-o-o. What have we here?" The deep, mellow voice had a hint of an accent. And more than a hint of derision.

I didn't turn around. Her reflection loomed in the

grubby mirror over the sink. Tall. Very tall, and wide, with a square face that had seen hard living, if those were scars I saw instead of streaks on the mirror. She had a strong jaw, wide mouth, high, broad cheekbones and dark hair cropped as close as mine.

Shuffling sounds and murmurs let me know she wasn't alone. Great. An audience. A face-off like this would have come up sooner or later, even if I didn't give a shit about proving anything or challenging anyone. My voice almost managed to stay neutral. "So-o-o-o. What are you looking at?"

"I ask myself that very thing. What, indeed, am I looking at?" A Russian accent, or maybe Ukrainian. A sprinkling of giggles was interrupted by other women pushing their way into the room, impatient to use the facilities. I'd been washing up with my sleeves rolled above my biceps. Without hurry, I rolled them down, turned, and jerked my head toward the mirror. "You want to look at something? Be my guest. Let me know how you like what you see in there." That might have been a good exit line if I'd been able to exit, but the crowd was now surging in force. The first arrivals, including my nemesis, moved well into the room, blocking my way.

"Yevgeniya Akhmatova, move your butt!"

"Yes ma'am!" Yevgeniya moved. So did her entourage. "For you, Miss Natalya, I move." Her sidelong glance made sure I didn't think she was getting out of the way on my account.

A space opened and a woman appeared: slight, silver-haired, with regal bearing, and a face so intricately lined that I itched to sketch her. She extended her hand. I shook it automatically, surprised to find my head inclining in a slight bow.

"Alexandra McKenna? We'll be bunkmates. Come along and I'll help you settle in." She steered me toward the door like a border collie with an errant sheep, but I cast back a long, assessing look at my antagonist and her hangers-on. Several of them returned my look with more than casual interest.

"A word of caution," Miss Natalya said back in our room. "That was Yev. I can call her Yevgeniya, but no one else dares unless they're looking for a fight. Which no one is. Not anymore."

"I'm not looking for anything. Just...getting by." My tone was bleaker than I'd intended.

"That's what we all do. But we don't have to do it alone." Her smile was warm, kind, and profoundly weary.

If Miss Natalya hadn't been enough to crack my shell, our two young bunkmates would have managed it. Detachment was futile. Miss Natalya was clearly a self-designated "housemother," easing us through the transition to prison life. The youngsters didn't know what to make of somebody my age coming in for the first time, but that didn't keep them from asking how long I was in for, what I was in for, and what I used to do on the outside. Miss Natalya's nod indicated that this was permissible prison etiquette, so I answered, briefly.

"Eighteen months. Conspiracy in a drug case. And I carve stone."

That last part baffled them. Ellie—skinny, freckled, sandy-haired—wrinkled her brow. "Stones? Like, gravestones?"

"Now and then. These days most headstones are engraved by machines run by computer programs, but sometimes people who can afford it want the handcrafted touch and custom artwork. Sometimes statues." People who could afford it also wanted custom-carved decorative stonework, indoors or around their elaborate grounds, and sometimes that stonework masked the entrances to secret spaces where illegal substances and profits could be hidden. Which was why I'd landed in prison. I didn't feel like talking about that.

Ellie and curvy, dark-haired Paula—more reserved or maybe just shy—sat with Miss Natalya in the dining hall at dinnertime. So did I. Might as well get that particular "first" over with, and I'd skipped lunch. I nodded in response to introductions up and down the table, and made the best of the food on my tray; mushy mixed vegetables with carrots the only identifiable objects, some kind of processed meat, and mashed potatoes dense enough to model into the Devil's Tower. I pushed the potatoes idly around for a while, until Ellie leaned closer, looked down, and said loudly, "Hey, you drew a face in your potatoes!"

"What face?" I mashed my spoon across the plate to wipe out lines I'd made without conscious thought. A square face, strong-jawed.

"Alex is an artist," Ellie announced to those closest. "She writes on stone, and makes pictures, too. Right, Alex?"

The kid was enjoying the attention this got her. "Yeah, sometimes," I said. "Hold still, Ellie." I smoothed the dingy white mass into a flat oval and drew one line, then another, looking up at her face now and then. A few women got up to watch over my shoulder. It wasn't much, just a cartoon sketch, but if you already knew it was supposed to be Ellie, you'd recognize her.

"Now do Paula!" Ellie said. Somebody behind me gave a low chuckle. Paula reddened. Maybe she read my mind. If this were a gathering in a bar, I'd say in my most seductive tone, "Ohhh yeah, I'd do Paula, any time."

But maybe she really was just shy.

"Another time." I stood up. The pallid fruit cocktail had minus appeal. "Is it okay for me to leave for the lavatory?" Miss Natalya had been telling me where we were allowed to be, when we were allowed to be there, and the consequences of a misstep if the correctional officer on duty wasn't in a forbearing mood. She glanced toward the door and then nodded.

"Ask the guard politely. Don't push it if he says no."

I turned around and saw, with no surprise, that the chuckler behind me had been Yev. Up close, she didn't look quite as tall, but still with maybe fifty pounds on me, plenty of it muscle. I nodded as though we'd been formally introduced and went toward the door to try my luck. For once, I had some.

But not for long. At least Yev had the grace to wait until I was out of the stall and at the sink before confronting me.

"What are you doing here? The truth."

"What does anybody do here?" I kept my tone light. "We've got to stop meeting like this. The guard must already think we're up to more than the ordinary bathroom routine."

Her fierce glower wavered and almost let a smile through. "Nothing is out of the ordinary here. Nothing. But tell me what you are here for. In this prison."

"Haven't my details spread through the grapevine yet? I'm here for eighteen months. Conspiracy in a drug case. I make...made my living as a stonecutter. Anything else you want to know?"

"I want," she said harshly, "to know how good a liar you may be." I'd thought her eyes were a hazel close to green, but now they were steel gray.

"Pretty damned good. I'm not hiding anything now, though. Just doing my time, staying out of trouble. No poaching on anybody's turf. Okay?"

The eyes were still hard, but there was something else in their depths, a spark that sent heat through my body somewhere decidedly south of my eyes. "Maybe you hide nothing," she said after a long pause. "But I will be watching you."

I would be watching her, too, against my better judgment. I just shrugged. The after-dinner surge swept through the door. I edged my way through it, and out.

Two weeks of learning the routines, chafing at bureaucratic injustices and avoiding the pitfalls, left me more and more bored. I spent several days sketching Miss Natalya in various moods, and a few hours each on Ellie, who chattered the whole time, and Paula, who'd begun tentatively to flirt with me, which I ignored. Some others asked for pictures to send to their boyfriends or children. The requests from a few who came on to me with more expertise than Paula—including a female guard—I politely declined.

I was going stir-crazy. Too much idleness made it hard to keep from sketching, if only in my mind, the face and body and shifting expressions of someone I saw only across the dining hall. Someone who watched me as intently as I watched her. Enemy or not, she couldn't be ignored, and something about her got through to me in ways no one had for years. I had dreams of measuring her for a portrait not with my eyes, but my hands. And my mouth.

Once in a while, I caught Yev looking at me as though she had similar thoughts about me. She'd be jovial, teasing, or stern with the girls who flocked around her, and then look up, frown as though I were some puzzle she needed to solve, and look away.

I tried to solve Yev, too. Finally, I gave in to the urge to sketch her, from memory, just quick line drawings of her jogging in place in the yard or passing along some corridor. Not in the lavatory. It turned out that her room was in a different block and she shouldn't have been in our bathroom at all. She'd been there on purpose, to harass me. Or assess me.

That's when my subconscious took charge of my fingers and told me a thing or two, not about Yev's body—I'd already noticed plenty about that—but her body language. The set of her head on those wide shoulders. Tension in the muscles of her back. She was hypervigilant, always aware of who was where, how close, who approached her. And wary of me most of all. Not about being hit on, so about...what? An actual hit? Did she think I was a hit man? If a prisoner knew somebody wanted them out of the way in case they might tell things better left buried, an inmate like me would bear watching. I wasn't sure how I felt about that. The hitting-on part had a dangerous appeal. But no. Just get through this prison thing with no complications, no drama. Detached. *Yeah, right.*

Finally being assigned to a job was a relief. Not just any job; one that would let me work outdoors, under the sky, even though brick walls still surrounded the place.

"The grounds crew?" Miss Natalya said. "Yev's the muscle on that. New inmates aren't often given clearance to work in the outer perimeter. She must have requested you."

So much for relief. Boredom, however, wouldn't be a problem. "C'mon, you know more than you've told me about Yev. What's up with her?"

"I know more about many folks than I tell, Alex. Including you. Leave it at that."

Miss Natalya was too damned perceptive.

The grounds crew assembled behind the sprawling garage. In the front section were the warden's vehicle and those of the chief correctional officers. The back part held what could have been a hundred years' worth of tools in one section and a couple of mowing machines, the sit-on kind with wings of rotary blades extending six feet or so on each side, in the other. Neither machine was less than twenty years out of date.

There were five of us on the crew, but it was clear right away that Yev, not the official CO, Mr. Haynes, was in charge. Haynes mostly left us to ourselves, staying in his office above the garage, but I'd occasionally see him gazing out the window, watching Yev. There was some weird vibe going on there. I already knew that women who had "special relationships" with guards or COs got extra perks, and I'd noticed that nobody in charge ever messed with Yev. Maybe it wasn't just because she could have tied any one of them in knots. The thought that she might have something going on with Haynes made my insides boil, for reasons I didn't want to examine too closely—even as it stoked a raging curiosity.

"McKenna!" Yev snapped that first day, after she'd set the others to sweeping the front section and trimming the token shrubbery along the sides of the building. "You know machinery?"

"Pretty well. What do you need?"

"Number one mower hit a rock, bent a blade. It must be straightened and sharpened. You can do that?"

"I'll give it a try." The challenge in her eyes was getting familiar. Either she hoped I'd fail at the job, or she was tired of wondering and decided to see what I'd do with dangerous tools in my hands. I looked along the jumbled shelves and racks lining the walls, then picked out a heavy hammer, a mallet, and an assortment of files. Yev took a set of wrenches. We weren't even allowed to take knives and forks from the dining hall to our rooms, but here we were with a potentially deadly arsenal of mostly blunt instruments. "Lead on."

I looked forward to a close rear view of those powerful haunches and thighs, and I couldn't even convince myself that sketching them was my first concern. Yev, though, had no intention of turning her back on me.

"Over there." She jerked her head toward the other room. I led the way, my own butt tingling with the sense of being watched. It didn't occur to me until we reached the mower that maybe I should be worrying about Yev's heavy metal wrench case. She might have a preemptive strike in mind.

I survived the walk, and we pushed the mower out into the sunlight. It took both of us to get the bent blade out, Yev loosening the bolts with a powerful grip on the biggest wrench, me steadying the blade and hauling it free. Seemed like as good a chance as any to get chatty.

"How come they let us use all this stuff? There were even wire cutters hanging over there. Don't you ever think about trying to escape? I guess Mr. Haynes is watching us from a distance, but still."

At the mention of his name, her grip on the wrench tightened until her knuckles went white. "They want to get plenty of work out of us." She bore down with a grunt. The rusty nut turned just a bit. "But some might feel more safe inside the walls than out." The nut moved more. She turned that steely gaze on me. "Or not."

I met her eyes squarely. "So what's out there? What's your story?"

"You don't know?"

"Miss Natalya told me to mind my own business when I asked."

She steadied the mower while I tugged at the bent blade and edged it out. "So, what is your own business?"

"I'll tell you mine if you tell me yours. I'll even go first. Just let me get this done first."

The sun was hot. I shucked my baggy prison-issue shirt and went to work with the hammer, working up a sweat that made my sleeveless undershirt cling to my torso. I trusted she appreciated the view.

When the blade was as straight as it was ever going to get, I stood up and raised the hammer. Yev tensed but didn't shrink away. I tossed it into a double flip in the air, caught it, and knelt again to work on the blade with a file.

"My business is using mallets and chisels and drills to etch words and pictures into stone, and sometimes to carve figures in bas-relief. Once in a while, I'll do freestanding figures, but I'd rather let most of the stone speak for itself."

"And how does this get you imprisoned?" The arch of

her brows indicated skepticism.

"Only very rich people can afford my work. It's not my business how they get rich. And if they want me to carve a stone garden bench that conceals the entrance to a secret vault, it's not my business what they hide in it. Having a dragon-and-treasure motif on the backrest was a bit obvious, but still, not my business. I did find out, though, and at their trial I wouldn't lie and say I hadn't known just to save my own skin, so here I am."

"No more than that?" More skepticism, though no less appreciation of my back and butt as I bent over my work.

"Not much. Except the police wanted me to tell them who else I'd done jobs for, and who else I thought might be hiding contraband. I didn't know any others for sure, so I wouldn't talk. Finally, I told the prosecutor the cops could do their own damned detective work. Which they will. And in the process they'll destroy some of my best work. They left my dragon in shards. Maybe nobody else will turn out to be guilty, but I'll never be able to work in Bar Harbor again. Or anywhere in the northeast."

"Bar Harbor?"

"Way up in Maine. Big old family mansions, some on private islands, owned now by newcomers. Mountains rising from the sea, hundreds of yachts coming and going in the harbor...so much space, and sky..." My arm slowed. I looked up at the brick walls, then quickly down. "I'll miss it."

A big hand touched my shoulder gently, then not so gently. For an instant a fierce current of magnetism flowed between us. When Yev snatched her hand back, my skin ached with the loss of that heat.

I tossed aside the file. "Now for your story. I showed you mine. You show me yours." I lay back on the grass, propped up by my elbows.

She leaned against the riding rig of the mower. "Fair enough." For a second, she reached down. I thought she was going to shed her shirt as I had, but she looked slantwise up toward the window of CO Haynes's office and changed her mind, instead rolling up her sleeves as far as they'd go. I could tell that beneath the shirt she wore a binder that couldn't quite conceal the swell of full breasts. I had too little in that department to bother binding, but enough to make a sweaty undershirt interesting. The fact was not lost on Yev. And, possibly, CO Haynes.

"I, too, would not speak at my trial. I have family yet in Chechnya...if indeed they still live." She was silent for a moment or two. "There was a time, long ago, when I imagined a different life. Just need a little while, I thought, to save up money. But to work as bodyguard to a Chechen drug lord is a road to nowhere but destruction, even in America. He enjoyed humiliating men by having a woman rough them up. For a few, who liked very much to have a woman rough them up, he used me as a reward—and then blackmailed them. If I tried to get out..." She shrugged. "Now he is dead, but I could tell more than is known, and there are men still free who would pay much to have me dead as well."

I nodded. Yev's level gaze acknowledged our mutual attraction without diminishing her suspicion one bit. I gave it a try anyway. "If somebody put out a contract to get rid of you in prison, wouldn't a cute young femme be the natural choice? Plenty of them manage to get close to you. A blade between the ribs or a contrived accident wouldn't take much muscle."

"Pah! Those children. Them, I can read. If not, they do not get close. But you...either you tell the truth, or you are very, very good at what you do."

"Why not both?" My wry grin coaxed one from her. I turned back to the mower. "Come on, let's get this rust monster put back together."

Crouching together, conscious of being watched from above, we worked quickly, not touching, not needing touch to feel each other's heat.

"Yev?" One of the crew members peered around the corner of the garage. "Fifteen minutes until count!"

"Go, then. Shoo, shoo." She waved an arm. "You, too." Yev could probably get away with not being in her assigned room for the thrice-daily count by the guards, but I couldn't. Her big hand gripped my ass hard before shoving me in the direction the others had gone. I let her get away with it. Anyone else would have had that wrist in a sling for at least a month.

At dinner we kept to our opposite sides of the dining hall, casting the usual enigmatic glances at each other. A shadow of a knowing smile drifted across Miss Natalya's face.

The next day, Yev and I mowed, while the others trimmed the hedges along the drive. I stopped and got off at the rock that had bent the blade. "No digging out this one. There's a whole lot more of it down there, like an iceberg. Was it sticking up this much last year?"

"A little more each year I have been here." She saw the question on my face. "Three years. Six more to go."

"By then, they might as well just make a rock garden here and stick some kind of plaque on this."

"You could kindly offer to carve words into it. Fine lines about the greatness of prisons."

"I could do a wreath made of coils of razor wire around the edges. And in the middle...hmmm...there's a verse I inscribed on a marble mantelpiece, for a rich guy's bedroom. Lines from an old poet, Andrew Marvell. They've been on my mind lately." I paused for dramatic effect.

"So tell!"

I basked in Yev's impatience as I sat on the newly-mown grass. And I told:

> *"Let us roll all our strength and all*
> *Our sweetness up into one ball,*
> *And tear our pleasures with rough strife,*
> *Through the iron gates of life."*

The words hung between us. "Is that how you like your pleasures, McKenna?" Yev said at last. "With 'rough strife'?"

Something about her expression told me to tread carefully. A hot, sweaty bout of rough strife with Yev had certainly been on my mind, but I remembered how her old boss had pimped her skills. And what about her new boss, if Haynes could be called that?

"It depends," I said, glancing back toward his office window, but it was out of sight around a corner.

"It does." Yev slumped to the grass beside me. "Sometimes..." Her voice was so low I could scarcely hear it. "Sometimes one does things to protect others." She jerked her head back toward where I'd looked. "Yes, he found out, somehow, and wanted some of that for himself. Humiliation, punishment, the usual. But he has a wife and cannot afford visible injuries, so he asks for other things. And, of course, he provides his own...implements."

"Pegging?" Even as I said the word I was trying to shake that image of Haynes out of my mind.

Her laugh was harsh and abrupt. "There is a better word for that in Russian. But yes." She shrugged. "The hardest part is not leaving bruises, or more, on him. But he leaves others alone and does all he can get away with to please me, for the moment. No more need be said."

She stood and climbed back up on the mower. "But what about you, McKenna? Alex, the girls call you when they speak of you, which is often. You did not give me much of an answer. It depends on what?"

"On being equally matched," I said. "Strength for strength."

Her wide grin was wolfish now, and genuine. "Perhaps I should have mentioned my silver medal in Olympic wrestling."

"Thanks for the warning." I looked her over. "I'd sure like to meet whoever won the gold."

"Ah, Anneliese!" Yev rolled her eyes in remembered bliss. "We still correspond. Even here she sends me letters now and again. Who knows? Maybe someday you will have the pleasure of meeting her. She lives in Norway. Where mountains also rise out of the sea." Her mower sputtered into life, and she drove away.

By the time I caught up we were back at the garage and I had to bolt for the damned count.

The next day, it rained. Thunder rumbled in the distance. The grounds crew worked inside the garage, washing and polishing the vehicles. Yev roamed restlessly between the front section and the back while I worked with the others, chatting and joking. A burst of general laughter brought her, frowning, until she saw the elaborate dragon I'd drawn in streaks of polish along the side of the warden's black car.

"Write something under it," one girl said.

Yev made an effort to lighten up. "Just do not scratch it into the finish."

"How about 'Puff, the Magic Dragon?'" somebody piped up.

Yev nearly smiled, but got back to business. "How about 'Puff the Disappearing Dragon?' All this must be cleaned up before count time. Go as soon as you finish. The storm is coming closer. You, McKenna, stay to chip rust off some of the tools out here."

In the back, she bolted the connecting door and resumed pacing while I dutifully chipped away at rust and filed dull edges. A paint-streaked tarpaulin heaped in a corner caught my eye. I filed it in my mind for future reference.

"You look like a caged lioness," I said after a while. "That marble mantelpiece I told you about had a lioness crouched above the poem, looking ready to spring." If she didn't spring pretty damned soon, I would. The thunder grew ever louder, heightening the sense of urgency.

Yev didn't spring, exactly, just took one long stride. "So, you like your pleasures with rough strife?" Her growl vibrated into my ear, no distance at all between us now, bodies moving against each other slowly to savor the rising heat of friction. Her arms wrapped around me, mine around her, grasping each other's butts, pressing into each other—but I raised my hands and bent my torso back just enough to yank my shirt off first. I hadn't bothered with an undershirt.

"Nothing up my sleeves." I gasped. "But you'd better make sure I'm not hiding anything down below."

Instead of pulling my pants down, she tightened her grip, lifted me off my feet, and shoved me up against the locked door. Her knee came up between my legs, supporting my weight, while she gripped and squeezed and probed every inch of my hips and thighs. Visions of magnificent bruises flitted briefly though my head, vanishing in the urgent need to feel more of her. I rode her knee, bent my head to bite along her shoulder through her shirt, then lower, respecting her binder, yet coming back again and again to leave damp spots with my tongue where I knew her nipples were swelling into soreness.

When, for balance, I had to grab Yev's shoulders, her own mouth got busy with my breasts, telegraphing more and more wild need into my cunt, until I pushed off, landed on my feet, and got my fingers inside her waistband. "Fuck rough strife!" I panted. "Just...just fuck!"

Yev was panting, too, and maybe swearing—some of it was in Russian, some didn't sound like words at all. With a twist of my body that she could easily have countered, but didn't, I got her to the tarp and we dropped down onto it, rolling over and over each other for the sheer joy of it. Knees, hands, mouths pressed into whatever warm hollows they found until the need for more focused intensity overwhelmed us.

Yev pulled my pants down and off with expert speed while I was still fumbling with hers. I gave up the attempt, lay back, and let myself be swept along by her mouth working hard at my clit and her big fingers demanding more and more space inside me. My hips arched upward for even deeper penetration. I clutched at her short hair, trying to tug her head down harder against me, but she refused to be forced past the point where her tongue could move freely. She kept my desperate need mounting and swelling until my screams of frustration surged into incoherent cries of pleasure. Only in the afterglow did I realize that the full force of the storm had just passed over us, and Yev had perfectly orchestrated my climax to match the fiercest blasts of thunder.

When I had enough breath, and some control of my body, I rolled on top of her, streaking her bare thighs with my wetness as I slid between her legs. I couldn't remember how her pants had come off, and didn't care as long as I could get into her musky heat to torment her for at least as long as she had done it to me.

But Yev wouldn't let me get away with that. Her powerful scent and taste demanded more than teasing licks, and the hands pressing my head hard against her were too strong to resist. I managed to make room for my own hand to work deeply into her heat, and set up a pounding rhythm of thrusts.

Sounds more growls than moans rumbled from Yev's throat. Her walls clenched harder and harder around my fingers, her strong thighs gripped me until it hurt and her hips bucked so fiercely that I had to brace myself to stay with her. I managed to hang on, not easing up, riding her peak as growls became one long, rising howl, then descended gradually through harsh gasps to mere panting. By that time my head was pillowed on her belly, rising and falling with every deep breath. When I couldn't resist any longer and moved my lips across her sweaty skin, over her binder, and up into the hollow of her throat, I felt as well as heard the words she muttered low in Russian, then English.

"So long...such a long damned time..."

I knew exactly what she meant. It had been a long time since I, too, had opened up to sex this intense. And it wasn't over yet. With very little rest we worked each other into another burst of glorious spasms, and then, taking my time, I stroked and nibbled and licked her to yet another, only slightly more gentle. The sounds she made were enough to give me aftershocks.

We lay there, nearly comatose, until I said, "We've missed count. How screwed are we?"

"Maybe a lot, maybe a little. So what?" She was quiet then for so long that I thought she was asleep, until she opened her eyes and grinned at me, more wolf than lion now. A supremely satisfied wolf. "You have not quite managed to kill me yet, although you came close. I have decided what you must carve on my tombstone, just in case. Yevgeny Yevtushenko, now there's a poet!" The lines she recited in Russian meant nothing to me, though the resonance of her voice stirred both my mind and body. Then she translated, stumbling over a word or two:

"Sorrow happens. Hardship happens. The hell with it, who never knew the price of happiness, will not be happy."

"Carve it in Russian," she said cheerfully. "There are better words for everything in Russian."

It felt just then as if words in Russian, whether I understood them or not, would forever zap me with surges of lust. How could I argue with that?

Sgt. Rae

Sgt. Rae was so strong she could carry me at a run through gunfire and smoke and exploding mines. Two years later, she's that strong again. With just one hand, she can keep me from getting away, no matter how hard I struggle. Even her voice is enough to stop me at a dead run, so it doesn't matter that she can't run anymore. And anyway, I'd never want to run away.

I'm smaller, but I've got my own kind of muscle, even if it doesn't show. A mechanic in an armored tank unit has to be strong just to handle the tools you need, and if you're a woman doing the job, you need a whole extra layer of strength. I'm not an army mechanic anymore, but I can still use tools. Sgt. Rae isn't an army Sgt. anymore, but she'll always be in charge. At the town hall where she's the police and fire department dispatcher, they tell me she's got the whole place organized like it's never been before.

In our house, or in the town, I'm supposed to just call her Rae these days, and mostly I remember. I'm just Jenny. In the bedroom, we don't need names at all, except to wake each other when the bad dreams come, and whisper that everything's all right now. Or so close to all right that we can handle it, as long as we're together.

Out here, though, on this trail I've made through the woods and across the stream, we play by my rules, and that means I'm Specialist 2nd Brown and she's the ball-buster Staff Sergeant, even though neither of us has any use for balls.

She'll be coming along the trail behind me any minute, coming to see what new contraption I've constructed. What she expects is something like the exercise stations I've built for her in every room in the house, chinning bars and railings and handgrips at different levels, and in a way that's right, but with a different twist. She expects I'll want her to order me to drop and do fifty push-ups or sit-ups, or run in place until I'm panting, but this time I want something else.

I check the gears and pulleys one more time, even though I already know the tension is set right. It's my own tension that's nearly out of control. The posts and crossbars are rock-solid, while I'm shaking in my old fatigues, so nervous and horny that I can't even tell which is which.

I hear the motor now. I could've made it run quieter, but if you've been where I've been, where we've both been, you want to be sure you know who's coming around the bend.

She's crossed the rocky ford in the stream where no regular wheelchair could have gone. I salvaged tracks from old snowmobiles at the repair shop where I work, and they're as good as any armored tank tracks, even though they're made of Kevlar instead of steel. Fine for this terrain, and even the steel kind got chewed up in the desert sand in Iraq.

Mustn't think about the desert now. Here in New Hampshire, green leaves overhead are beginning to turn orange and red. This stream flows into a river just beyond our house, and we can watch canoes and kayaks pass by—no desert in sight. This is home. We're together. Safe. Except that safe isn't always enough, when you've known—had to know—so much more.

Now I hear Sgt. Rae veering back and forth through the obstacle course, steering the mini-tank around trees, stumps, boulders, right over small logs. With a double set of the tracks on each side, the only way to steer is by slowing one side while accelerating the other, and that takes strength. I think of her big hands on the levers, the bunched muscles of her arms and shoulders, even stronger now than in the army because she insists on a manually powered chair anywhere but in these woods. Gloves help, but her hands get calloused from turning the wheels. Calloused, and rough, even when she tries to be gentle... Anticipation pounds through my body.

I kneel on the ground, close my eyes, try to clear my mind—but on the distant bridge over the river, a truck backfires, and in spite of the leafy dampness, the desert flashes around me again, the clouds of dust, the explosions, the machine-gun fire on that final day. I think of Sgt. Rae's powerful voice, how it cut through the pain and confusion and kept me breathing when I didn't think I could last another second.

"Brown!" she bellowed, again and again, coming closer to where the shattered truck cab trapped me. "Brown, damn you, report!" That sound gripped me, forced strength into me, so that I moved, just a little, no matter how much it hurt, and she found me.

I never remember what happened next. I don't think Sgt. Rae does, either, but somebody told me later they found a bent assault rifle barrel nearby, and maybe she levered the truck cab up enough with that to drag me out. I just remember being slung over her shoulder, feeling her run and swerve and run some more, and hearing her voice drilling right through to my heart in a tone I'd never heard before. "Jenny, Jenny...hang on..."

Right then, with bullets still screaming around us, it was like I'd died and woke up to a new world. Ever since the day we met, Sgt. Rae had mesmerized me, obsessed me, and I'd worked to hide my foolish longings behind hard work and casual jokes and chatter. But in that moment, as her strong voice shook, a window opened in the midst of hell and gave me a glimpse of a heaven better than anything they'd ever preached about in church.

I passed out when she set me down behind a sand bunker some of our guys had piled up in a hurry. Maybe I heard somebody say another soldier was still out there, or maybe I just heard later how she went back into that hell. Either way, I know she went.

It was a month before I saw Sgt. Rae again. I was still bandaged, but up and walking. She wasn't. At first, when I stood beside the hospital bed, I wondered whether she was really there at all, inside, until she saw me.

"Jenny?"

I could scarcely hear the word. But then strength came back into her voice, and the power I'd always felt surrounding her was there again, as though a light had been switched on. "Specialist Brown, report!"

So I did, listing my injuries and treatments and recovery, even though her half-smile softened the formal order. Later, when she'd had her meds and fallen asleep, I pumped the nurses about her injuries and prognosis, and from that day I was never away from her for more than a few hours. There were some rough parts, and sometimes I had to be the strong one to get her through. A nurse or two caught on that there was more to it than just that she'd saved my life, but they never made any fuss. It helped that I could fix mechanical glitches in the orthopedic ward's equipment, and even make some things work better than originally designed. I think somewhere along the line, they claimed me as an adjunct physical therapy technician.

The dampness of the ground soaking through my jeans brings me back to the present. Sgt. Rae is coming around the clump of hemlock saplings. It's time, and now I'm ready, in position, on my knees, hands clasped high above my head, ropes wrapped around my wrists, head bowed.

"Brown!"

I can't salute in this position, but I try to sound as though I were doing it. "Sergeant, yes, Sergeant!"

"What do you think you're doing, Brown?"

"Sergeant, I'm kneeling, Sergeant."

"I can see that. But do you know what you're doing?"

Without looking, I can tell she's surveying the situation. A pair of leather-wrapped rings hangs right where she can stretch up and reach them. The system of gears and pulleys is rigged to offer just the right amount of resistance and stability for her to pull herself to a standing position, brace with forearms at chest level on a crossbar, and then lower her weight slowly back down. Three of the doorways in our house have similar setups, but this one is more complex—and in this one, the counterweight is me.

"Sergeant, yes, Sergeant, I do know what I'm doing."

There's the slightest of creaks as she begins to rise. The ropes tighten, and I rise, too, until I'm dangling in the air, helpless—or as helpless as I can make myself seem. My wrists are padded just enough to keep the circulation from being cut off. I could thrash, and kick—I fought off rape a time or two in the army, before I got to Sgt. Rae's squad, where you'd better believe no woman ever had to fear attack by fellow soldiers—but now I'm sinking into sub space, wide open, vulnerable.

"What's got into you, Specialist? What do you think you want?"

She knows, of course. By now we know almost everything about each other. My face is level with hers, a rare treat, and I try to focus on her features through my fog of obsession. The hair that was mostly dark two years ago is more salt than pepper now, and brush-cut even shorter. There are lines around her eyes from more than the desert sun. The squareness of her face, so like her father's in the picture I've seen, is softened just enough by the graceful curve of her cheeks that I want to stroke it with my fingers and then my tongue, if I could only earn that privilege.

Sgt. Rae shifts so that her weight is mostly on the crossbar and slides one hand free of its ring. "Speak up, Brown!" She grabs my brown ponytail, yanks me close, and then shoves me away so that I spin one way and then the other as the ropes twist, untwist, and twist again. When I sway close enough she swats me across my ass, or as close as she can reach, and I feel it all the way from my buttcheeks down between my thighs. She does it again, and then again, until the heat flows so deep inside me I think I might explode.

With all her weight on the crossbar through her chest and armpits, she reaches out to grip me by the shoulders, hard, hurting me just the way I like it. Then her big hands slide under my armpits so she's partly holding me up. My upstretched arms raise my small breasts. She rubs her thumbs across my nipples so hard and fast they must be standing out like bullets, and when she pinches them, sharp pangs of pleasure shoot down through my belly.

She knows where the worst of my scars are, and works around them down my sides and ribs, trying not to be too rough even when I squirm and squeal and try to get even harder pressure from her fingers. I'm not silent any longer. It doesn't matter how I sound, what's pain and what's pleasure. All that matters is getting more and more.

Sgt. Rae's the one who has to use her safe word first. "At

ease, Brown!" She grips the rings again and sinks slowly back into her chair.

My feet touch the ground. My arms drop, and I loosen the rope loops with my teeth, getting free just in time for her next order.

"Get over here, Jenny, stat!"

So I leap to straddle her lap, and she lifts me tight against her shoulder, right where I belong. Her free hand kneads my butt hard enough to make my crotch grind into her. I could come from that alone, but she needs more, more of my skin and heat and wetness, so she gets my pants down and sighs approval when I'm slippery enough for her calloused fingers to move easily between my folds. Back and forth, teasing, pressing deeper, a knuckle nudging my clit on each forward stroke. I want it all now, now! But I have to wait for her to drive me even harder, higher. This isn't just for me.

"Now." Rae's voice is strained. "Feel it. For both of us." I'm rocking with her thrusts, howling with need, taking everything she can fit inside me, and when the pleasure bursts through all control, I shout my joy to the treetops loud enough for two hearts, two bodies.

She holds me tight while my breathing slows toward normal. When I raise my head I see a tear trickling down her cheek. This doesn't scare me the way it used to. I've figured out that it's her own release of tension after she's made me feel what she can't feel anymore except through me. Being strong when that's what I need makes it safe to be vulnerable afterward. Besides, now's my chance to lick the tear away, kiss my way all across the face I love, ending with the lips that say more this way than words ever could.

Rae sets me gently away sooner, though, than usual. "Jenny, there's something... Well, something that needs saying."

Now I'm scared. Hasn't everything already been said?

"You gave me back my life," she says, and pauses to search for the right words. "And I know you think I saved yours. So, you could say there's no owing anything on either side."

I couldn't say that at all, so I just look at her. She sees my expression, and strokes my face with such tenderness that fear melts away.

"I didn't mean... It's just that whatever we do, it's by choice. Maggie Burnside stopped by my desk today and asked, out of the blue, when we were going to get around to making things legal."

"Maggie the town clerk? Old Maggie Graniteside?"

"She's not so bad when you get to know her. And I guess she's come around to thinking we're not so bad, either. Or maybe she's decided to catch up with the twenty-first century without being dragged there."

"So, what did you tell her?" I snuggle back against her side.

"I said the piece of paper might be nice to have, but it couldn't make us any closer, so I'd just go home and ask my wife."

"We might as well humor her, then. Set a good example."

There'll be more to say later, and plenty of time to say it. Now, the afterglow of lovemaking intensified by the vibrating hum of the motor, we don't need words at all, as the mini-tank I built carries Sgt. Rae, and Sgt. Rae carries me home.

The Pirate from the Sky

In Seok-Teng's dream, a great pale dragon twined through a labyrinth of shifting clouds. Opaline scales shimmered through intervals of sunlight, slipped into invisibility, then flashed out again in dazzling beauty. Its long, elegant head swung from side to side, tongue flickering like sensuous lightning.

A distant hum arose, a subtle, tantalizing vibration that teased at Seok-Teng's mind and flesh. A song? A warning? A summons? In all her dreams of dragons, never had she been aware of sound. She strained to hear, to understand. But the hum became steadily louder, swelling to a growl, tearing her from sleep into darkness and sudden, stark awareness. If the roof of her captain's cabin had been high enough she would have bolted upright.

Still the sound grew. This was no dragon, nor yet thunder, nor storm winds. The sea spoke to Seok-Teng through the ship's movements as it had to her forebears for generations beyond counting. Tonight it gave no cause for alarm. Japanese patrol boats? She had taken her crew far enough out of the usual shipping channels to avoid such pursuit. No, she had come to know that sound all too well. This one was different—yet not entirely unknown.

The cabin's entrance showed scarcely lighter than its interior. Now it darkened. Han Duan, the ship's Number One, squatted to look within.

"An aircraft," Seok-Teng called, before the other could speak.

Han Duan grunted in agreement. "Not large, but low, and coming close. Who would fly so far from any land?"

"It is nothing to do with us." Seok-Teng wished to resume the dream. She wished also to avoid resuming discussion of why a pirate ship would sail so far from any land, when it was accustomed by tradition to plying the coasts along the South China Sea.

"The Japanese have many planes," Han Duan said.

"And better uses for them than pursuing us this far. We are very small fish indeed." That was a tactical error, Seok-Teng realized at once. Evading a Japanese navy angered by the plundering of several small merchant ships off Mindanao had been her stated excuse for sailing so far to the east.

The small islands and atolls of the Marianas and Marshall groups were technically under Japanese control, but surely the eye of Nippon was bent too fiercely on the conquest of China to pay much attention to every far-flung spit of sand. On some of those islets distant relatives from Seok-Teng's many-branched heritage still lived, and on others, there were no permanent habitations at all. Good places for her crew to find or build a refuge while the world at large descended into war and madness—if a refuge was what they truly wanted.

She herself was torn by the desire to take part in the battle, to join forces with China's defenders, as pirates in the past had often done. In her small packet of private belongings was a photograph, cut from a newspaper, of Soong Mai-Ling, the beautiful wife of Generalissimo Chiang Kai-shek and a leader in her own right. Seok-Teng longed to serve her in some fashion, but the way was not clear. The old pirate practices might suffice for the harrying of merchant ships, but the modern military craft of the Japanese were another matter.

Han Duan grunted again and stood, with just enough of a stoop to clear the low roof. The plane was nearly overhead now. Seok-Teng slid a hand under her pillow, ran a finger delicately along the undulating blade of her *kris*, then gripped its hilt. Both blade and hilt were warm. The dream, then, had been no accident, but a promise—or a warning. Seok-Teng would have spoken to the dagger if her Number One had not been present. Instead, she rolled from her bed into a crouch, pressed her brow to the weapon in mute homage to the ancestors from whom it had come, and, still stooping, emerged onto the deck of the *She-Dragon*.

Han Duan's head tilted back as she stared upward. Seok-Teng straightened and stepped to the rail. Along the eastern horizon lay a faint hint that day would come, but overhead, a low, sullen cloud cover obscured the stars. The airplane, now directly above them, could not be seen, though its roar seemed so tangible that Seok-Teng raised her hand, whether to grasp or fend it off she did not know.

She had even forgotten that she held the *kris*, which now pointed into the sky.

"Would your demon blade lead us now even into the heavens? Let it fly, then, by itself!" Han Duan raised her voice to be heard over the noise of the plane. Her scarred face seemed demonic in the light of a single swaying lantern.

The eight crewmembers with their bedrolls on deck, already roused by the turmoil, watched this drama with great interest. More heads emerged from the hatchway, jostling for a view. Some couples preferred the privacy of the hold for their sleep or other nocturnal pursuits, but they were still alert for any excitement from above.

Seok-Teng allowed her arm to descend very slowly, while the blade pointed ever toward the unseen aircraft moving away into the distance. Her tone was harsh as steel on steel. "Has my *kris* ever led us to less than a rich prize?"

"Not yet." Han Duan's fierce expression relaxed into a wry grin, defusing the conflict. "And if you can contrive to fly after this target, then so can I. So can we all. Just as soon as you leap aloft and lead the way." A few muffled laughs came from the bedrolls. She leaned closer to Seok-Teng and spoke in a lower tone. "But your demon has always led us to women, as well as treasure, to be restored to their families or taken into the crew. You will find no woman in a ship of the air."

"Who knows? Many would be even more certain that a pirate ship could not be crewed by women." Seok-Teng's hand dropped to her side, but still she gazed into the eastern sky.

"Well, what will come, will come," Han Duan said. "For now, that craft has passed beyond our reach. Perhaps we will yet come upon it crashed onto a coral reef, laden with gold and gems and a princess worth a great ransom. Enough even to buy our peace with Madame Lai Choi San."

Seok-Teng frowned. A subtle motion of her head led the other to follow her back into the cramped cabin, where they reclined on woven floor mats. Whatever speculations might entertain the crew, these days the two old shipmates shared the low bed only during the fevered revels that followed each successful—and profitable—raid. Too long an interval since the previous occasion might well have something to do with the tension that had shortened tempers in recent days. Han Duan had many an eager outlet for her energies among the crew, when she chose, but Seok-Teng's authority as captain of the *She-Dragon* depended on a degree of aloofness. Beyond that was an unspoken truth between them. Only in each other could their deepest needs be met.

"With enough booty, our crew, and even you, might purchase old Mountain of Wealth's pardon," Seok-Teng said, "but no treasure will ever cause her to let me live. More passed between us than I have told, though you may well guess. Better that our youngsters do not know how fiercely her hatred of me burns. They have seen Japanese soldiers only from a distance. The fury of the Dragon Lady of Bias Bay is far more real to them."

Han Duan drew a long breath and blew it out slowly.

"So, it is not only the Japanese we flee. I thought as much, though not that you had fallen from Madame's favor so far that gold could not pave the way back."

They sat in silence, both thinking of the woman they had served. Lai Choi San ruled the most powerful pirate fleet in Macao with an iron hand untempered by any velvet glove. Most of her wealth came from "protection" schemes and ransomed captives, who, if their families were slow to pay, would return with fingers or ears missing, but her influence extended far beyond the coasts of Hong Kong and Guangzhou.

Smaller fleets and individual ships in which she held a share cruised as far as the coast of Vietnam to the southwest and Luzon in the Philippines to the southeast, sending her tribute and perpetual interest on her investments. One of these had captured the young Seok-Teng in her own small smuggler's boat on the waters of Vinh Ha Long, Bay of the Descending Dragon, where China gives way to Vietnam. The girl had fought so valiantly and viciously, and her beauty had been of so a fierce a nature, that a wise captain had seen in her a value beyond the ordinary, and taken her to Macao to offer to Lai Choi San herself. He had even presented her captured *kris* along with her, knowing well that the spirits with which such blades were imbued could bring luck only to their rightful owners and fatal misfortune to others.

Seok-Teng sighed, wishing she had not been reminded of those times. She had, indeed, risen high in Madame's favor. For several years, she had served as one of two *amahs*, companions and bodyguards to their pirate mistress. There had been rare moments of kindness, and much education in the ways of pirating, as well as occasional instruction in service of a more intimate nature. And there had been Han Duan, who had come to the same position by a different route, passing as a man for years on the Macao waterfront until one day she overheard plotting among rival pirates and came before Lai Choi San to warn her.

"Duan, old friend, why did you follow me?"

In the dimness, only shapes and movements could be discerned. Han Duan's bowed head would have hidden her expression in any case. Seok-Teng pushed on.

"Madame would have given you your own ship, with the pick of captured women to sail her. Indeed, this entire crew would have joined you, given the option. Or she would have given you the management of her fan-tan casinos in Macao. I know she offered."

Lai Choi San had been practical enough to know when her strong-willed *amahs* had reached the limits of service to a domineering mistress. She had agreed to finance a ship for Seok-Teng, crewed by captured women who had experience on fishing boats, and were in any case too unattractive or combative to be sold to the floating brothels. As long as enough profit came her way, what did it matter whose pillaging had procured it? Besides, it amused her at times to pit the female pirates against men she wished to humiliate. This aspect of their duties had not, however, amused Seok-Teng, and had driven her to range farther and farther until her ship had become independent in all but the payment of more than adequate tribute.

Even that had come to an end. There was no going back to Bias Bay and Macao now, or to any waters under the influence of the Dragon Lady, after the last bitter clash of wills. Seok-Teng would no longer be a party to the sale of captured women into slavery. Far to the east now, beyond the Philippines, the Marianas, and nearly to the Marshall Islands, Seok-Teng had no regrets save that her closest friend might have done better to stay behind.

Han Duan looked up with a grin, and the early rays of dawn through the cabin's entrance glinted on white teeth. "How could I leave my guns and cannons to your bumbling care? No one alive knows the ways of ships and the sea as you do, but when it comes to any weapon beyond a blade, you might as well be gambling at fan-tan yourself." Then she sobered, glancing sidelong at the ancient *kris* lying on Seok-Teng's pillow. "Yet I would follow you even without the guns. Yes, even though you steer by dreams sent through a blade. Such a captain might be thought to traffic with demons or djinns."

"Or to be insane?"

Han Duan shrugged. "Nearly as dangerous." She looked past Seok-Teng to the cabin door. A sleek young girl had just knelt to set down a tray with the morning meal, tea and bowls of rice flavored with dried cuttlefish. Her long wet hair was evidence of an early swim.

"Thank you, Amihan," Han Duan said formally. The girl ducked her head and backed away, smooth cheeks flushed with more than reflected sunrise. A sidelong glance at her captain as she left deepened her rosy glow.

"So you've had the pair now?" Seok-Teng was glad of the diversion. "Dalisay was blushing last week, I noticed."

Han Duan considered it one of her duties to "initiate" any new recruit who was receptive to such things. Not until they had become accustomed to their surroundings, and none more than once, to avoid an appearance of favoritism that would interfere with discipline, but it had become a tradition. Even those who were at first not so inclined often came to indicate an interest, even if only out of curiosity or communal sentiment, and none seemed disappointed when they emerged from her closet-sized cabin in the bow of the hold.

"I do not fault your blade's taste in women," Han Duan conceded, though Seok-Teng knew that her friend did not believe that their good fortune in finding crewmembers was truly due to the influence of the *kris*. The pair of young pearl divers from the Sulu Islands between Borneo and Mindanao had been fleeing their slavemaster, and the trader's ship on which they had stowed away and been enslaved again was, after all, a natural target for a pirate ship. Its cargo of pearls had been well worth taking. The sacks of rice and coffee and cacao beans among which the jewels had been hidden would have their uses, as well, if the pirates had need of passing for legitimate traders.

Still, it had been Seok-Teng who set that exact course, and Seok-Teng's *kris* had shown her the way. In that dream, a pair of small, lithe dragons, the blue-green of shallow tropical seas, had twined about each other in a wheel like the yin and yang, spinning through the sky toward a point farther south on the horizon than she had intended to steer.

How Amihan and Dalisay would perform in battle was yet unknown, but they had taken at once to life on the pirate ship. Both learned quickly to race up the lines and masts to tend the great ribbed sails, and often amused themselves by diving from those high perches down into the ocean. There they frolicked like merry dolphins and, when commanded, swam beneath the ship to assess the state of its hull. At all other times they moved about the deck nearly as closely entwined as in the dream, and even more closely pressed together in their shared bedroll.

"I was surprised that you did not have them both together, for variety," Seok-Teng said between mouthfuls of rice.

"Variety is the enemy of order," Han Duan answered with mock sternness. "You as captain should understand the importance of unvarying ritual. Not," she admitted, "that I wasn't tempted, but the girls needed to learn that they could not always cling to one another, and besides, that tiny rathole of mine can barely hold two bodies at once, the more so if both are breathing heavily."

Not for the first time, Seok-Teng felt a pang of regret

for her vow of abstinence when it came to her crew members. Any of them would be more than willing; the new pair clearly idolized her. She fought down visions of smooth young bodies writhing in pleasure, then returning the joy with sweet mouths and slender hands. Even harder to suppress was the remembrance of Han Duan's strong, skilled fingers, her skin with the taste of salt and sun and gunpowder, and the acquisition of bruises to be savored for many days.

No. It was necessary to maintain authority and a mystique of infallibility. Even with Han Duan, Seok-Teng's defenses against vulnerability could not be easily breached, and never when the *kris* drove her onward to conquests yet unclear.

Suddenly both young girls were kneeling in the doorway, struggling, in their excitement, to speak as one.

Authority took clear priority over desire. "Silence!" Seok-Teng barked. "You, Dalisay, begin again."

The taller girl blurted out a few words. "Ship...far..." And then, at a stern look from Han Duan, touched her forehead to the deck, straightened, and drew a deep breath. They had been quick to pick up the pidgin language in use on the ship, a blend of all the tongues of the South China Sea and some from beyond, but it was not yet second nature to them.

"Captain, ma'am, Gu Yasha has sent to inform you that a ship of the air is in sight, far to the east."

"Return to Gu Yasha and tell her that we will come at once. Go now!"

They went, tugging each other along. Seok-Teng, after thrusting her *kris* into its ebony scabbard and swiftly buckling it to her belt, followed just far enough behind to maintain her dignity. Han Duan, half a step back, muttered, "It takes no dream for me to foresee the day when the skies will be as crowded with vessels as the seas."

Gu Yasha stood at the prow, shading her eyes with a hand as she stared just to the north of the newly risen sun. Without turning she pointed toward a silver glint barely large enough to be recognized as flashing from the wing of an airplane. "The craft was flying toward us when the lookout spied it, but now it has turned slightly southwest."

Born far inland, north of Hangzhou, Gu Yasha had learned the ways of water on the great Yellow River, which took her at last to the sea. Like Han Duan, she had passed as a man on many waterfronts and coastal barges. Her dragon, in Seok-Teng's dream, had been a golden amber, and she was worth more than her weight in that precious resin. Tallest and strongest of the crew, she drilled the others in battle skills and was leader of any boarding party.

"See, Captain, it veers again southward. When it has passed beyond the glare of the sun, we may know its course better, but I do not think it will fly any closer to us."

There was no reason that it should, and no cause to connect this sighting with the cloud-muffled craft that had come so close in the night. As Han Duan had said, airplanes would soon become more common over great stretches of ocean, and it was not impossible that even the small islands in the Marshall group could have a landing strip or two now. If so, it would be Japanese planes that used them.

Seok-Teng felt a hollow pit of misgiving in her gut, and fear for the crew who had followed her so faithfully and so far. They had been offered a chance to stay behind, and bounty enough to lead independent lives, but only a few had chosen that course.

She sent the others about their business, directing Gu Yasha to keep the ship on its eastern course, then stood for long minutes at the bow watching the tiny distant arrow through her spyglass. Gradually it banked due south, and southeast, in a great curve, as though inscribing a circle in the sky. When the heading reached due east, the plane's profile was too narrow to be seen at all, as though it had blinked out of existence.

It could not be the same airplane. And yet Seok-Teng was certain that it was.

Han Duan came up behind her. "They search for something, those in that sky craft. Or perhaps they are lost."

Seok-Teng said nothing. Her hand was on the scabbard, and she could feel the spirit of the *kris* emanating from within. Han Duan waited a few moments. Finally, as though she had never expressed a single doubt, she said, "The finding of this one will be a far different adventure than any we have yet seen. Perhaps variety does have its virtues, after all."

Even the fastest sailing ship must journey at the will of the winds and the seas. They could never overtake that sleek silver machine with its roaring engines, not if it continued to fly. And if it did not continue…well, nothing yet devised by men could long withstand the will of earth's gravity. The plane would either land on some island of coral and sand, or crash, possibly into the sea. Without the continued stirring of the spirit in the *kris*, Seok-Teng would have given up hope. But she did not give up, and Han Duan did not try to dissuade her.

They sailed steadily eastward and then a few degrees to the northeast, plotting their position when possible from the stars by night and the sun by day. The same vessel that had carried the young pearl divers had provided two other treasures nearly as valuable—a modern compass, though Seok-Teng would not rely wholly on such an instrument, and a set of charts more extensive than any she had been able to procure in the South China Sea. Such storms as they encountered were centered to the north or south, affecting them only lightly, yet were violent enough in the distance that if the need arose they could plausibly be blamed for blowing the ship off course unusually far to the east.

In the ten days that followed the crew worked through their daily routine with an added pitch of excitement. The captain had a new goal. There would be adventure and riches ahead. Even those who still doubted the existence of land so far to the east did not doubt their captain's unerring instinct for prizes. If it were steered by a demon blade, all the better and more certain.

Any tedium to the voyage was dispelled by the antics of Amihan and Dalisay. The young pearl divers had set their sights on Gu Yasha, since the captain was clearly out of reach, and her Number One had made it plain that they would get no more special attention from that quarter. Gu Yasha, the next in authority, and the tallest woman they had ever seen, was a most worthy and intriguing object of desire. Gu Yasha, known to restrict such recreation to stays in port, played the game by seeming not to notice their ploys.

In this, as in all else, the pair worked together, coming at her from two directions.

One would look upward with wide eyes and ask an innocent question, pressing so close that her target must step back to avoid contact, while the other came silently up behind in order to be bumped, and take the opportunity to rub seductively against Gu Yasha's rump. Or, holding hands, apparently in deep conversation and paying no attention to where they went, they would stroll right into her and then divide, each wriggling seductively along her body while they made profuse apologies. In either case she would set them aside with scarcely a nod, her face impassive.

Crew members placed wagers as to whether and when Gu Yasha would react, and, if so, how. Odds were highest that the girls would achieve both less and more than they bargained for. Seok-Teng stayed aloof, but with a keen eye on the proceedings. Soon, whatever lay ahead, there would be no time for such distractions, however amusing.

On the ninth day, Han Duan, with a sidelong look and a jerk of her head, signaled to the captain that matters were about to reach resolution. Amihan and Dalisay had clambered aboard naked from their morning swim, and knelt close to Gu Yasha. They had been issued blue cotton shirts and trousers, which they often "forgot" to wear, and now they made no attempt to clothe themselves but used the garments to dry wet hair and bodies. Their long sensuous strokes and posturings displayed every feature of their lithe bodies, while they peered slyly upward to assess what effect they might have.

Gu Yasha, with a single barked word, grasped an arm of each and yanked them upright. She propelled the girls, stumbling, to the rail, and bent them across it. Han Duan unhooked a long net deftly from the ship's side and tossed it over the girl's heads and torsos, entangling their arms, leaving their rounded rumps even more blatantly naked by contrast.

Gu Yasha struck first, with a hand that could easily span both of Dalisay's buttocks at once, but focused on one and then the other. Han Duan set up her own complex pattern of smacks on Amihan's wriggling posterior. The girls squealed, and writhed, and gasped each time an especially sharp blow landed, but neither begged her assailant to stop, even when red streaks marked their smooth skin.

The entire crew gathered to watch and cheer. Some clapped their hands in a futile attempt to match the varying rhythm of strikes. When squeals and gasps intensified into sobs, and ultimately to frantic, wordless pleas not for mercy but for something beyond pain, many a watcher would have been glad to step forward and supply the need, had that not been the clear prerogative of Han Duan and Gu Yasha.

A prerogative that they did not claim. Both stepped back in unison and viewed their handiwork in the manner of calligraphers assessing their brushstrokes. Han Duan surveyed Dalisay's flesh, and then Amihan's, both now aglow like coals in the galley brazier. She frowned. Three more openhanded blows, with accompanying yelps from Amihan—and Han Duan was satisfied.

The pearl divers, still far from satisfied, wriggled their way down out of the entangling net and watched Gu Yasha stride away to climb up beside the captain in the high prow. Han Duan paused for a few stern words, pointed down into the hold, then joined Seok-Teng as well.

The two girls, each with an arm about the other's waist and a hand fumbling in her own wet crotch, limped to the hatch and disappeared below.

"What did you say to them?" Seok-Teng asked Han Duan.

"Shape up and tend to your work, unless you wish to find yourselves in a floating brothel that caters to Japanese soldiers."

A rare smile lit up Gu Yasha's face. Seok-Teng herself yielded briefly to laughter. Then she handed her spyglass to Han Duan and indicated a point in the eastern sky.

"The aircraft?" Gu Yasha shaded her eyes and stared in that direction.

"Birds," Han Duan said. "Land is not far off."

Word spread like a freshening wind through the crew. Land to the east, just as the captain had promised. The afternoon's entertainment receded from their minds, to be recalled in many a bedroll that night, but for now eclipsed by a flurry of preparation.

With the first distant sightings of fishing boats, the graceful *proas* of the ocean islands, everyone on board knew even more surely that they were not alone on an empty sea. Land, some land, was very near.

They did not, for the present, intend to act or be seen as pirates. The large guns along the sides remained retracted and concealed. When fishing boats became more frequent, the *She-Dragon* approached to a non-threatening distance and Han Duan, more able to pass as a man than ever as she grew older, took their small boat to intercept one and ask for news.

From the first vessel she was waved onward to a larger one, where, as she reported on her return, she and the crew members with her were able to cobble together enough fragments of mutual languages with those aboard to communicate at a reasonable level.

"We are indeed among the southernmost Marshall Islands, and already to the east of several. I asked, in passing, if they ever saw airplanes so far out here in the ocean; we had heard one and been surprised. After some hesitation they told me that Japanese planes were often seen to the north, and indeed large airstrips had been built on some islands. I could see that there was more to tell, so I offered silver coins for their trouble, and finally was told that stories had spread of a plane, not Japanese, crash landing on a coral reef in the Mili atoll. Further, it was said that a Japanese ship, large but not so large as some, was refueling at the major island of Jaluit and would then go to the harbor of Mili Mili to pick up the wreck and a survivor."

"Survivor." Seok-Teng pondered the news. "And how did they know the plane was not Japanese?"

Han Duan shook her head. "The way news travels here, I think that they did know more, or suspect it, but I did not press further. That same swift flow of news could bear suspicions of us to quarters we would rather it did not. I did, however, get directions to the Mili atoll, and when I inquired about a place where we might put in to a lagoon, work on some repairs, and replenish our fresh water supply, all without disturbing local residents, I was told of a much smaller uninhabited atoll not far from Mili, called Nadikdik."

Seok-Teng spread out her charts, and between them they determined where they must be. As to where they should go, Nadikdik and Mili seemed the natural choices.

The winds were favorable. At times Seok-Teng even felt that some force beyond known wind and current sped their ship onward. The crew, aware only that their captain was rushing them toward some new adventure after so many weeks of nothing but empty sea, and that in some way a mysterious ship of the air was involved, worked smoothly and well.

A new scattering of fishing boats appeared as they neared other islands. Seok-Teng was reassured to see a few vessels junk-rigged in the Chinese fashion, like the *She-Dragon*; they would not stand out as much of a curiosity.

Han Duan sailed again for information. Now gossip about the downed airplane was widespread. The survivor was said to be white, and there were whispers that the pilot was, incredibly, a woman. She was dressed like a man, with short hair, but someone's cousin's son had heard a high scream when a Japanese official struck her. She was now imprisoned in Japanese headquarters at Mili Mili, the chief town, and a naval ship would be in the harbor by late next day to take her away.

A woman! And perhaps they were in time, but in time for what, Seok-Teng could not say. Her ship could not take on an armored military vessel in open combat.

The Nadikdik Atoll was easy to find, and not hard to approach once a fisherman's son was paid to show them the safe entrance between islets of sharp coral into the center lagoon. Besides a silver coin, they gifted him with a small bundle of coffee beans and a sack of rice, as much to establish their credentials as legitimate traders blown off course as to reward him. In further negotiations with his father, they purchased a slim, fleet *proa* to more easily navigate among the reefs of both Nadikdik and Mili, ten kilometers to the north.

"What is your plan?" Han Duan asked that night. "We are not exactly hidden here, and news of us will have reached Mili Mili by now."

Seok-Teng had no plan except to be in the right place at the right time, whatever that might be.

"We must see the harbor, the town, how everything

lies," she said. "At dawn you and I and the two pearl divers will sail in the *proa* to the harbor at Mili Mili. A harmless family of traders. If the Japanese ship is not yet in sight, we will dock, and you may even go about the town to purchase a few supplies and listen for gossip."

Fishing boats were heading out of the harbor as their *proa* was going in, but enough boats were still at the docks to keep them from being conspicuous. Han Duan went about the town, returning with packets of tea and sweets and a sack of breadfruit. The crew back in the lagoon would be gathering wild coconuts and filling barrels of water from small springs on a few of the encircling islets.

"There is no approaching the guardhouse," she said. "No one dares look toward it directly. There is a current of curiosity and fear throughout the town. And danger."

Danger was closer than they had known. Once out of the harbor, they could see, across the great lagoon to the northeast, the gray bulk of a naval ship close to a line of reefs. Seok-Teng did not dare bring out her spyglass where she might be seen, but the ship seemed to be anchored there. She recalled that it was expected to retrieve the wrecked plane, as well as the flyer.

On the way back to Nadikdik, Seok-Teng muttered to herself and to Han Duan, trying to form a plan of action. "The naval ship is not huge, but too big to dock in the inner harbor. They will have to bring the prisoner out in a smaller craft. Our ship might just manage to pull up to the longest dock, but we could not maneuver quickly in the

harbor. We must not be trapped inside. We have the *proa*...
and our small boat..."

As the sun slid below the land, the Japanese vessel, the
wrecked body of an airplane bound to its aft deck with
heavy cables, eased through the inlet into the harbor and
anchored where the water was deepest. The large, junk-
rigged ship that had been standing half a mile offshore
began to drift almost imperceptibly inward. The pirates'
proa and small sailboat were already inside the harbor,
blending in with other boats as innocuously as possible.

The naval ship lowered an engine-driven boat, which
carried four armed soldiers to the main dock, already
cleared of onlookers. Another military party met them,
opening formation to reveal a manacled prisoner, who was
swiftly and roughly taken aboard by the others.

Seok-Teng, in her small sailboat, could not see the prisoner clearly, but she was swept up in the moment, certain
what she must do. Even in its scabbard her *kris* vibrated
against her thigh.

Dusk came quickly. When the boat with the prisoner
was underway toward the Japanese ship, a bright crimson
rocket burst into the sky from close to the huddle of docked
fishing vessels, and at this signal, the boom of cannons
sounded from the ship just outside the harbor.

In the confusion, Seok-Teng's boat moved toward the
prisoners. Gu Yasha's rifle sent one guard and then another
tumbling, and splintered the steering mechanism. One figure struggled to stand. In the fading light, a pale, ghostly

face looked directly into Seok-Teng's own. And then there was a loud splash. The prisoner had dived over the side, manacles and all.

This had not been planned for, but the possibility of sinking the boat had been considered. Behind Seok-Teng, Amihan and Dalisay slid soundlessly into the water. In less than a minute, while Gu Yasha continued firing from first one rifle and then another, Seok-Teng was pulling the prisoner into the boat while the two girls pushed from beneath.

More cannon fire, right into the harbor's inlet, and some wild shots from the naval ship. Now the *proa* slid alongside Seok-Teng. The two pearl divers had already climbed aboard it. With scarcely a glance at the prisoner— but she was, indeed, a woman!—Seok-Teng passed her over to the lighter boat where other hands gripped her securely. Then, swift on even the lightest breeze, the slim craft darted across the harbor. The cannon fire had ceased.

Other boats began to move, and at least one motor coughed into life. While Gu Yasha continued to shoot, their slower sailboat moved toward the far side of the harbor, Seok-Teng using all her skill at making the most of what air current there was. Gu Yasha paused briefly to set off another rocket, and at once Han Duan in the *She-Dragon* ordered the big guns to be fired again, this time lofting their cannonballs over the heads of the fleeing pirates so that no one dared follow.

Just outside the harbor the proa waited. Seok-Teng and Gu Yasha leapt across from their boat, the *proa* caught the wind again, and in scant seconds cannon fire blasted their small craft, left behind in jagged pieces. Two pursuing vessels hit the wreckage and were wrecked in turn, effectively blocking the exit.

This part of the plan, or something greater than a plan, had succeeded.

On the ship, freed from her manacles, the prisoner was half-carried to the captain's cabin, stripped of her wet clothing, and lain on the bed, so limp and drained that Seok-Teng thought again of ghosts. The flickering light from a whale-oil lamp did not dispel the notion.

"You are safe here," she said, trying several languages before the colonial French she had learned in her youth in Vietnam got a response. The white woman's accent was odd and her vocabulary limited, but they were able to communicate.

"Yes, safe," Seok-Teng reiterated. "For a while, at least. They cannot follow us for at least a day, and by then we will be far away."

In what direction, she had not yet decided. Questions swirled in her mind, but the other seemed too exhausted to answer yet. Suddenly, though, she jerked to half-sitting, pulling the thin blanket up around herself, eyes blazing in defiance. "No!"

Han Duan had come in.

"All is well," Seok-Teng said soothingly, though she had a nervous impulse to laugh. "She is one of us. Look again. We are all women on this ship."

After a moment, the other lay back. "And all pirates, I

suppose," she said. "On a ship. With cannons." Her eyes closed then, and her face relaxed. Soon she was asleep.

Seok-Teng, her cabin occupied, shared Han Duan's small retreat that night. There was scarcely space for a slim young pearl diver to lie beside Han Duan on the narrow bed, much less the tall, sturdy captain of the ship, but the fever of victory burned all the hotter for being delayed, and they came together in a clash of flesh and will in which side-by-side had no meaning, only above and below.

Seok-Teng's naked body pressed down fiercely on the length of Han Duan's. Han Duan pressed upward with equal force. Friction of breast and belly and loins, hands and lips and teeth, fed the desperate hunger for more, and more, harder and yet harder, until the tiny hidden dragon Seok-Teng visualized between her folds tensed its coils and raised its head in a triumphant roar that shook her to her core.

Han Duan waited mere seconds before lurching to the top position and thrusting violently against Seok-Teng's pubic mound. In a few seconds more great shudders and groans of pleasure wracked her, subsiding into gasps and finally to silence.

In the captain's cabin they would have fallen apart then, to lie side by side in satiated companionship. Here, though that would have been just barely possible, they rolled instead until they were face to face, still closely pressed. Seok-Teng worked a hand free and stroked gently across the old scars on Han Tuan's face. "Tomorrow," she said, "Our guest must move to this cabin. You and I will maintain the proper management of the ship in the captain's quarters—unless you choose otherwise."

Han Duan's hand rose as by right to Seok-Teng's face. "Wartime calls for sacrifice," she said, though her gentle touch belied her dry tone. "I will follow you even there. You and your demon blade."

Hands moved along then to other places, in explorations more languorous than urgent, until sudden urgency resumed command. There was space after all for bodies to reverse and tongues as well as fingers to find tender places aching to be filled; and bodies found room to arch and strain and thrash when driven by need only a strong and deeply probing hand could satisfy. It was long before they slept.

Next morning, in Seok-Teng's spare clothing and with a meal of rice and breadfruit inside her, the flyer started right in with her own questions before they could ask theirs. No ghost now, she was alert and affable, with still an underlying watchfulness. Her looks were strange to them, especially her light, unruly thatch of hair, but her thin body seemed strong and healthy except for dark bruises so recent that they must have been inflicted by the crash. Or her captors.

"Real pirates? Where did you come from? Where are we going? Why are you here?"

Han Duan answered the first two questions in general terms, but knew better than to deal with the third. *We are here because an ancient demon blade sent dreams of you, but we do not yet know why.* Impossible to tell her that.

"Where we go now depends on you," Seok-Teng said.

"We could sail south, to Kiribati—the Gilbert Islands—where I think the British are still in control. Are they your people?"

"I know them," the white woman said. "When I was lost, I searched for those islands, hoping to land there."

"Then we will go there. They can send word, at least, to those who must search for you."

"I...let me think for a day." The ghost-mood had reclaimed her. She looked hollow, shadowed, even in the sunshine on deck.

They set a course to the south, and let the flyer have her day. That night, in the cabin, Seok-Teng pressed her again.

"We must know where you came from, what we should call you, who you are, where you should go. We have our own course to follow, after all."

The woman raised her head. "It seems so simple, and yet it is not. I am... I do not know. Once I was the woman who thought she could fly around the world. Now..." She was silent for a while. Then, haltingly, she said, "They said I was a spy. They...beat me. And more." A shiver swept through her. "I never hated before, never believed in violence. But now... I don't know who I am. I think I could willingly kill."

Another silence. "I was not a spy, but now I know things they wanted to hide. That huge airstrip, fortifications...that much the British and Americans must somehow be told. But I am not ready for my old life."

Seok-Teng said, carefully, "We are changing our ways as well, still pirates, but bending all our efforts to harrying and blocking the Japanese warmongers. We will sail far from here, since too much is now known of us, but always we will work against them, and may well die in the attempt. Our way is not yet clear." On impulse, she unwrapped the protecting oilcloth from her private papers, drew out a photograph, and proffered it. "If only we could gain the trust of Soong Mai-Ling. We could be her secret eyes and ears."

"Madame Chiang Kai-shek. I have met her several times. She takes a great interest in airplanes." The flyer pondered for several minutes. "It could be...if I were to give you a letter signed by me, recommending you to her attention... But I am not ready to be *discovered* yet. Perhaps written as though we had met earlier, in New Guinea, before I took off from Lae."

"If you are not soon gone from us," Seok-Teng said, managing to conceal her awe of this woman, "you must darken your skin and hair for safety, and even then act a part so well that none can guess."

Han Duan had said nothing, but now broke in. "You asked for a day. Do you wish a week, a month, some longer time, with no promise that you will have such a chance at safety and your old life again? Who would you be, if you could have another life?"

"I would be...I *will* be," the former pilot said, with scarcely a moment's hesitation, "a pirate."

Seok-Teng touched her *kris*, and felt it quiver, and fall still. The plan was accomplished.

The Dragon Descending

"My first woman? As well ask if I recall my first dragon." Seok-Teng scarcely realized she spoke aloud, still afloat in the ebbtide of the fierce coupling that followed battles won and prizes taken.

Han Duan lay intensely still beside her. When she spoke again, her tone was a study in idle curiosity. "Your first dragon, then. Surely not old Mountain of Wealth?"

"Blasphemy!" Seok-Teng managed a chuckle. "With a tentacle in every profitable pot, Madame Lai Choi San should be called Old Octopus rather than the Dragon Lady of Bias Bay." Best to pursue this much safer line of conversation. "And you know well that I was no more a virgin than you when we met as her bodyguards."

"Yet even I," Han Duan admitted, "learned much from her beyond the managing of pirate ships."

"Is that how you formed your knack for domination of our young crew members?" Seok-Teng relaxed, confident that the dangerous topic had been circumvented.

Han Duan held firmly to disbelief in her captain's visions of dragons, yet as second in command she followed with complete trust wherever Seok-Teng led. Seok-Teng, and her *kris*, the short, undulating blade passed down through generations of her family until a woman was the only heir. A demon blade, Han Duan would say, in a tone that meant she did not believe in such things. But demon or no, the *kris* had bonded with its inheritor according to the old traditions. Always, after Seok-Teng's dragon dreams, the *kris* would point the way her ship must sail, where they would find women skilled in the ways of the sea, or captives on their way to slavery, who would gladly join such a pirate crew.

Seok-Teng did not wish to speak now of dragons. "Our rescued sleek young pearl divers are certainly eager for your domination." Dalisay and Amihan should be good distractions.

But Han Duan would not be distracted. Not this time. "What color were their dragons, in your dream?"

For once, Seok-Teng would be open. Han Duan deserved that of her, and more. "They were the blue-green of shallow southern seas, twined about each other in a wheel like the yin and yang, spinning through the sky."

Han Duan nodded, but pulled Seok-Teng closer against her lean body and murmured into her ear, "And what of your first dragon?"

A shuddering sigh swept Seok-Teng. Whatever the cost, she would be open at last with the comrade and lover who had been her lifeline for so many years.

"My first dragon was my first woman as well. Not a dream, nor yet a vision, unless visions leave scars."

"Ah! These?" They knew each other's bodies as well as

they knew each inch of their ship. Han Duan moved so that her fingers could trace the line of short pale ridges along Seok-Teng's sides from armpit to hip. "Truly a dragon of a woman!"

"A woman who was truly a dragon," Seok-Teng said flatly. "But take it as merely a tale, if you wish. A tale worth hearing."

Ha Long, Bay of the Descending Dragons.

Seok-Teng had heard of its beauty and legends, but never seen its labyrinths of vertical, time-carved islands until the day she sailed her small boat through them in pursuit of her father's killer. No time then to stare at its wonders, only to maneuver among them, searching always for the motorized vessel whose lines were etched indelibly into her memory.

Rival smugglers who resented her father's incursion this far north, they had come in the night, while he slept. Only chance kept them from finding Seok-Teng, whose younger energies had sought outlet in a night swim, naked, of course. If they had seen, they could not have mistaken her for the adolescent boy she pretended to be. She saw their boat from a distance, and the first flames of the fire they set as they left. But all she could do when she reached her floating home was to put out the fire, weep and curse over her father's body, and take up the ancient blade he had not had a chance to grasp.

The *kris* was cold to her hand. Such blades descended from father to son, bonding to their owners, tradition said, and a danger to any other who would try to wield them. This time there was no son. Seok-Teng swore, though, that she would sink the blade into the bodies of his murderers, and as she raised it in the direction they had gone, she felt a subtle vibration, an almost imperceptible warming, that gave her hope. For this revenge, at least, she must trust the weapon to accept her right to hold it.

Twice she had found the killers moored in tiny villages, and twice she had swum from her boat, now repaired and disguised, and slit a smuggler's throat. One remained. One terrified killer now fleeing from what he thought to be a demon. Perhaps he was right.

Once in Ha Long Bay, it should have been impossible to find one small boat hiding among the thousands of limestone islands with their caves and grottoes and thick pelts of greenery clinging to sheer walls. Impossible for a man— or even a girl with a warrior spirit—but not for the *kris*. It showed the way, through three days of a winding course.

On the third evening, the blade took on a glow that told Seok-Teng her prey was so close that she must approach with caution. She anchored and waited through the night. This time she would make sure her prey saw his doom coming.

At last, the dawn mist began to dissipate, the islands took shape, and the sun's first rays struck the leafy crest of the nearest island in a blaze of emerald flame.

Seok-Teng slid into the water wearing nothing beyond the *kris* belted to her naked hip. The boat she sought was there, just beyond the island, perhaps fifty feet away. When she reached its side, she listened for several minutes until she heard the man stirring, moving slowly about, then standing on the lee side and, by the sound, relieving himself into the sea. The perfect moment.

She was up over the side, *kris* unsheathed and raised, before he could turn. Yet, even at such a time, he had kept a dagger in his hand, and parried the longer blade. Seok-Teng spun and struck again, knocking his weapon this time from his grip. He grasped her knife wrist so tightly with his other hand that it took all her effort to keep from dropping the *kris*. Or almost all. Her knee tensed, began its upward strike toward his groin—but he fell back before it connected. She had only a fleeting glimpse of his eyes, widened in horror as he looked at something beyond her, his face as contorted as though her blade had pierced his belly.

Seok-Teng stumbled, unbalanced, and still managed to slice the *kris* across his throat before he toppled backward into the sea.

She swung around and saw what he had seen. A golden eye gazed down at her from the island's greenery, and then two eyes, in a long, elegant, emerald-scaled head that lifted to regard her full-on.

"I had him! He was mine!" The blood-madness ran still so hot that Seok-Teng felt no fear, no amazement that a dragon such as she had seen only on painted screens or the prows of festive longboats was here before her in the flesh. If indeed dragons were made of such. "I needed no help!"

The dragon seemed to laugh, though what difference there might be between a dragon's laugh and its snarl Seok-Teng did not know. Indeed, as her blood slowed, she scarcely knew whether she herself dreamed, or imagined, or even lived. She held the *kris* upright, flat between her breasts, as talisman rather than weapon; it quivered, but gave off no heat.

Heat of another sort did warm Seok-Teng's flesh as the dragon's gaze moved slowly along her body. Did dragons lust after human women? She had never heard such tales, but after all, she herself lusted after women, though so far only in her dreams.

"Why not?" The voice was not her own, yet unmistakably female—and it spoke from inside her head. "Who can know so well how to please a woman as another woman?"

A dream, then. That sort of dream. Already Seok-Teng's loins stirred with longing. Her bedroll would be damp and tangled when she woke. If only this dream would take her far enough for relief!

The boat she stood upon had floated nearer to the island. Seok-Teng looked full into the golden eyes, not flinching when the dragon's green coils, their scales textured to resemble leaves, loosened from the rough limestone enough that its neck could arch outward above her and descend. Even when a flickering forked tongue, impossibly long, darted across her belly, Seok-Teng held her ground, though she could not suppress gasps and jerks at the tantalizing sensations it aroused.

"Set aside your noble blade," the voice said, "if you would taste of more tender delights."

She sheathed the *kris* but kept it belted at her hip. This time the dragon's laughter echoed inside her head, drowned out soon by Seok-Teng's own cries as the deep-coral tongue lapped at the paler coral tips of her high breasts, teasing and tweaking at them until they hardened and darkened and sent bolts of pleasure close to pain down through her belly into her cunt.

"How brave are you, girl? Enough to follow me?" The voice seemed uneven now, almost breathless. The long tongue reached down between her thighs and slick lips to find the jewel of pleasure there, and a low, rough moan was wrenched from deep in Seok-Teng's throat, followed by a keen wail as the stimulation ceased.

"Come, if you dare!" The dragon launched suddenly from the rock, leaving it nearly bare, and dove into the water. Seok-Teng followed so swiftly that the wake of the great long tail swept her briefly off course. Attuned from birth to all the motions and secrets of the sea, she was back on course in a moment, and when the waters stilled beside an island much larger than the first, she dove unerringly through an underwater passage to come up in a pool within a grotto infused with green light.

On its far side, stalactites hung nearly to the floor, chiming like bells as the dragon's emerald scales brushed them. Nearer, an arc of sandy beach edged the water.

The voice came again. "One more challenge, if you are truly brave." But this time it felt more like a plea than a dare. "Your blade…will you trust me with your blade?"

The *kris* was extended in Seok-Teng's hand before she could even recall drawing it from the sheath. "The blade chooses for itself, always," she said. "It appears to have done so already."

"Place it between my teeth."

Seok-Teng advanced along the beach. Fear, which she had not felt until now, weighed on her like anchor chains. The dragon's rows of sharp teeth could easily take off her arm—she would have parted with that rather than lose the weapon that embodied the soul of her lineage, but indeed the blade had chosen. She watched in amazement and horror as the bright undulating curves of metal slid, seemingly of their own accord, down the dragon's throat. Her hand jerked upward as though reaching out to reclaim the *kris*, whatever the cost, but it was too late.

"Turn away!" This was a desperate plea and a command, all in one. "Go below the water!"

Seok-Teng turned, not quite in time to miss the sight of her sacred blade's tip slicing through the emerald scales from within; then she dove into the pool.

She could always hold her breath for several minutes. This time, she waited even longer. When hands—human hands!—reached down to pull her forth, she was too dazed to brush the water from her eyes, and when she did, the vision before her seemed no more believable than an erotic hallucination caused by lack of air.

The woman was taller even than Seok-Teng herself, and as strongly built, with hair as wild and dark, but glinting with green highlights. Her curves were both voluptuous and graceful, while her face, like Seok-Teng's own, would have been as beautiful on a man as on a woman. In the grotto's subdued light, her golden eyes were muted to amber.

The womanly parts swept away all thought of other matters. They came together on the beach, heat sparking wherever skin met skin and spreading like a raging fire. A very human tongue found Seok-Teng's nipples, and a human mouth tugged and sucked them to peaks of glorious soreness. Her own mouth yearned to taste the other's flesh, but for the moment hands sufficed, filling with sweet, bountiful breasts and tweaking coral nubs that grew ever harder in their demand for more, and yet more.

Someone whimpered. Someone moaned, long and low. Voices had better uses than mere words. Seok-Teng's hunger grew, and her hands left the other's breasts to explore the further delights of a female body not her own. What her fingers had often done for herself, she tried on this dragon-woman, with the same effect and more. So soft, and yet firm—wet, slick to enter, then clenching, hips thrusting forward for more, until the need to taste her sent Seok-Teng to her knees and her mouth to those demanding folds and depths. Her own tongue felt as long as the remembered dragon's tongue, thrusting deeper, deeper, while hot sea-flavored flesh pressed and ground against her face and her thumb worked the jewel of pleasure to its peak. The woman's cries rang out so loud and high that the stalactites chimed again in unison.

Seok-Teng held on until she could stand it no longer, then rammed a hand against her own aching cunt. In moments it was knocked away, replaced by a mouth and fingers infinitely more skilled than hers. They teased, tormented, swept her to the brink and left her hovering there, time after time—until, when at last she tangled her fingers in the dark hair and held the mouth fiercely against her need, she was allowed to plunge over the edge. Her body reverberated like a temple gong, subsided for a moment, then reached for new heights and plummeted into new depths, over and over, until at last she had not enough breath for further screams, or even whimpers.

"Rest for a bit," came the voice. "Regain your strength. You will need it all, for there is yet more that I must have."

So, of course, Seok-Teng's strength surged once more, with scarcely more than time for her breathing to recover. "I am ready," she said, "for anything. But first," and she dared to place her hands on the beautiful face leaning above her as they sprawled on the sand, "tell me now who you are, and how this comes about, for I may die of pleasure before I can ask again."

"You may choose your tale. They are plentiful enough." The woman paused for a long minute. "Have you not heard how, long ago when China first threatened this land, dragons were sent by the gods to protect it? They spit out gems that became the tangle of islands, and found the bay so beautiful that they stayed for a time. The mother dragon's children stayed in their turn, some becoming islands themselves." The dragon-woman shrugged. "As good a story as any. There are few of us now, and we sometimes sleep for eons as men count time, but I will tell you this one true thing." Her laughter rang in Seok-Teng's head. "A woman like you is so rare a gem that her approach will always wake me."

At this, Seok-Teng wrapped arms and legs about the other, and they grappled again in a delirium of lust and laughter, bodies finding joy in any contact, any stroke or pressure.

Gradually, laughter ceased, and hunger surged again. The dragon-woman rolled on top, face and body tense. "You must be strong now. I must...there are no words..."

She moved as they had moved before, but harder, pummeling Seok-Teng's body with her own, grinding into her until it seemed that bone must break bone. Her face twisted, became wilder, neither human nor dragon, only savage passion personified.

Seok-Teng thrust back in response, adding her own strength and savagery, heedless of pain even when the hands gripping her hips and sides spread farther and claws sprung forth that pierced her skin. When the voice roared in her head with the fury of a great volcano, her own voice followed as closely as any mere human voice could.

Sound, pain, pleasure—it was all too much. Blackness closed in around Seok-Teng.

When she woke, the daylight filtering through crevices in the limestone had faded almost away. The grotto was deserted, except for herself, and the faintly glowing *kris* beside her.

She sat up and grasped the blade's hilt. There was a wetness on the blade. When she touched her tongue to it, the taste was of sea salt and blood.

Outside the grotto, catching the last reflected light of sunset, her own boat lay anchored, though she had left it some distance away. "Thank you," she thought, for her body was now stiff and aching and bleeding from her punctured sides, and she was glad to be spared the swim.

A faint, far voice answered from within. "You owe me more thanks than you know. Since you have tasted my blood, some day, when you have need, dreams of dragons may lead to warriors with spirits like yours, just as you came into my dreams."

Seok-Teng's story ceased. She wondered, for a time, whether her tale had put Han Duan to sleep. That might be just as well.

But Han Duan stirred. "So, you dreamed of Gu Yasha, too, and many others." Gu Yasha, the strong, tall gunner as silent as her cannons were loud, had appeared in a dream as a dragon of golden amber.

Seok-Teng heard the hurt in her companion's voice, and knew where this was going. "Yes. But I have never lain with any as I do with you, and never will." She turned toward Han Duan and stroked the weathered face that moved her more than any beauty. "I had no dragon dream of you, because there was no need. You, I found for myself, as you found me. That makes all the difference."

And that was enough.

Meltdown

"Some piece of work you got there." Sigri jerked her head toward the door. Or maybe she was just flicking a trickle of sweat out of one eye, since her hands were occupied with hammering a rod of red-hot iron into submission. She'd been wearing goggles but shed them when we came in. "Ought to keep a shorter tether on your toys, Roby."

It was just as well Maura had already flounced out in a snit when she realized that we weren't going to focus on her—although Maura's every movement was far too elegant to be termed "flouncing." Even when she'd knocked over a short trollish creature built using trowel hands and garden-rake teeth, tried to right it, got those long auburn waves that had sold ten million crates of shampoo tangled in another contraption, and knocked that one over, too, her taut ass was as elegant as it was enticing. She could have been modeling those stretch ski pants for a fashion spread in Vogue. Probably had been, in fact, when she'd been here in New Hampshire in October for an autumn leaves photo shoot. Now, in January, the outfit suited the snow coming down outside.

Sigri's boi, Rif, edged deftly among the metal sculptures, righting the ones Maura had knocked over, touching some of the others as though they were friends. Or lovers. In their shadows, her slight body and pale short hair were nearly invisible. She hadn't spoken a word since I'd been here. Now, at a gesture from Sigri, she followed Maura out of the barn.

Maura needed to be the center of attention. Someplace deep inside, being in the spotlight terrified her, but she still craved it. She didn't know how lucky she was that Sig and I had been ignoring her, catching up on old times and our lives over the past twenty years. She'd brought us together for her own convoluted purpose and pushed me over the edge of anger into rage once I knew what she was up to. Could have been part of her plan. Maura's plans were never straightforward. I didn't care whether she was listening outside the door or not.

"I'm not her goddamned keeper!"

"No? Somebody sure ought to be, and I get the impression she thinks it's you."

I perched gingerly on the seat of an antique hay baler stripped of its wheels, waiting its turn to be cannibalized into parts for the scrap metal beasts and demons Sig sold to tourists and the occasional high-end craft gallery. "Not a chance. Don't tell me she hasn't been trying you on for size."

Sig concentrated more intently than necessary on the metal she was bending across the edge of her anvil. "Trying is the word, all right." Her hammer came down hard. "The magazine crew was doing a photo shoot down the road with my neighbor's big black Percheron mare close by and sugar maples in the background. Rif hung around watching, kind of dazzled by the glitz, I guess, so when Maura asked about the weird iron critters out front here, Rif dragged her to the barn to see more. I knew you'd worked with her—Rif keeps some of those fashion mags around for some strange reason, and I don't deny taking a look now and then. Just to see whether your name's in the small print as photographer, of course. Not for those skinny-ass models." That brazenly lecherous grin was just the way I remembered it.

"Yeah, Maura has a thing for sharp scary things, the weirder the better. So, I guess one thing led to another?"

"One thing led to—zip! Nothing but some crazy maze of 'yes…no…wait, maybe…' Does she have any fucking idea what she wants? Won't negotiate, won't submit, won't bend, likes to be hurt but mustn't be marked anyplace it would show when she models bikinis. I tell you, Roby, I don't have the energy anymore for games like that. No topping from the bottom." One more hammer blow and a curse, and then the warped metal was cast into a tank of water where it hissed as it cooled. From what little I'd glimpsed, I didn't think it had turned out as Sig intended.

"She doesn't know what she wants until she gets it," I said. "Looks like just now, she thinks she wants it from you." *And she has the gall to want me to show you how to give it to her.* I'd given in to Maura's pleas to come back with her to the Mount Washington Valley in New Hampshire for a long weekend visit with my old friend Sigri, which did sound tempting, and then just as we arrived at the farm-house, Maura had told me casually that she wished I'd teach Sigri the right way to hurt her. I had never come closer to hurting her in all the wrong ways.

"Screw it. I wouldn't have bothered at all if Rif hadn't been all for it." Sig pulled off her heavy leather apron and straddled a wooden bench. "Why'd she drag you here, then? Not that I'm not glad to see you. Every time I see your name on one of those photo spreads in a nature magazine, I think about getting in touch, but somehow I never get around to it." She considered me for a moment, the fire from the forge casting a red glow over her square, sweaty face and muscular arms. "Good thing you moved on from the fashion ads racket. Your stuff is too good for that."

"The fashion biz pays better." I didn't quite meet Sig's gaze. "I still do it once in a while."

"You didn't come when Miss Fancypants threw a fit last October and insisted they had to get you because she wouldn't work with anybody else. So why now?"

"I was in Labrador on assignment from the Sierra Club magazine. And next month, I head for Patagonia. In any case, I do have my limits. The guy they had here was good and needed the work." I looked her full in the face—a face I've seen in my dreams through the years more often than I'd like to admit. "This location is a big draw, though. So many memories..."

"Ohhh, yeah!" Her smile this time was slow, reflective, and genuine. I wondered what she was remembering. My second most vivid image from those days was Sigri's fine broad, muscular butt in tight jeans twenty feet above me on the face of Cathedral Ledge.

We'd been casual friends, members of a fluctuating group of dykes renting this very same farmhouse for a few weeks in the summer while we hiked and climbed, and again in the winter as a ski lodge. Both of us usually had a girlfriend in tow, but when it came to rock climbing, we trusted each other and no one else. Even on easy climbs with iron bolts not more than twenty-five feet apart, when you take the lead with a belaying rope and call "Watch me," you damned sure need to know that when your partner on the other end answers "Go for it, I've got you," she has absolutely got you, her end of the rope firmly anchored, and will hold on if your grip fails or a rock edge breaks away and you start to plummet down the unforgiving cliff face.

We'd only admitted to figuring in each other's fantasies back then as mead companions, playing at being Viking warriors ravaging villages side by side as we bore off not-unwilling maidens. She still wore her yellow hair in that thick Viking braid down her back; I couldn't tell in this unreliable light whether there were silver strands mixed in with the gold. My own dark cropped hair was still more pepper than salt, but not by much.

"Well, you're here now, and I'm glad. No need to let that glitzy bitch spoil things." She put away her tools and adjusted the damper on the furnace to let the fire die down. "Think we could make her sleep out here in the barn?"

"Not unless we made it seem like her own idea. Which isn't impossible."

"Never mind for now. Rif'll show you your room, and once you're settled in, we'll eat dinner. She'll have it in the oven by now."

"Rif sounds like a real treasure."

"More than I deserve, that's for sure," Sig muttered, almost too low for me to hear. She made for the door. I followed, admiring that rear view the way I used to when no one was looking. Just a bit broader now, but even more muscular since she'd turned to blacksmithing. The front view had been admirable, too, but harder to enjoy covertly. Back then, butch buddies did not openly ogle each other's chests, and things hadn't changed in that department. I could tell now that it was still remarkable, even hidden behind the leather apron shielding her from any runaway sparks or splinters of metal.

Snow was building up fast along the short path from the barn to the house, piling the existing banks along the sides even higher. Good thing we didn't have to drive anywhere tonight. Maura had damned well better not make me wish we could get away.

Dinner was maple bourbon-glazed salmon with hot cornbread, mushroom risotto, and tossed salad with pecans and dried cranberries. Perfection. Rif was perfection, too. Maybe too perfect. Her cooking was excellent, and her serving of it—well, let's just say she epitomized service in more ways than one while managing to sit for long enough to eat her own food. Quiet, efficient, never speaking without being spoken to, anticipating our needs, all with downcast eyes, at least whenever I glanced at her. Just the same, I could feel her gaze on me from time to time, and I was pretty sure she was sizing up Maura, too.

Maura was sizing up Rif right back, maybe taking notes on how to appeal to Sigri. At least she was putting on a pretty good demure act. Sig and I were wallowing in nostalgia, swapping recollections of cliffs we'd climbed, mountains we'd summited, ice walls we'd conquered, and après-ski orgies we'd enjoyed the hell out of.

Finally, when we were about done eating our desserts of individual pumpkin custards and sipping Rif's excellent coffee, Sig turned to Maura like a good host. "How about you, Maura? Done any climbing?"

"Oh, yes, I've been on some jaunts with Roby out in the Sierras." She gave that trademark toss of her head that made strands of chestnut mane drift across one or another of her perfect breasts. Her navy silk shirt was conservative but clingy in all the right places. "You know how it is, though, hiking with somebody so much older, having to take things slower than you'd like."

Sig shot me a "what the fuck!" look.

Okay, Maura was asking for it. I smiled, genuinely amused, but also irritated as hell. "Got a mouth on her, hasn't she. Don't worry. It's just that insults are the best Maura can manage as foreplay."

"So how does that work out for her?"

Maura's glare in my direction was weakened by her belated realization that Sigri was just as old as I was.

"Depends on the circumstances. The last time she called me too old, she was already spread-eagled, tied to the four corners of a tent frame, and demanding to be gagged."

Rif's eyes flashed wide open for just a second. Sig nodded judiciously. "I can see getting a little something out of that."

"What I got was a bent tent frame. What Maura got was my mark in a place even a bikini won't reveal."

Maura apparently decided to go with the flow. "Isn't it cute," she said with a sultry smile, "the way old folks' memories get so fuzzy?"

Sigri leaned forward and looked from Maura to me. "More foreplay?"

"Well, she seems to think so. It'd be cute if it weren't so juvenile."

Sig almost asked another question, thought better of it, pushed back her chair, and stood up. "Rif, how about you kids go take a walk while Roby and I have a nice chat about grown-up matters."

"Is it still snowing?" But I knew perfectly well that it was. "They could just stroll around inside the barn, and Maura could decide which sharp-edged, long-toothed demon there she'd most like to fuck her in her dreams."

Maura managed to stifle a smartass retort. Rif stifled a smile, then went to stand beside Sig with head meekly bent, speaking softly, before leading Maura away. Sigri and I moved into the cozy living room to sit by the fire and savor our after-dinner port, like any Old Country lords of the manor. Except that, instead of port, we savored excellent home-brewed mead a friend had given Sig and Rif at Christmas.

While Sig bent to pour a little of the golden elixir into my genuine bull-horn cup set in its own wrought iron stand, I felt her closeness with a jolt that startled me. In the old days, no matter what girl I was with, if Sig was in the room, I was more aware of her than of anyone else. Comradeship, sure, but I couldn't deny that there'd been an intensely sensual element as well. Now she was so close I could have reached out and touched her breast, guarded now only by flannel instead of the leather apron.

"Your work?" I switched my gaze quickly to the elaborate Celtic swirls of the cup stand. "And this?" I ran a finger over the spiraling dragon shape carved into the horn cup in exquisite detail.

"The metalwork, sure. The carving is all Rif's, though. She's an incredible artist, hands steady, fingers strong and flexible, every stroke precise..."

Sig might or might not have seen the slight quirk of my eyebrow. The reddening of her face might or might not have been due to a sudden flare-up of the fire. She went on in a hurry, "She did these in the tenth-century Norwegian Ringerike style, but she can do just about anything."

"She's really amazing, isn't she? I hope Maura isn't giving her a rough time."

If Rif had been dazzled by the October photo shoot and

"all for" some D/s play between Sig and Maura, it would be a shame if Maura's rudeness shattered her fantasies.

"Don't worry. Rif can take care of herself, and then some. She—" Sig shook her head. "Well, enough about that. Tell me more about Maura. Did she really let you make a mark on her precious skin?"

"You might put it that way. It's not just vanity. Her agency takes out insurance on every inch of her, and at the slightest marking, the agency collects and she gets fired. It's a clause from the days before everything and anything could be photoshopped, but they still demand it. Sometimes she really, really wants to be marked and hurt, to feel like a real person instead of a very expensive commodity. Even dreams of a scar on the face that the world sees so it will be all her own again. But she doesn't want any of that enough to give up the life she has, and she trusts me to take her almost as far as she wants to go without going over the edge."

Sigri was shaking her head by the end of my revelations. I picked up my drinking horn and took a sip of mead. "As you said, that's enough about that. Too much, in fact." Another sip. "Hey, this is really fine stuff! Smooth and intense. Wish we'd had something this good back in the day."

"Nah, we'd've been too dumb to appreciate it." She sank down on the couch by my side, took a longer sip than I had, licked her lips, and looked slantwise at me. "We were too dumb to appreciate a hell of a lot."

"No kidding." I raised my horn. Hers met it halfway. "Here's to our wasted youth."

A few more sips of mead later, I was on the verge of blurting out a maudlin confession, but Sig beat me to it.

"That pool." She looked into the fireplace, not at me. "That day…"

I finished for her. "We bushwhacked off the Slippery Brook trail, discovered that huge gorgeous pool, and went skinny-dipping. The goddess place, I called it, and you told me not to go all woo-woo."

"But you did. And you scrambled naked back up that rock to where we'd left our stuff before we jumped off, got your camera, and yammered on about how the rocks on each side of the little waterfall looked like spread thighs, and the knobby stone in between with moss on it was the pussy, and the—the water of life, I think you said, was pouring into the sacred pool."

"Yeah, I guess that's what I said. And you dived into the deepest part and came up with handfuls of pebbles that you kept throwing at me while I tried to get pictures from just the right angle."

"Well, maybe I was as bad as your Maura at foreplay when it came to somebody like you. Girly types, no problem, but you? I figured you'd either laugh in my face or punch it if I made a move."

I shook my head in self-disgust. "And I just kept on yammering to keep from jumping you and getting slammed for it. Talk about dumb kids. When you got fed up and left, I was desperate for the chance to jerk off, fantasizing about what it would feel like to be in a clinch with you."

"Hah! I only made it to that other stream coming out of the beaver pond before my hand was in my pants. If you'd caught up with me then…"

I reached for the decanter of mead, poured us each a little more, and raised my horn again. "Well, here's to the years of steamy dreams inspired by the sight of you naked in that pool."

Just as well not to reveal that I'd snapped a picture of her from behind that day, right when her muscular body arched, butt high, into the dive that got her those pebbles to throw at me. I'd carried a print of the photo around with me until I literally wore it out.

We were half facing each other by that time, up close. Somehow my left hand had reached over to her nearest thigh, and her right hand had done the same to me.

"You know that time when we arm wrestled a couple of nights later?" Sig's grip on my thigh tightened. "The only time you ever beat me? Shouldn't count as a win. I only lost because I was so distracted remembering how you'd looked naked, like a tougher, stronger version of those nymphs in old paintings. But I paid for that round of drinks anyway."

"No kidding? I thought I only won because I was so mad at myself for thinking of you in pretty much the same way, and the adrenaline gave me extra strength."

"How about—"

"A rematch? Not a chance. I've been hiking and toting my camera gear over some pretty rough terrain, but you've been hammering iron. No contest." I set my cup back on its stand on an end table to free up a hand so I could grip her bicep for emphasis—and for something more. But Rif's dragon carved into the horn seemed to be looking right at me. I paused. "Rif..." I said uncertainly, and as though the name worked a magic spell, the outside door opened and Rif herself came in. A brief gust of cold air blew right through the entrance hall, past the dining room, and into our cozy fireside haven.

She came right to Sigri, looked for a moment as though she were going to kneel before her, then thought better of it and just bent her head. "Excuse me, but Maura thinks it's getting too cold in the barn with the forge turned so low, and anyway, I started up the fire in the sauna hut a while ago, like you said I could, and it should be getting nearly hot enough."

"You still use the sauna? Great!" I hadn't moved my hand from Sig's thigh, so I gave her a squeeze, which she returned with interest. "All those rocks we dragged up from the river and the logs we cut."

"We've upgraded it a bit since then, but yeah, the same old place. We use it quite a bit, and this time I'm pretty sure Rif thinks it'll be the easiest way to get Maura's clothes off."

Maura herself came in just in time to hear that last part. "The fastest way, at least," she said companionably, and from the look she exchanged with Rif, I figured they were up to something. If it got us all naked in the sauna, it was definitely a step in the right direction. And if they were in it together, I didn't need to worry. Right?

"Upgraded" was an understatement. Besides the structural improvements, there were birchwood benches with armrests carved like voluptuous mermaids, leering gargoyle heads at the ends of the towel bars, and the coatracks, where we hung our clothes, looked like giant sets of antlers with minidragons twining through them. Not that I noticed all these details right away in the shock of coming into intense heat out of the cold and snow outside, and then the delirious distraction of such a variety of naked bodies.

Maura's delectable form was, of course, familiar to me, far more than it was to viewers of her photos even in bikini ads. Rif's slim body seemed more graceful in the freedom of nakedness than it had clothed; she could easily have been a sprite or nymph out of mythology, and her open smile and gleaming eyes gave her face a kind of elfin beauty.

Sigri... I'd seen her naked often enough in this same sauna years ago, but now I hardly dared look at her, and when I did, a flush of heat beyond anything the fire pit could produce swept through me. We'd both changed over the years, Sig with somewhat more flesh and a lot more muscle, me with some shifting of what flesh and muscle I had in spite of gym workouts when I'd lived in the city and strenuous trekking once I'd switched my focus to wilderness themes. But I'd never needed so intensely to get my hands on her. And in her. I could already feel her eyes on me, sharing that hunger.

But we both glanced toward Rif, who stood between Maura's spread legs gazing down at the shaved, smooth pussy on display. "That's the mark?" Rif said. "What does it mean?"

Sig went to look, too, with a lingering stroke across my flank as she passed me. I knew what they saw on that triangle of smooth skin just low enough to be covered by the skimpiest bikini bottom—four tiny curving arcs, not quite meeting, formed a delicate circle like a secret mandala. Maura just smiled mysteriously and leaned far back, her long hair flowing downward, her face clean of makeup, beads of sweat beginning to show between her breasts, looking more beautifully alive than any fashion ad could ever show.

We were all sweating by then. Rif took down two of the birch switch bundles hanging on the wall, laid one across Maura's lap, then approached Sigri with bowed head. "May I be of service?" she asked in a low, formal tone. Sigri looked toward me, shrugged, and took a position facing the wall with her hands braced against it. Maura was suddenly there beside me with her own bundle of switches, gesturing at me to do the same. I went along with it. We'd done this same sort of thing in the old days, ratcheting it up well beyond the traditional therapeutic usage. The idea of letting Maura use the switches on me was a bit disturbing, but at least it might distract me from the urge to shove Sigri hard against the wall and rub myself against her.

Apparently, Rif knew all about the ratcheting-up part, and so did Maura. The sting of the pliant birch twigs went up and down my back, lingered on my ass, then traveled down my legs and up again, over and over, more stimulat-

ing the harder they struck. All I could think of beyond my
own throbbing backside was how red Sigri's must be, and
how hot to the touch.

Sweat ran down my face, between my breasts, along my
spine, between my ass cheeks, and down my inner thighs,
although I couldn't be sure how much of that last substantial trickle was sweat and how much wild arousal. Any second, I would pull back, turn around, get to Sig—but just
before I tensed to move, another movement distracted
me—Rif darting between our arched bodies and the wall.
Suddenly a rope was pulling me toward Sig and winding
around her as well while Maura shoved me from behind so
that I faced Sig and Rif tugged at the crossed rope ends so
that Sig faced me.

We had to clutch at each other to keep from stumbling,
and then the clutching seemed like such a good idea that I
dug my fingers into the clenched muscles of her butt while
she yanked me by my shoulder blades hard up against her
big breasts. Resistance was so futile, it ceased to exist.

The girls wrapped more of the rope around us, but we
scarcely noticed. Sigri's mouth tasted of fine mead, and
mine must have, too, but however intoxicating that contact
was, there were other places that needed tasting. I licked
sweat from the hollow of her throat and then down between and around her breasts while she kneaded my back
and as far along my birch-switched ass as she could reach
until she pushed my torso back enough to work her tongue
and teeth down my chest to my belly.

Standing ceased being an option. The rope loosened, and a burst of steam swept over us. Someone, probably Rif, had poured water on the white-hot stones of the fire pit. As the steam cloud rose upward, Sig and I rolled on the floor, where there was slightly more air, first one on top, then the other, one knee thrusting and sliding between the other's sweaty thighs until the positions reversed. Finally, Sig growled "Dammit, Roby!" and held me down with her greater weight. What the heck, she was the host here. I let her big hand work into where I needed it most, arching my hips to meet her thrusts with equal force. A wave that had been building for over twenty years swelled, crested, and crashed down over me, through me.

In its ebb, still quivering and scarcely able to breathe, I swung above her, grabbed onto her wide hips, and went at her with tongue and mouth and teeth and, for all I know, nose and chin until she was as spent and breathless as I was. With all the meager strength we had left, we pulled each other upright, hands sliding along our sweaty bodies, and made for the door.

The snow was powdery, deep, and searingly cold on our superheated flesh. Just what we needed. We rolled together, still hot where our bodies pressed together, melting mystical runes into the white surface touched by our backs. When we finally chased each other back into the lingering heat of the sauna hut, Maura and Rif passed us, laughing, on their way out. Whatever they'd been up to, which wasn't hard to guess, they'd clearly had a fine time.

Later, dressed again and heading back toward the house, Maura tugged me aside along the path to the barn. "Don't you want to know which demon I picked for my dream lover?"

The others followed us into the dim space, now only slightly warmed by the embers in the forge and lit only by a single naked light bulb by the door. Maura proceeded along rows of strange figures made even eerier by the shadows. She paused once in front of a creature with a horned helmet, long braid made of straw-colored rope and sled-runner arms holding a shield made from a woodstove door embossed with a dragon silhouette, considered for a moment, then shrugged and moved on.

She stopped at last before a figure in the corner, limbs constructed from tent poles, one hand a saw-toothed adze blade used in ice climbing, and the other with a single digit, seven thick inches of spiral-machined, nickel-plated steel rod. She touched the tip of her own delicate finger to the tip of that rod where four tiny curving arcs of metal, not quite meeting, formed a delicate circle like a secret mandala.

"I might as well stick with this one," she said casually.

"An ice screw. I knew it." Sigri muttered behind us. Rif tugged at her gently and led her away, maybe thinking Maura and I would have some kind of tender interlude.

What actually happened was that Maura said, almost as casually, "I got a call yesterday from my agent, right before you picked me up at the airport. She said I got that movie role I was after. Not a lead, just the 'bad girl' character, but terrific exposure. We'll be shooting mostly on location in France and Switzerland."

"Good going, kid," I said, and put a comradely arm across her shoulders. We didn't have anything close to what Sigri and Rif had, and that was fine with me. Maura three or four times a year was about all I could handle, and if she really needed me in between, she knew that I'd come. Even from Patagonia.

Pulling

Don't look. DON'T LOOK! Keep your eyes on the horses, the judges, anything else. Anything but the bad girl of your dreams in her fuck-me-if-you-dare outfit. If you look, you'll never be able to look away.

But she *was* there. She'd really come. And it hadn't been just the garish lights of the midway last night. Even in the noonday glare Carla smoldered, like an ember about to ignite dry leaves. The thought of stirring up that blaze made me sweat. Except, it damn sure wasn't all sweat.

"She's here!" Cal said urgently. "Over by the fence!"

"Eyes front, or you're dead meat." I snarled, just low enough not to startle the horses. The loudspeaker announcing my team drowned out my voice.

"...Ree Daniels out of Rexford, Vermont, driving Molly and Stark, with a combined weight of..."

I backed them out smoothly enough and drove briskly down the drawing ring, grip on the lines steady, attention fixed strictly on the 4200 pounds of horsepower surging ahead of me. Two great glossy black rumps pumped in unison, two muscular bodies slowed and began their turn— and Cal stumbled on my right, just managing not to drop the evener bearing half the weight of the two single trees.

Ethan, craning to see, wavered on my left. He sped up—got into position—and the clang of the steel evener dropping onto the stone boat's hook sent the horses lurching forward with all their strength. The heavy sledge began to move. Shoulders bunched, hocks straining, hooves the size of pie plates chopping at the dirt, they pulled a load twice their own weight across the ground, responding to my hollered commands without really needing them, until the last few feet of the required distance. Training and heart were what mattered most, not driving skill, but I still wouldn't let either of my brothers handle my team in competition.

Not that Cal hadn't given it his best shot last night. "C'mon, Ree," he'd pleaded, "she said she might come on her lunch break. And I sorta let her think I'd be driving."

"You think she cares about anything besides the bulge in your britches?" I whapped his butt right across the wallet pocket. "You can strut your studly charms all you want tomorrow night. If you get lucky enough to have a chance at slipping something inside those tight panties of hers once the midway shuts down, you can even borrow my pickup. Tonight you get to bed all sober and early and solitary, 'cause tomorrow morning your ass is mine from dawn to whenever the pull is over and the horses rubbed down and stabled."

Cal couldn't make up his mind whether to sulk or grin. He'd have looked even younger than his eighteen years if he hadn't been six-foot-six, square-jawed, and built like somebody who'd grown up tossing around fifty-pound bales of hay. My "little" brother towered over me by four inches, which still left me six-two of height and plenty of bale-tossing capacity of my own.

I almost felt guilty at letting him get his hopes up, but I sure as hell wasn't about to tell him why.

If any slipping inside Miss Carla-from-Boston's panties was going to be done, I had a bet with myself that he wasn't going to be the one doing it. Not Cal, nor any of the other young punks—and some not so young—who hovered around her booth and pretended to be interested in throwing darts at balloons for cheesy prizes, while they watched her working her ass and tits and dark, light-my-fire eyes.

Cal and sixteen-year-old Ethan hadn't been hard to locate last night when I cruised the fairgrounds. Both white-blond heads, streaked hot pink and green and purple by the midway lights, loomed above the crowd. I hung back for a while near the balloon-dart booth to get an idea of what they were up to, hardly able to see the carnie huckster through the wall of testosterone-pumping adolescents between us. I could hear her slick come-on, though, and the sly, seductive tone of her voice sent hot prickles across my skin. Just food for fantasy, of course, but damn, she was good.

"C'mon folks, I'll rack 'em up again. See how Cal, here, got one right in there? Popped that cherry good? Here y'go, show us what y'got." I caught just enough movement to know she was tossing her long dark hair and twitching her hips for emphasis. "Stick that ol' dart right in! Ri-i-i-ght in there!"

"Right in where?" asked a wise guy. "Show me again!"

"If you can't find the spot on your own, hot stuff," she shot back, "maybe you better go home and practice some more on your favorite sheep."

Whoa. Considering the concentrated beer fumes in the area, she could be asking for trouble. I moved closer and squeezed in next to Cal just as the guy hurled his three darts too fast to be aiming much, and one balloon popped with a satisfying crack.

"There y'go, I knew you could hit the spot," she purred. "Prize from the first row, or wanna try again and get an upgrade?"

"How many hits to go all the way?"

His leer was unmistakable.

"Sorry, Bud, my ass isn't sittin' up on the prize shelf tonight." She tossed him a big purple plush snake and moved away. "Who's next?" Her sultry gaze lit right on me, and maybe she figured it was safer not to pitch to another guy right then.

"How about you, honey? I always like to see a lady show the guys how it's done." She put one foot up on the low barrier across the front of the booth, leaned an elbow on a sleek, black-stockinged knee and rested her chin on her hand. The top three buttons of her red satin shirt were unbuttoned, giving me a prime view of peach-tinted flesh barely held in check by a lacy black bra. Her mini-skirt was hitched up so high I caught a glimpse of matching garters and tender thighs. "How about it, darlin'?"

She sure as hell knows just how it's done. Question is, does she mean anything by it?

"Nobody here I'd call a lady," I said, looking her straight in the eye, "but I'll have a go at it anyway." I shrugged off my denim jacket and handed it to Cal, shoving him back a bit to give me room. All I wore underneath was an old white tank top smelling of sweat and horses. She handed me three darts, took my money, leaned a little farther forward, and tucked the bills loosely into her cleavage. The clueless males watching didn't seem to have any doubt that her show was for their benefit.

I raised my arm to pitch the first dart. The gaze of half the guys switched to the movement of my heavy tits—but her gaze was all that counted. And it was all I'd hoped for.

My first throw hit a red balloon, just making it bob sideways. "A real teaser, huh?" Her tone was impersonal, but a sidelong glance at my face and then my big hand hinted at more. I threw again, with a better idea of the angle required, and this time the balloon snapped and shriveled into a limp dangle of rubber. My inner tension built. When I popped the next one, too, the pressure exploding out of it seemed to pump me up right where it mattered most.

"Way to go, girl! Second-shelf prize," she said. "What'll it be?"

I stifled the impulse to ask if she was still so sure her ass wasn't on that shelf. "Go on to the next guy and let me think on it a minute, okay?" I said, and she nodded, so I got down to business with my brothers. Not that I wasn't thinking on my prize real hard.

"You two go on ahead," I muttered, hauling them away. "We have to get going early tomorrow morning. Tell you what, order us all some apple crisp with ice cream down the way at that church booth, and I'll meet you there in a minute."

"Rather have some fried dough," Cal grumbled.

"Okay, whatever, anything but those damned fried onion sunburst deals."

Cal took the money I passed him, still looking longingly back at the balloon game. Ethan looked, too, but more shyly.

"Her name's Carla," Cal said. "From Boston." As if her accent, its nasal edge a notch beyond our own upcountry twang, hadn't been a giveaway. "Isn't she hot? I told her about the horse pull tomorrow, and she said she likes to watch the big ones."

"I'll bet she does," I said. "Move your butts along, now."

And they went. Every time they do what I say I figure it may be the last, but this time I was paying them well to help with the team, so they were less inclined to argue.

When I turned back, a girl who'd been looking for her boyfriend was making a scene at the other end of the booth. Under cover of the distraction, Carla leaned close to me. "Your brothers?" she asked, jerking her head toward Cal and Ethan's retreating asses.

"'Fraid so," I said. "You got a thing for big dumb farm boys?"

She shrugged, clearly aware that the movement made her

shirt gape farther open, and that I was enjoying the view. "Not when there's a big farm girl around to distract me."

"You forgot the dumb part."

Carla looked me over slowly and thoroughly, her gaze moving down over my substantial midriff to rest on the crotch of my faded jeans.

"I'm not noticing any dumb parts," she drawled.

Damn! But attention was swinging back toward us. "So, how about my prize?" I asked. "You choose for me."

She reached for a cluster of long ropes of Mardi Gras beads, slung them over my head, then swished them back and forth across my chest. My nipples responded with visible enthusiasm. "Here's a first installment," she murmured. "You gonna be around later?"

"Not tonight. Got an early wake-up call coming and a busy morning." Which wouldn't have held me back if I hadn't known Cal would come looking when I didn't show up at our RV to sleep. "Maybe tomorrow night."

"Will you be at that horse pull deal the boys were talking about?"

"Wouldn't miss it." I pulled the hank of beads off over my short pale hair and handed it back to her. "How about you hang onto these until I see you again."

A couple of customers were waving money at her by then, but Carla stuck with me for another few seconds. "Okay, but keep this one." Before I could see what she was up to my wrists were tightly bound together by a strand of purple plastic beads. "So you won't forget."

Then she was playing to the crowd of men again, hips swaying, mouth sassing. I got my own mouth closed, stepped back into the shadows, and watched for a minute. What was it about her? She was good-looking, but not gorgeous, and not really all that young. Which was fine with me. More than fine. What she was, was…knowing. "Hot" pretty well covered it. Hot, and on the verge of bursting into flame. Something in the way she moved, as if the stroke of her clothes along her body kept her always turned on, hinted at sexual expertise country hicks at county fairs could only imagine.

I looked down at my bound wrists and imagined plenty. Breaking the fragile string would have been easy, but I wriggled loose with care, just in time to hide the beads in my pocket before Cal and Ethan came back to find me.

My imagination kept hard at work a good part of the night, too, which might have happened even if a strand of purple beads hadn't been nestled deep into the warm, wet heat between my thighs. I wasn't a dumb farm girl, not anymore, but whatever I'd got up to with girls at UMass and then in postgrad at UConn, it hadn't been much like this. I don't say that no femmes go for veterinary medicine degrees, but I sure hadn't come across anybody like Carla. The way she flaunted her body, and teased mine with her eyes, the thrust of her breasts and sway of her hips, offering and daring both at the same time… Well before dawn, I had to get out of the RV and find a place to do some serious solitary teasing and flaming of my own, and even that only slowed me down to a simmer.

In the morning, the horses got me back on focus. Molly and Stark had been pulling in competitions all summer, and knew what was what. They were about as psyched up as Percherons get, and maybe more than most. The huge black horses have been bred for double-muscling for centuries, but they have spirit and heart as well.

By noon, they'd come through the first few elimination rounds and hardly broken a sweat. This last load had been more of a challenge, but they'd handled it well. There were only four teams left in competition, and two of them I knew we couldn't beat without straining hard enough to risk injury. My pair were relatively young, full-grown but without all the heft a few more years would give them, and Molly would never quite achieve the muscle mass her brother could. Letting a mare pull was, in fact, pretty rare. I got a lot of flack from old timers for it, but she had the spirit, and I'd decided to give her one more year before breeding her and complicating her life with motherhood.

I watched the loader piling another 1500 pounds of concrete blocks on the stoneboat. So far, I'd never set the team at a weight I wasn't sure they could handle. Should I drop out at this stage and settle for an honorable fourth? Would I quit now, if I didn't want so badly to impress somebody who was watching?

Hell no!

Molly nudged me hard with her big velvety nose and blew as though in agreement. I whacked her shoulder companionably, turning my head a few degrees—and there was Carla right in my line of sight. Her mouth hung open and her eyes were wide with something that might have been fear. I grinned and nodded. Her cocksure, seductive expression from last night took over again right away, but she still eyed Molly warily.

Then Cal waved, and called to her, and I had to whack his shoulder to get him back on task. The first team of this round was trotting toward the loaded sledge. I was sure these huge Belgians were up to the weight, but their driver's helpers didn't get a secure hook before the horses bolted forward, and missed on the second try, too, so that by the time they did get a good hook, the team was too flustered to pull together. I elbowed Cal meaningfully in the ribs.

The second team gave it a good try, but stopped a few feet short in spite of all their driver's yelling. Then we were up. I bent for one last feel of each horse's hocks to be sure there was no tenderness, straightened from between enormous equine legs—and the quick flash of horrified awe in Carla's eyes sent a jolt of power crackling through my cunt.

Wow! But...no time for that now. No time for anything beyond keeping control of the eager horses while Cal and Ethan hustled to drop the evener onto the hook, and then the team's surge of power when I sent the order through the lines. The loaded stoneboat moved, caught, moved again, slid a few feet, slowed—"Hup! Hup! Hup!" I hurled my voice at them like an extra ton of muscle, of breath, of heart, and they took it all and gave back more, struggling onward just because they refused to stop. And then the judge signaled that they'd made the distance, and the boys released the sled.

My gorgeous pair of black, sweat-flecked treasures pranced back to the far end of the arena, proud, hyped by the applause, and, I knew from their gait, just slightly sore from the strain on their hocks.

After the last team made its distance, I waved off the next round. Second place was fine for now. Molly and Stark would give me everything they had, but I didn't need to make them find their limit at the risk of injury.

When the event was over and the rosettes awarded, I drove them out into the warm sunshine, keeping an eye out for Carla. Cal and Ethan had been headed off by a gaggle of cheerleader chicks, just the types that always give me flashbacks to the horrors of high school. The boys were welcome to 'em.

There she was, keeping a safe distance. "That was... something."

"Sure was," I agreed. "I need to get them rubbed down now and tape their legs. Want to come along and make their closer acquaintance?"

"I have to get back...I'm late already...but I close down tonight at ten." Molly's inquisitive black head swung toward her. Carla stepped back in a hurry.

"Then ten is when I'll be there," I said, riding a wave of confidence.

Carla tried for a note of command. "You'd better be."

She turned away, her fine ass eloquent with an assumption of power. But I'd seen some cracks in her eat-my-attitude self-possession, some fear and awe, maybe even excitement. And I'd enjoyed the hell out of how it made me feel. Those beads tight around my wrists—well, they'd sure sparked a tingle of anticipation and curiosity, and there was no denying that I'd go along with a lot just for the promise of some hot, wet, sweaty sex. Still, power was such a rush... It was going to be an interesting night, to say the least.

I was there, in fact, at eight, and at nine, just passing by, in range of her voice but not in her line of sight. Cal caught up with me in the next row at nine thirty and groused that Carla had turned him down.

"She's prowling around like a cat in heat, but says she's got other plans, and that's that. Didn't exactly tell me to fuck off, but close enough."

"You can still borrow my pickup," I said generously. "I'll probably just keep an eye on the horses tonight in the barn. What about those girls who've been trailing you around all day? I saw a couple of 'em hanging with Ethan over by the Tilt-a-Whirl."

He shrugged, but grabbed my keys fast enough and took off toward the rides with a fair show of enthusiasm. Good thing he was too full of what filled his own pants to notice how his big sister was prowling around.

At ten sharp, Carla was shooing the last few customers away. I stepped up, unlatched the front canvas flap and started to lower it. "Closing time, Sport," I said to the last reluctant straggler.

He started to object, tilted back his head to look up at me, paused reflexively at my chest, finally saw my expression, and decided he had business elsewhere. I dropped the flap to close us in and stepped over the low barrier, and into a role I was making up as I went along.

Her back was turned while she unclipped balloon fragments from the backboard. She'd shot me a little smile when I arrived, but there was something tentative about it, wary. Or maybe even nervous. I kind of liked the idea of making her nervous.

"So, what does it take," I asked, pressing right up against her ass and putting my hands on her hips, "for a big old farm girl to distract you?"

She turned right around into my arms and did a slow grind against me. "It's been a while since I got that lucky," she said against my chin. "What do you generally have in mind when you pick up slutty carnival hucksters?"

"Once I pick 'em up," I said, digging my hands into her round asscheeks and raising her so that her breasts rested above mine, "my mind doesn't have all that much to do with it." Which was pretty much true. "But I've been known to offer to buy a girl dinner. To keep her strength up."

She grabbed onto my shoulders and pushed herself higher. My nose was right in her cleavage and her musky scent telegraphed messages all the way down to my dampening cunt. "If you're hungry," she teased, "I have better ideas. If you think you can keep your strength up."

Well, I had better ideas, too. Like digging my teeth into the lace of her bra where it peeked through her unbuttoned shirt, and tugging. One nipple was about to pop free from constraint. "Hungry" didn't begin to describe it.

"But not here," she said, digging her knees hard into my midriff and straining away. I whoofed, groaned a complaint, and let her slide gradually down. One bent knee ground deliberately into my crotch as it went past, forcing out a different tone of groan.

"Think of the show we're putting on for anybody watching our shadows through the canvas," she said, once her feet were on the ground.

"We could just turn the damned light off," I said. "Or, what the hell, sell tickets to the show."

Carla scooped up a handful of the metal clamps that had held balloons to the wires strung along the backboard. "Nope." But she did turn out the light. "For what I have in mind, we'd knock the whole booth over, if you're as strong as you think you are."

That got my attention all right. So did the clamps. "So, where are we going?" All I had to offer was a few not-so-clean blankets in a horse trailer, or a bunk in an RV that might fill up with randy teenagers at any moment. Smooth. *Really smooth, Casanova.*

"To my cheap, tacky motel room. Where else?" She edged through the canvas flap into the night, still bright with streaks of garish, colored light from the rides, and

throbbing with the heavy beat of music. I followed, choos-
ing strong-and-silent over the distinct possibility of making
a fool of myself.

Her car was battered and dented. Prying open the pas-
senger-side door might have been a test of strength in itself,
but, if so, I passed. Carla's skirt was hitched up so high in
the driver's seat that I didn't refuse the invitation to explore
beyond her garters, in the process making sure I'd know
how to either unhook them with one hand when the time
seemed right, or to work right past them. I couldn't recall
anyone at vet school ever wearing garters.

From the pungent wetness of my fingers when we
reached the hotel, I knew Carla'd been more distracted than
any driver should be, but when I tried to clinch just inside
the door, she pushed me away. "My room, my rules," she
said sternly.

"We'll see," I said, leaning back against the closed door.
Skin flushed, lips full and moist, heat practically radiating
from her thighs, Carla clearly wanted it as much as I did.
"What've you got in mind? Something like 'The bigger they
come, the harder they fall'?"

"And the harder they come," she said, her purr verging
on a growl. "Get on the bed."

Well, what else was I here for? I strode over, trying to
look like it was my own idea. Then, I saw what was fastened to the metal posts of the bed. "Wait a minute, aren't
those the strings of beads I won?"

She reached into her purse. "Plenty more where those

came from." Her voice became a falsetto caricature of a Mardi Gras reveler. "Hey, baby, show me your tits and I'll throw you some beads!"

I laughed, and shrugged out of my jacket, making sure the small tin of horse lube from my vet kit didn't fall out of its pocket. Then I plopped down on the bed. "Show you my tits? If you can't find 'em on your own, baby, maybe you better go back and practice on your balloons."

She launched herself forward. I was flat on my back, jeans unzipped and yanked down past my ass, shirt pulled way up and nipples firmly twisted between her fingers, before I could do more than grunt.

"Spread 'em," she ordered, kneeing me without mercy. "Arms, too." She let go of my tits to push my hands toward the corners of the bed, which, of course, let her tempting breasts hang right above my mouth.

I went along with it. "You're going to tie me with just those flimsy strings of beads?"

"That's the plan." She got right to it. "Sure, you're thinking you can break free any time. But if you do, you lose out. The challenge is to hold still, no matter what I do to you." She reversed direction to work on tying my ankles. Now her crotch, skirt pushed up to her hips, was right above my face. So much for getting into her panties—she wasn't wearing any. I breathed in her scent hungrily, but didn't try to arch up toward her. I definitely didn't want to lose out.

So, I lay still, if not silent, when the clamps came out. She moved them along my flesh like crab claws traveling across a dune, digging into my belly, my ribs, the lower swell of my breasts. Anticipation became as sharp as sensation, until my nipples seemed to be straining toward the promise of pain. When the metal bit into my tender peaks with cold fire, my stifled scream had as much of relief in it as anguish.

My shoulders clenched, my chest heaved, but I managed to keep my arms and legs nearly still. Carla watched my face, and bent to chew my lips when they twisted with the effort to be silent.

"Not bad," she muttered against my mouth, "for starters." Her tongue nudged at my gritted teeth until I relaxed them and let her probe deeply. The sheet under my hips grew hot and damp as I imagined that supple tongue probing elsewhere.

Carla finally reared back and released the clamps. Pain flooded back into areas that had become nearly numb. Then I felt the procession of crab pinches travel up my inner thighs. "How're we doing?" she asked cheerfully, bending her head to watch her handiwork.

"Next time," I gasped, "How about a room with a mirror on the ceiling?" Her head was dipping lower. Was that brief pinch on my pussy lips from metal, or fingers? And was that…oh, God! Hot, wet, thrusting deep, and deeper, her face hidden between my thighs… My hips arched, my cunt grasped at the pressure, but Carla's tongue retreated, flicking my clit enough to swell it to desperation, but not quite to ignition.

"Don't move." she said, and kept at me, teasing with darting tongue and pinching fingers until my throat was raw with groans and curses. But I must not have moved hard enough to break the strings of beads, because they still hadn't snapped.

Until suddenly she pressed harder, and deeper, hands under my ass pressing me upward toward the mouth that gave me everything I wanted, everything I could take. My wrists and ankles tore free as I forgot everything but the fierce, consuming bite of orgasm.

"Is that what you call losing out?" I said faintly, when I got enough breath back.

"You did okay," Carla said. "Look at your wrists."

They were scraped and bleeding, and so were my ankles. The damned strands of beads hadn't been so easy to break after all. "Looks like...looks like I didn't meet your challenge as well as I thought."

She shrugged. "Those suckers are tougher then you'd think. Nylon string, knots between each bead. There's a fastener on each necklace that just pops open, but once you release that and tie 'em like rope they're really strong. Don't go thinking something's flimsy just because it looks tacky and flashy and cheap."

"I don't see anything here tacky and flashy and cheap," I said, looking straight into Carla's startled eyes.

She froze for a second, then leaned back and spread her thighs. The garters and belt had disappeared somewhere along the line.

"Show me what you got, then, big girl," she said, "and tomorrow I'll meet any challenge you name. Even if it means getting up close and personal with horses as big as elephants and twice as mean."

So I did, with hands that were hard where she was softest, leaving bruises that would linger. Finally, my fingers slicked with the horse lube, I worked my way deep into the first cunt I'd known that could swallow me to the wrist and clamp hard enough to give me bruises of my own. Not that I noticed those until much later, or the marks of her nails on my shoulders.

And Carla did meet her own challenge. Molly's broad black back will never look more glorious than it did when a dark-haired, seductive, naked Lady Godiva rode her through the horse barns one unforgettable midnight at the county fair.

Finding Carla

"Keep your skanky hands off me!" The words sliced through drifting aromas of coffee and pancakes and bacon. "Touch me again, and those fingers won't even be able to fuck your own sorry dick!"

I'd know that voice, that attitude, anywhere. A truck stop where Vermont slopes into New Hampshire wasn't high on my list of places to look, but how much, really, had I ever known about Carla? Apart from the way she sounded in hip-swishing, femme-top command of any situation— or with her hips so entirely out of control she couldn't shape gasps into words—or steeling herself to mount my huge draft horse. We hadn't had much time for the getting-to-know-you parts.

I couldn't see into the dining area past the family with fidgety kids ahead of me. Getting by without trampling them didn't seem likely, but I was giving it a try anyway when a skinny whirlwind shot from around the cashier's counter and whacked me from behind.

"Ree Daniels, move your butt!" The manager forged her way through the milling kids like an icebreaker. I was twice Lyddie Brown's bulk and a foot taller, but I followed in her wake anyway.

It was Carla, all right, her pot of scalding coffee poised right above the hastily withdrawn hand—and the crotch—of a middle-aged truck driver I'd seen around before. On the scuzzy side, usually on the make, but Carla could've handled his kind in seconds with a sly quip, back when she'd been working arcade games on the county fair circuit.

Now her face and body were tense, brittle, close to panic. She looked as near to being spooked as any horse I've ever handled. What the hell had got into her? And what was she doing here?

It was my turn to shove Lyddie aside, with a look meant to convince her I knew what I was doing. "Hey, Carla." I moved in close. "Let me help you out with that." My hand curled around her fingers on the coffeepot's handle. My body edged hers away from the customer. "Let's put it down over here, okay?"

The wildness in her dark eyes mellowed into recognition, and something I hoped was deeper. That last morning, while I was still asleep, she'd cleared out without any clue as to how to find her, and for nearly two years I'd figured all she'd seen in me was just a hot enough two-night stand to pass the time with. If she'd thought that was all I'd seen in her, she'd been dead wrong. Okay, I lied about the getting-to-know-you bit. Two days and nights was enough for me to discover the vulnerability behind the bravado, the steel determination that overcame fear—and to want to know more.

"Sure," she said now, "anything you say, big girl." Her voice shook, but the old low, intimate tone was still there.

Remembered lust surged back in a rush. Carla had always radiated sparks of bad-girl eroticism. Even with her waves of black hair confined in a knot and her waitress uniform just skimming her curves, she shot off pheromones that could pierce a Humvee. I'd have felt some sympathy for the driver if he hadn't started to bluster.

Lyddie rolled her eyes, jerked her head toward the office, and went into damage control mode.

I got Carla to the coffee station and deposited the hot pot. In spite of interested observers at every table, my hand settled into the sweet spot where waist curves to hip as I steered her into the office and kicked the door shut.

She was shivering when I put my arms around her. I'd never imagined Carla so shaken. Physically wary, sure—my big horses had scared her before she'd discovered the delights of naked bare-back riding at midnight—but nothing like this melt-down. "Oh, honey, what's the trouble?" I used my soothing-skittish-fillies tone. "It'll be all right." I stroked her black hair, glossy as my Percherons. It came loose from its prim knot, falling into the wild mane I remembered whipping back and forth over my sweaty torso as she rode me.

"No it won't," she muttered against my chest. When her head lifted I saw that the glitter of tears in her eyes came as much from rage as from despair. It was oddly reassuring.

"There goes another job. That bastard. But I can handle his kind without lifting a finger. Usually." Carla searched her breast pockets. I took pity and grabbed the box of Kleenex from Lyddie's desk.

I dabbed at her damp eyes. No makeup beyond a subdued shade of lipstick. She still exuded that seductive air that had grabbed me the first time I'd seen her, but something else as well that grabbed me harder, even as I shied away from examining it too closely. "So, what went wrong?"

"Me. I went wrong. 'Sorry, I'm not on the menu' didn't do the trick, but I could've just smiled and moved away. When he put his hand on my butt, though, I felt...I wanted...dammit, Ree, I needed to be touched so bad it hurt, but not by his kind."

I could recognize a mare in heat long before I earned my veterinary degree, and my experience of women had tuned me to the similarities. Women aren't as easily ruled by their hormones as mares, though. For Carla to go off the deep end, there must be as much turmoil in her head as in her body. Dangerous territory.

Just the same, my hand went to her thigh and would have traveled farther if Lyddie hadn't charged into the office just then.

Carla tried to pull away. I kept an arm around her shoulder.

"How's it going, Lyddie?" I hoped my grin still had the tomboy charm that used to get me extra pie as a kid. The manager had known me all my life, and my family even longer. We'd always stopped here when I was helping my dad transport horses to New Hampshire farms and fairs. The grin could have got me a whole lot more than pie if I'd been so inclined, once I'd grown up, cropped my straw-yellow hair short, and shown that I knew who I was and where I was going.

Lyddie looked us up and down, hands braced on hips, head shaking in exasperation. "Might've known you'd be acquainted. There's gotta be an explanation behind this, but I don't have the time or patience now."

"It's the old story," I said. "Farm girl meets carnival huckster at the county fair. The Lancaster Fair year before last, when my team was in the pulling trials." I realized too late that Carla might not have included the midway balloon/dart concession on her résumé.

"Judging by such a touching reunion, maybe you wouldn't mind taking Miss Volcano-mouth off my hands for a couple of days until all this drama blows over."

Carla stirred under my arm. "I'm sorry, Lyddie. I should just move on. Thanks for taking a chance on me, but I've always been bad news."

I wanted to shake the old arrogance back into her. On the other hand, if it had been just a shield, I wanted to know what was behind it.

Lyddie softened. "You're not bad, honey. You're just drawn that way."

Carla was right on it. "Thanks, Lyddie. Jessica Rabbit is my role model."

"You're a fine cashier and waitress," Lyddie added. "Never did figure out what you're doing in a place like this. You could make a lot more tending bar in the city or the tourist area over by Mt. Washington. At least bars have bouncers."

Carla'd begun to relax, but now she tensed and glanced away from Lyddie. "Can't blame a girl for wanting to try out respectability for a change."

I was tired of being left out of the conversation. "If riding in the cab of a horse van rates as respectable, I'd be glad of the company. I'll be back this way tomorrow or the next day. We'll see how things look by then."

"Just let me get out of this uniform and grab a few things." Carla wriggled out of my grasp. Lyddie and I watched her go, both our gazes fixed on her slender back and swaying ass, both of us exhaling when she'd gone. But Lyddie's sigh was somber.

"Can't get a job at a bar these days without a background check," she said. "A police record will shoot you right down. She's a whiz with numbers, too, took some accounting courses she says, but the same goes there."

"And what's that supposed to mean?" But I knew.

"Just something to bear in mind, Henrietta." Lyddie tweaked my butt and left the office fast. Just as well. I don't mind the occasional grope, but nobody gets to call me by my given name.

Carla met me at my truck. "You got Molly and Stark in there?" Face scrubbed, hair pulled into a flowing ponytail, jeans not too tight and plaid shirt managing not to gape across her full breasts, she'd still never pass for the girl-next-door type. Which was fine with me.

"Nope. Truck's empty. I'm picking up a couple of two-year-olds in Maine and bringing them back to my farm for training." I boosted her up into the cab, enjoying cupping her rump in my big hands.

"Haven't taken the team on the competition circuit

lately." I settled into the driver's seat. "Molly indicated in no uncertain terms last spring that she was ready to be bred, so all summer she got to laze around in the pasture with nothing heavier to pull than kids on a hayride, and this spring there's one more black Percheron filly in Vermont."

"A sweet little Molly!" Carla's smile wavered, and she turned her face away.

Dangerous currents for sure. It occurred to me that I did know, or at least suspect, something intensely personal about Carla. Something she didn't know I knew.

"Well, little is a relative term when it comes to draft horses." I pulled out onto the highway, wanting my bad girl back so hard that it was all I could do to keep from squirming in the dampened driver's seat, wanting even more to soothe whatever deep hurt gripped her.

"So, what brought you to a place like this?" I steered the conversation away from babies of any species. "When I didn't see you at the fairs last summer, I figured you'd gone back to the bright lights of Boston."

"I did go back to Boston." She was silent for a while, watching the scenery, the green hills, the Connecticut River as we crossed the bridge into New Hampshire. "But I had to get out again."

"Must be a story there." I tried for just a notch beyond casual, in case she felt like talking.

"Yeah, well, that's one way to put it." She shrugged. "Don't worry, there's no SWAT team out to get me. Nothing big-time. I just can't go back. Not yet."

I risked a bit of prodding. "Not until you get respectable?"

"Something like that."

Still no outpouring of personal drama. I decided to cut her some slack, opened my mouth to rattle off some lame anecdotes about the horses—and Carla turned with a smoldering look and a try-me tilt to her body that made my breath catch.

My bad girl was back.

"Don't tell me," she purred. "Let me guess. You're itching to know whether 'respectable' means no sex."

My lungs got pumping again. "So—does it?"

"Up until now," she said. "For the past...what's the date today?"

"Um, Tuesday?" I couldn't have told what year it was just then.

"May fifteenth," she said thoughtfully, and then, hardly missing a beat, "that's six hundred and thirty-nine days of no sex with anybody but myself."

She really was a whiz with numbers. I'm not, but that seemed like about two years. Just about how long since I'd seen her.

"Wow." I swallowed some smart-ass remark. "That's... well, seems like overdoing the respectability thing. No wonder you were getting kinda edgy."

"Edgy? You think?" She stroked her palms across her breasts, leaned her head back, and drew a long, unsteady breath. "My tits could puncture your truck's tires."

My eyes stayed fixed on the road ahead, neck cramping with the effort not to turn and stare. I knew a pull-off next to the river a couple of miles ahead, plenty big enough for the truck.

"How about you, Ree?" Carla knew she had me going. "You been getting plenty of action?"

"Haven't let anybody else tie me to the bedposts with Mardi Gras beads and then dare me not to break them, but I get by." I risked a sideways glance. "I still have some of those beads."

"So do I." Her wistful tone made me want to hold her close even more than I wanted to fuck her.

It was a good thing no fisherman was parked in my pull-off. A clash between a horse rig and a pickup would be no contest. And it was a good thing that a row of young birch trees, first tender green leaves unfurling, masked us from the road. Carla was on me before my truck stopped rolling. I grabbed both her hands and held her off, but she got a leg over my thigh.

"Carla, we have to talk. No fuck me and leave me this time. I mean it."

She tried to laugh. "Anything you say, big girl. But can't we fuck first and talk later? I promise I won't leave. How could I? You're my ride."

I guess I gave in, since suddenly my hands were on her hips and she was, quite literally, riding me. I leaned the seat back as far as it would go. Even so, her ass made the horn honk, so I squirmed sideways until my substantial butt was in the passenger's seat and we had just enough room to loosen our clothes in all the right places.

The sex was fast and furious, nothing fancy, with her knee in my crotch and my fingers in hers and our mouths hungry for whatever they could reach. We kept it up through wave after wave until finally Carla collapsed on my breasts sobbing for breath. It wasn't all that cold outside, but the windows were steamed up, making the space inside seem safe and intimate. Breathing our mingled scents, her skin pressed against mine, felt like coming to a home I'd just discovered.

It was a while before I realized that her sobs were producing real tears. "It's okay," I murmured, stroking her hair, my hand sticky with her juices. "Tell me about it."

"If only..." she nestled even closer against me.

"Tell me," I said, and then, on a hunch, "Girl or boy?"

She stiffened. "Girl. How did you know?"

"An educated guess." This was going to be tricky. "Okay, you know I'm a veterinarian."

"Yeah, so?"

I blundered along. "So, I have a problem. My hands are too big. Okay for delivering foals and calves, but not always for young ewes in trouble with their first lambing. Even with lube. In tough situations I need an assistant with, well, smaller hands." This wasn't going well.

Carla sat up straight and said it for me. "So, when I could take your whole hand that night, you figured I'd had a kid."

I shrugged. "Never found anybody who hadn't who could." No need to mention the faint stretch marks on her belly.

I thought a storm was brewing, but suddenly she grabbed my left hand and cradled it between her naked breasts. "Was that animal lube you used?"

"Horse lube. I never expected to get lucky at the fair, but I always keep some vet supplies in my truck, so…"

"Got any with you now?" This was the cocky, seductive Carla, even with a tear-streaked face.

"Maybe, but there isn't room in here for that much action. And you promised we'd talk." I draped her shirt around her shoulders and rebuttoned mine. "What's her name?"

"Josie. She's almost six." Carla took a deep breath, looked away, and let it all come rushing out. "She's been with my cousin in Boston since she was three. I…I couldn't be with her for a while, and when I got out, I couldn't find a job to support her, so I took whatever work I could get and saved up. It seemed like enough after the carnival gigs, but then my cousin said I wasn't a fit mother so she'd report me to social services if I tried to take my child. Now Josie's getting to be as wild as I always was, and they can't handle her, but my cousin still thinks it's her duty to try. And my cousin's husband comes on to me lately when I visit. So, I've been trying to get respectable—even got a job as a secretary, but of course my boss couldn't keep his hands to himself. I did some damage and had to get out."

No surprises there. What did startle me was my own sudden, certain determination. I turned her gently to face me. "Lyddie tells me you're good with numbers. Business paperwork fries my mind. Being a bookkeeper for a lesbian veterinarian might not rank at the top of the respectability chart, and I couldn't promise your boss would keep her hands to herself, but there's a farmhand's cottage you and

Josie could have to yourselves, separate from my house. It's yours if you want to give it a try."

A light flashed in Carla's eyes, then died. "Social services are such hard-asses!"

"It's the twenty-first century. Massachusetts and Vermont and even New Hampshire are getting better. And..." I played my remaining card... "I know a good Boston lawyer."

"Lawyers are expensive." Before my mouth was halfway open, she added, in her don't-cross-me tone, "No. You can't pay."

"No need. She does pro bono work for discrimination cases. And she owes me a favor."

"Oh?" Carla's expressive eyebrows arched. "I suppose you cured her horse, or something?"

"Her Great Dane. She has a vacation condo over toward Mt. Washington. I check up on the place now and then when she's not there. That's where we'll stay tonight, so we'd better get on the road."

"You must be real friendly with this lawyer," Carla said pointedly as we rolled along through the wide valley of the Ammonoosuc.

I just grinned, and took a while to answer. Spring was greening up the fields and woodlands. In spite of uncertainties, I was feeling pretty spring-feverish myself. "I have plenty of friends," I teased. "The favor she owes me is getting her together with another friend, a ski instructor at Wildcat."

"And now you're all pals together, right?"

"The condo does have a super-sized Jacuzzi," I countered. "Big enough for three, even if one is my size." She shouldn't assume I only wanted her because my opportunities were limited.

Carla got the full benefit of the Jacuzzi that night, but first she got the full benefit of me, and of my tin of horse lube, and a king-sized bed.

When we were finally so wrung out that even crawling into the Jacuzzi took an effort, we leaned back in it and let the interacting whirlpools and bubbles hypnotize us. At least I did, until Carla's foot nudged between my thighs, her toes pressed deeper, and suddenly all my focus was on where my cunt and her toes met.

She wriggled, teasing me, drew back, then thrust forward, harder each time. I'd fooled around in Jacuzzis before, but with Carla it felt different, the bubbles and swirling currents sensitizing my skin, her laughing eyes and flushed breasts rising like two peaked islands from the water, her demanding toes pressing against my clit, then sliding into my depths. If I'd ever wondered what an underwater orgasm felt like, I found out then. It turned out that my thrashing response sent waves over onto the floor, and then Carla launched herself out of the water and splashed more landing on top of me, so it was good thing the room had built-in drainage.

In the morning we enjoyed a brief steamy repeat. Then I left Carla still soaking while I called Attorney Cheryl Banks, Esq.

"Here," I said, back in the Jacuzzi room, "Cheryl wants to talk to you, alone. Lawyer-client privilege."

Ten minutes later, Carla came out, dark hair all damp

and curly, hips draped in a fluffy pink towel. She looked like a '40s pin-up girl. "Cheryl wants you now."

Cheryl never beats around the bush. "You're sure she's a keeper, Ree? Because the only really safe move is to marry her. If the cousin cries scandal then, it's a clear case of discrimination."

"I can't ask her to decide under pressure. But I want to get both her and Josie out of the city right away."

"It may be easy. The cousin's probably noticed her husband's shenanigans. Duty only goes so far. Well, go with the job offer, and I'll feel out my contacts in social services. Luckily, Carla never signed papers giving up custody."

I hung up. Carla got dressed without any attempt at distraction. "Ree, this doesn't have to be your problem. Don't decide anything under pressure yourself."

"I know what I want." Then, to keep it light; "And not just somebody to straighten out my bookkeeping."

"Cheryl says you can't even compute how much to tip a waitress. She also says if I hurt you, she'll hang me from a yardarm."

I laughed. "That's Cheryl for you. Besides skiing, she's into sailing, and likes slinging around nautical terms."

We didn't talk much more until the brown Belgian two-year-olds over in Maine were safely tethered in the truck and we'd headed west.

"What did that guy say when he slapped you on the back?" Carla's casual tone wasn't convincing.

"My cousin Jack. He said, 'Way to go, Ree!'"

"What will they say where you live?"

"Folks got bored talking about me years ago, which isn't to say they won't enjoy gossiping about somebody new. The Vermont tradition of minding your own business doesn't rule out knowing everybody else's, but most won't be outright mean, and some will be friendly. I took considerable flack when I was growing up—" I let a little bitterness show—"but even the guys who tried to date me in high school just because their dads wanted big strong grandsons are good friends now. Anyway, no farmer wants to piss off the vet he might need to call in the middle of the night."

"What about your family?"

"You met my big dumb brothers at the fair. Ethan's a nice kid, away at college in California. Cal's got a good wife now, and a baby on the way. If he lets slip that you worked on the midway, so what? A job's a job. And he sure knows from experience how you turned down all the guys panting after you at the fair. My mom's gone, and my dad...well, whatever he thinks, he won't be unkind."

At the truck stop I left her with Lyddie, who knew better than to try to talk me out of anything. She did issue a warning to Carla, though, in my hearing, pretty much what Cheryl had said about not hurting me, but in earthier terms.

Two weeks later Carla, with Cheryl's backing, reclaimed Josie. The cousin seemed relieved to have her hand forced. Carla and Josie stopped over at Lyddie's for the night.

Josie was the true test. If she couldn't adjust, Carla

wouldn't stay. I had a not-so-secret weapon, but who knew what a city kid would think?

I paced all morning. My dad, just as nervous in his way, drove the tractor up from his place and tinkered with harness repairs in my barn. He'd had a good idea of what I was up to on my trips to visit friends in North Conway and Boston and Provincetown, but this was the first time I'd ever brought someone home, and under complicated circumstances. I couldn't blame him, but I wished he'd waited.

By the time Carla pulled up in front of my house, I'd forgotten he was there. I had my arms around her as soon as she emerged from the car, and for a moment her head rested against my shoulder where it belonged. Then she straightened. "Josie's asleep. She's had a rough couple of days."

Over on the passenger side, a tangle of dark curls stirred, lifted to show a pair of drowsy blue eyes, and then a clear, high voice said, "You promised there'd be big horses!" Her tone clearly showed she expected to have been duped.

"Come on, I'll show you." Josie avoided my offered hand, squirmed out on her own, saw Molly and the filly in the paddock and trotted toward them.

"She doesn't trust anybody much," Carla said. "Especially me."

Molly's huge black head extended over the gate by the time Josie got close. The little girl slowed until we caught up.

"Hi, Molly," Carla called. Even after almost two years, Molly's ears pricked up at a familiar voice. She whickered softly as we approached, lowered her head to be petted, and Carla stretched up on tiptoe to scratch between her ears.

Josie tried to stroke the velvety nose, but couldn't reach. I picked her up and sat her on the fence too fast for her to struggle. Just then, the month-old filly came out from behind her mother, prancing on long legs she was still getting the hang of, and the two youngsters were face to face.

Josie reached out. The filly danced backward a few steps. "What's her name?"

An opportunity too good to pass up. "Maybe you could think of a good name for her." After all, her name in the Percheron registry book was too long for daily use. "And I was hoping you could help another way. She needs somebody young to be her friend. All the other horses are too old." I waved toward the Belgians and Molly's former teammate Stark, browsing in the next pasture.

Josie cocked her head, pondered half a minute, and announced, "Her name's Dancer. Right, Dancer?" She reached out again. By some miracle, or because the filly figured she'd been skittish long enough, nose and finger connected. On the child's face I saw the same thrill I'd felt long ago with my own first horse.

Carla was staring past my shoulder. For an instant she shrank back against Molly's sheltering neck, then stepped forward, hand extended with dignity and grace.

"Hello, Mr. Daniels." She met my dad's eyes directly. "I'm very glad to meet you, and happy to be here."

He'd taken to expressing his inner Viking with a shaggy beard since my mom died, but behind it a little smile twitched at his lips. He shook Carla's hand. "We're glad you're here, too. Is it okay to call you Carla? Any friend of

Molly's is a friend of the family. Lyddie Brown recommends you, but I value Molly's opinion the highest."

Carla's dazzling smile could have knocked a less substantial man back on his heels. "Any friend of Molly's is my friend, too."

"Look, Dancer is my friend now," Josie called.

Dad shot me a questioning look. I shrugged. "Don't worry. I won't team her with a horse named Prancer."

"Well, Miss Josie, that's a fine name for a fine filly." He moved up close. Josie still hadn't looked directly at me, but she tilted her head way back to look him over, the tall, thickset body, the weathered face, the graying blond beard.

"Are you a grandpa?" she asked suddenly.

Carla, embarrassed, started toward her, but Dad answered solemnly, "No, not yet, but I'm told I will be soon. Maybe you could help me practice."

"I don't have a grandpa," Josie said bluntly. "Or a dad, either." Her little chin was raised in defiance.

"I reckon you'd still know whether a grandpa should take a little girl to see a litter of week-old kittens, if her mother didn't mind. What do you think?" He jerked his bearded chin toward my barn.

"Kittens?" She hesitated. "Okay, but Dancer will still be my very best friend!" Her small fingers gripped his big, gentle hands, and she let him swing her down from the fence.

"Okay with you, Carla? Maybe after the kittens, I could take her down to see the young lambs at my place and share my mac 'n' cheese for lunch, while you get settled in. Back in an hour or so."

Carla tensed beside me. I squeezed her hand reassuringly and nodded as subtly as I could.

"Of course." she said. "How could I say no to a treat like that?"

She stared after them with an odd look on her face. "Josie's certainly hooked."

"Carla," I said nervously, "I didn't mean to make you feel trapped. I guess I got carried away with making Josie feel at home here."

"Trapped?" She tugged my face into kissing distance. After a brief moment of blood-stirring contact, she pulled back. "You want to know why I was at Lyddie's? After the secretary fiasco, I was all torn up. I'd failed Josie, failed everything. So, I just drove, and drove, not caring where. Lyddie's was where I ran out of gas, ran out of money, ran out of running. It wasn't till I had to stop that I knew I'd been running toward Vermont to find you." She hid her face against me, not before I saw the glint of tears. "Not to load you with my troubles. Just to be...closer."

"I looked for you all that time," I said. "You had me for sure by that second night. Or maybe that very first minute."

"Remember at the fair when I showed you how strong the Mardi Gras beads were," she said, "and told you not to go thinking something's flimsy just because it looks tacky and flashy and cheap?"

I held her even closer. "I said I didn't see anything there flashy or tacky or cheap. And I meant it."

"I know. That's when you had me for good. Even if I had to leave."

We clung together in silence for a minute, and then her body moved against mine in search of more than comfort. "Don't we have an hour now before we have to be respectable again?"

We didn't waste a second of it. When my dad brought Josie back riding on his shoulder, he approached the cottage whistling loudly, and didn't seem at all surprised that very little had been unpacked. "Quite a girl you've got here, Carla." He swung Josie down and escorted her into the cottage.

Josie called from her new bedroom, "Mom! There are horses on my curtains!"

Carla's head jerked. "She hasn't called me Mom in years."

My dad came back out. "Wouldn't mind for this grandpa thing to be permanent, if you and Henrietta should ever see your way to it." He strolled nonchalantly to his tractor and drove off.

"Henrietta?" I'd never seen Carla so taken aback.

"Family secret. He got away with it this time. But never again, unless we're in front of a preacher making honest women of each other. And that won't be until you see if you can stand rural life, and a Vermont winter."

"And be respectable enough?"

This time I did shake her, but gently. "Don't you go all respectable on me. Well, only as respectable as we need to for Josie's sake," I conceded, but my words were muffled by Carla kissing me so hard I doubted we'd wait all that long after all. Good thing I'd already put in an order for a Jacuzzi.

Flying the Prairie Lily

The curving staircase rose right up from Miss Lily's plush and gilded parlor in a sweep so wide, so elegant, I doubted there was another such thing closer than San Francisco. Miss Lily herself moved down it like she'd invented the whole notion of elegance, along with all the earthlier charms of a woman's body. I doubted there was another such sight as her to be seen, either, closer than San Francisco, and likely not even there.

She wore some sort of satiny dressing gown, open a good way down the front and clinging to all the curves not otherwise revealed. My embarrassment at calling so early, without taking into account the hours people must keep in an establishment like this, was considerable, but not so much as to make me regret getting such a view. While the pretty girl who'd fetched her had surely stirred my pulses, I was happy enough to see the back of her, and not just because of her mighty appealing rear view.

Miss Lily looked me over real slow, like I might be a saddle horse she contemplated buying. I was all too aware of how tight my brother's britches fit me in the butt. No hope in hell that she'd mistake me for him, even with my hair the same sun-bleached wheat as his, and chopped just as short. When her gaze lingered briefly on my crotch, I figured it was just as well I'd decided against that rolled-up sock I sometimes used to augment my privates. I had a notion she'd seen me before, stealing sidelong glances at her in the street, and like as not knew just who I was.

"Miss Lily," I said, trying to sound as cool and unflustered as anybody could expect in such circumstances, "I'm Maddy Brown, and I'm here to discuss a business matter."

The arch of her brows heightened a bit. The corners of her red lips might've twitched if she'd let them. After a pause long enough to give me time to curse myself for how that must have sounded, she said, "And just what kind of business did you have in mind, Miss Brown?" She sank down onto a plumply cushioned settee, leaned forward, and motioned for me to take a chair.

Well, what I had most urgently in mind right then was wondering how much farther down into her very low-cut satin bodice I could see if I moved a step closer, but I sat down. She leaned back, an arm raised along the back of the settee, which lifted one full breast until it seemed like its nipple would surely spring free from the barely confining cloth. My own modest nipples tingled under their homespun binding.

I cleared my throat. "Well, ma'am, what I need is to purchase a large amount of silk fabric. I was told by Miss Ballingham, the seamstress, that you order bolts of cloth direct from your own source in San Francisco, and then she makes it up to suit you and your—your young ladies. She doesn't get much other call for silk around these parts."

"Very true," Miss Lily said. "But now you feel the need to...to expand your wardrobe? Quite extensively?"

Her eyes gleamed with amusement beneath lowered lids. She knew well enough, I guessed, that dresses were not what I had in mind.

"It's not my wardrobe that needs expanding, Miss Lily," I said coolly, damned if I'd let her fluster me any more than I could help. "Do you know anything about hot air balloons? Montgolfiers, folks call them sometimes, after that Frenchman."

"Ah," she said, sitting up straighter and looking more alert. "You're Teddy Brown's niece, aren't you, God rest his soul. You do favor him considerably—although," with an openly wicked perusal of my legs, "he'd never have done such justice to those doeskin trousers." She leaned far forward to lay a hand on my thigh, and between the heat spreading from there to my belly and the truly remarkable view I got of her splendid bosom, I came close to forgetting what I'd come for.

Then she stood up. "Well," she said briskly, "if you're planning on launching Teddy's Prairie Lily, you'll get all the help you need from me, for old time's sake."

I nearly knocked over the chair as I lurched to my feet. In all the time I'd known Uncle Thaddeus, which was roughly the first fourteen years of my life, it had never occurred to me that his airship might be named for anyone, much less the madam of the most elegant whorehouse between Kansas City and San Francisco.

"Come along," Miss Lily said, a touch impatiently, as she moved toward the stairs. "How much silk do you need? Just for patches, or major reconstruction? I suppose the poor thing has been jumbled up in the corner of some barn for the last six years, since Teddy died."

"No, ma'am," I said indignantly, "not jumbled. I did my best. But he didn't use it much those last few months, or fix it up after the barn roof caved in on it during a blizzard."

Uncle Ted had finally succumbed to the recurring fever he'd got while he was away at Mr. Lincoln's War, flying airships with Colonel Lowe's aeronauts and keeping the Rebel troops under surveillance.

"And then my Pa made me promise I wouldn't try to launch it myself till I turned twenty. Which I just did." I followed her up the stairs, my breath coming a bit faster by the top, not so much from exertion as from the tantalizing effect of satin sliding over well-rounded buttocks just inches beyond my nose.

In the upper corridor a row of female heads poked out to watch us. Some were two to a room, and the girl I'd seen downstairs, a tousled redhead, had her arm around a taller, copper-skinned girl with long black braids. When she grinned at me, and winked, I found myself giving a moment's thought to the benefits of working in such a place.

Then I followed Miss Lily into the front bedroom, all rose and ivory and crystal, and couldn't think of anything at all except the fact that she was untying the sash of her dressing gown.

"Well, Maddy Brown," she said, gesturing toward a little room opening off to the side, "I don't suppose you'll mind if I take advantage of my bath water while it's still hot. You caught me just as I was about to step in."

I was amazed she'd agreed to see me at all, in that case, and even more amazed at what she was letting me see. Her rose and ivory body was reflected in two long mirrors, but I kept my warm gaze on the real thing and watched sharply for some cue as to what was expected of me. At the very least, I might learn a thing or two of use in the future.

When she raised her arms to pile her red-gold hair on top of her head, her breasts lifted and seemed to challenge my hands to weigh them. The curve of her rounded belly led my gaze downward to the darker gold cluster of curls at the junction of her thighs, and as she began to turn toward the waiting bath, already afroth with rose-scented bubbles, I had a startling urge to catch her round the hips and press my face into those musky curls before she got too clean. I stored away the thought to dream on.

She stepped into the big copper tub and settled languidly into the steaming water. "So, Maddy," she said, spreading soap froth over shoulders and breasts getting rosier by the second from the heat of the bath—and just maybe, I hoped, from the heat of my gaze. "Why do you think I brought you up here?"

"To scrub your back?" I asked cockily, if a bit breathlessly.

Not many could look severe in a bubble bath, but Miss Lily managed it. She sat up straight and water sluiced over her curves like syrup over preserved peaches. "Just you turn yourself around, girl," she said, so sternly I obeyed without a murmur. I could feel my face glowing as pink as her soap-slicked flesh. "Now open the bottom drawer of that chiffonier."

I did as I was told, feeling, when I knelt down, as though my brother's britches had grown even tighter than before. I had to tug to get the drawer open. Then I saw the folds of ivory silk filling it, and reached out to touch the smooth fabric with something like awe.

"Sheets," Miss Lily said behind me. "The finest quality, never used. Teddy always preferred the French weave, on the bed or in the air. How many do you need?"

I most definitely did not want to imagine Uncle Teddy sprawled on Miss Lily's sheets, touching her silken skin, but I surely wished I could be there in his place. Which reminded me what else I was determined to do in his place. I wrenched my mind back to business.

"I can get by with three or four, depending on how much they cost," I said. French weave might well be beyond my means, but I recognized by the feel and heft that this silk was the perfect match for what was left of the Prairie Lily.

"Take six," Miss Lily said. "I'm willing to barter."

So, I filled my arms with folded sheets, stood, and turned back toward the tantalizing vision of Miss Lily in her bath. She was sponging her shoulders and breasts, and then, eyelids half lowered as she watched me watching her, she dipped her hand beneath the water and reached down between her thighs. "Set them on the bed, girl, before you drop them," she murmured in a low, purring tone. I stumbled into the bedroom, dumped my load, and couldn't keep from touching myself some before I turned back, which made my borrowed britches feel all the tighter. And damper.

"All right," I said, when I was back beside her. "Let's barter. What's your price?"

I knew by now she was toying with me, and I wasn't quite cocky enough to think that what she wanted was what I'd have paid half my savings to provide, and let the Prairie Lily wait another year or two to fly.

"Take me along," she said, no hint now of seduction in her voice. "Take me up with you when you fly her." She stood right up in the bath, looking like that picture of the goddess standing in a seashell, but even more bountiful. When she gestured toward the bucket of water for rinsing, I hustled to lift it and pour it over her, struggling to keep a steady aim at her shoulders while my gaze followed the downward flow of the water over the ins and outs of her lush curves.

She stepped out onto a fleecy sheepskin mat as I was bending to set down the bucket, so that for a moment my face was on a level with the triangle of wet curls between her thighs. I came close to falling to my knees to explore those glimpsed delights, and maybe even to rouse a muskier aroma to spice up the scent of roses rising from her skin, but she took down the biggest, softest towel I'd ever seen from a nearby hook and wrapped it around herself. I stood and stepped back.

"Well," I said, struggling to remember what we'd been talking about. "So that's all?" I wiped the sweat from my forehead with my sleeve. The little room had got mighty cussed warm. "You want to go up with me? You're that sure I know what I'm doing?"

"You just run along now, Maddy Brown, and don't worry," Miss Lily said, turning her back to me and letting the towel slide away from her fine, round, taunting buttocks. "I know enough for both of us."

I had no doubt of that at all.

Turned out Miss Lily knew a good deal about ballooning, too. She loaned Miss Ballingham two of her girls who were good hands with a needle, and drove the three of them out to the ranch in her own wagon when the seamstress had finished as much stitching as could be done on her treadle sewing machine. While they worked to insert new panels into the huge silk bag spread out on the carefully swept barn floor, Miss Lily grilled me on the rest of the project. When she'd inspected the wicker gondola and the heating device, mounted on steel rods in a way that let it swing to stay level, like a lantern on a ship, she seemed satisfied. I was relieved she didn't question the necessity of using buffalo chips for fuel, charcoal being pretty much out of the question out here on the prairie, and tanks of gas even less affordable.

"You must have flown a good deal with Uncle Ted," I said, for conversation, as we leaned against the paddock gate outside. I tried my best not to be too obvious in how I was looking at her. Ranch hands kept finding excuses to wander by, and I figured it was none of their business if my eyes devoured her with the same avid hunger as theirs. Her severely cut jacket and no-nonsense skirt just made my memories of her naked, glowing flesh all the more vivid, and the row of tiny buttons down the front made me itch to undo them, very slowly, and find out what she wore underneath. If anything at all.

"Just a time or two, since I came West," Miss Lily said. She looked past the colt being schooled on a long rein into some far distance of her own thoughts. "I don't suppose Ted ever told you that we knew each other before, in the war. I was a nurse in a field hospital."

Now I could guess at some of what she saw in that distance. Uncle Ted, like so many others, had caught his fever in a hospital tent, where he'd gone for a simple broken leg after a wind-botched landing. "So, you flew with him some back then, too?" I asked.

"Oh, that would have been against regulations," she said solemnly, but a smile twitched at her carmined lips. Then I started, as she reached out a gloved hand and pinched my rump firmly. "Don't think you're the only girl who's ever borrowed a pair of trousers," she said, with mock severity.

I wanted to ask more, but she started back toward the barn. I watched her undulating walk, and speculated on whether her fine, wide hips had been less bountiful back then. It was pretty common gossip that Miss Lily had come West to be a schoolmarm, and decided she might as well make men pay for what they were bound and determined to have anyway. Some still referred to her as the School-marm, in fact, which might have had more to do with her expertise with the customized whip she wore now coiled at her waist than with any actual schoolroom. Gossip also had it that there was no limit to what some men would pay for. I preferred to imagine her soft, and alluring, and naked, but the notion of watching her lattice some whimpering cattle baron's pale hairy butt did have a certain amount of appeal. I was speculating a bit on being the one holding the whip—and then, just outside the barn, she stopped and turned to me.

"So, Maddy Brown, what are your plans for the future? I'll wager you have more on your mind than just getting the Lily in the air."

Well, I did. More even than getting the original Lily right up naked against me, though that part seemed mighty urgent whenever she got close. And when I lay alone in the middle of the night. And whenever I had a moment to daydream.

"I plan to move on," I told her, "to someplace with more people, more sights, more choices. San Francisco, for starters. Around here there's a few folks might pay to fly in a balloon, like the hunters who come by train to shoot buffalo, but I'm not of much mind to help them find what few herds are left. In San Francisco, though, folks are always coming and going, some with plenty of money, and there are fairs and celebrations of all kinds. Could be a living to be made by an experienced aeronaut, and plenty of other work besides. And more to see than here, and more kinds of people."

Miss Lily nodded, knowing well enough what I meant, what kinds of people I hoped to find. "So, you've no ties keeping you here but family?" she asked. "No young man?"

I could tell she thought she knew better than that. "Oh, I've had one," I told her nonchalantly, "a time or two. Just to try him out. But I made him let me tie him to a fence post first, and not interfere too much. The first time he sputtered a bit, but by the second time he was all for it. After that I figured I'd learned pretty much all he had to offer, and sent him on his way."

She laughed so hard she had to lean against the barn. I thought I might have to open up her clothes and loosen her stays so she could catch her breath, but that was mostly wishful thinking. "Maddy, Maddy!" she said, when she could finally speak. "If ever you want such employment, at my place or in San Francisco, just say the word!" And she tweaked my rear again and sailed on into the barn to gather up the seamstresses for the ride back to town. I firmly resolved that the next time she laid a hand on me—and I'd surely give her every chance—my own hands would get busy, too.

Miss Lily was all business from then on, though, right up until the still, chilly dawn a week later when we met for our first ascent. Her approaching carriage was visible between wisps of mist rising from prairie grasses silvered with dew, as I made sure of all the final details. The chase wagon was ready to follow where the wind took us and retrieve us when we landed. Ranch hands stood beside tethers staked to the ground, ready to add their weight when the slowly swelling silk envelope reached positive buoyancy.

My body felt a slow swell of anticipation, too. Some of the feeling was familiar from when I was twelve, and Uncle Ted had first let me soar aloft with him, but now my senses had learned vastly more about how intensely my flesh could feel. Miss Lily's approach made me tingle with awareness of how much more I might yet learn. She reached me just as the balloon jerked, and lurched, and rose erect to quiver above us, straining at its tethers like a colt born to run.

My blood quickened. Something deep inside me lurched and quivered, too, and I could swear my private parts rose just as full as the balloon, and strained as hard to run their course. Flying and Miss Lily were all bound up together in my elation, and from the way excitement glowed in her eyes and made her face seem near as young as mine, I knew she understood.

Face to face in the wicker gondola, a few feet above the ground but still tethered, we both said at once, "Are you sure you're dressed warm enough?" or some such thing. Then we both laughed. I knew how cold the air would be up high, but at that moment I couldn't imagine feeling anything but heat in her presence, all the more so when she turned her back to me and lifted the skirt of her woolen dress up so far, I could see her knit silk long johns all the way up to the curve of her buttocks. She had sent me a similar set of underwear, and I knew Uncle Ted had considered knit silk the warmest for the weight, so I was wearing mine, too, and had been savoring the smooth friction as if it had been her touch. Now I didn't miss the chance to savor her flesh through her underwear and the rawhide of my glove, and, far from objecting, she pressed backward into my touch.

"Let 'er rise," I called down to the men at the ropes, and reached overhead to feed more buffalo chips into the burner. The earth sank gently away beneath us—and we were aloft, free, rising almost straight up until a light wind at a thousand feet caught us and swept us slowly toward the distant Bighorn Mountain range rising abruptly to the east.

To the west, the prairie seemed endless, the high Rocky Mountains only a long, blue smudge along the horizon. Far, far, beyond, to the southwest, the earth curved onward, I knew, to San Francisco and the sea. But for now, there was nowhere I'd sooner be than drifting above a sea of grasses licked with flame-color where the Indian paintbrush bloomed, Miss Lily beside me in our own private universe.

By the time we'd reached two thousand feet, the wind had dwindled until we were barely drifting eastward. A hawk soared just above and to the side, riding the same air current that bore us. Miss Lily watched with interest as I reached into a sack and brought out the precious store of high-grade charcoal I'd managed to trade for; enough, arranged just right amidst the embers, to keep us aloft without much effort or attention for at least half an hour. She knew just what I had in mind.

"I suppose, you young vixen, you think you've got me at your mercy up here," she said, looking not the least bit reluctant.

"What's mercy got to do with it?" I sounded a bit more cocky than I felt, but entirely determined. She hadn't brought her trademark whip, which was just as well, considering the close quarters and the burner overhead. "But I do feel responsible for keeping a lady warm enough when I take her for a ride."

"Why, Miss Maddy," she said teasingly, "I do believe I'm so warm now that I must have a few buttons loosened, or I shall swoon," and she raised a languid hand to her high collar.

That was all the encouragement I needed. I moved close against her, shucked my rawhide gloves, drew her warm cloak aside, and embarked on the glorious task of unbuttoning every last pewter button down the front of Miss Lily's dress. And the shell buttons down the front of her silk underwear, too.

Every few inches I paused to explore the territory revealed, slipping my fingers under the fabric to feel, at first, her smooth shoulders, and on down to burgeoning breasts that filled my hands to overflowing, and then filled my mouth, too, with demanding nipples. Wordless sounds of approval vibrated through her flesh into mine to let me know just what my lips and tongue and teeth were doing right. I might never have proceeded onward if the warm scent rising from below hadn't grown more and more insistent. When I first tried to move along, she moaned and held my head tightly at her breast for a long further minute. Then she urged me downward.

I bent and savored the soft flesh of her belly with such fervor that I left marks. Her long underwear, like mine, was open at the crotch, a construction I had noted with interest. I slid my hand along between silk fabric and silkier skin until short curls coiled around my fingers, not obstructing my progress but rather luring me farther into her damp, musky heat.

My probing was met with great enthusiasm, and thrusting forward of hips, but I wanted more. I wanted to see Miss Lily, in all her naked glory, in the clear light of a prairie morning. The hand that wasn't deep between her thighs had a firm grip on her luxurious hindquarters, and neither hand was inclined to shift position, so, with a quick assessment of altitude and the balloon's state of inflation, I dropped to my knees and applied my teeth to the problem, tugging her long johns all the way down to her ankles.

If Miss Lily's gasp was of indignation, it surely wasn't reflected on her face. I glanced up, saw her head thrown back and her arms raised so she could grip the ropes connecting basket and balloon. Then I glanced back down, looking my fill at the deep, glistening pink of her nether lips. A demanding wriggle of her hips inspired me to look closer, and closer, until taste took over from sight.

Glory beyond imagining, to be high and free and pressing my mouth into Miss Lily's heat! I licked the salt-sweet tang of desire from her crevices, probed and sucked at flesh both rigid and tender, and felt my own flesh tauten and my juices flow. Her voice rose, her breathing quickened into a storm of rough gasps, and, though I yearned to see her face in such extremity, I kept at her until a cry so long and keen it could have come from the hawk cut through the air, piercing through her body into mine.

Much later, skin chilled but still warmed to the core, we waited on the prairie for the chase wagon, wrapped close together in Miss Lily's cloak. Though our clothes were demurely re-buttoned, lessons in the subtler aspects of seduction went forward, and I paid close attention indeed.

Later still, I knelt beside the copper tub of steaming water, this time free to let my hands slide over Miss Lily's rosy flesh wherever my fancy led them, and to join her, at last, in the bath. On the bed in the next room, a contraption of harness and padded leather waited, teasing me with intimations of how much I had yet to learn from the Schoolmarm, but the intoxication of skin on skin, of Miss Lily's glorious body naked against mine, kept me from being in a hurry to move on. Until suddenly, urgently, I was.

And so began the next lesson.

In the Flesh

The fuchsia-topped cupcake was still there in the morning. Worse, so was I. No homicidal tendencies in her as far as I could sense, but I could hope I'd been wrong. Some darkness all too close to my own roiled beneath the surface of her mind. I didn't care enough to probe.

Waking up was all I could handle. Waking from dreams of Allison, vibrant, sensuous, her breasts warm against mine, her thigh teasing my crotch.

But Allie was gone. Forever.

The message light pulsed in counterpoint to the throb in my head. Last night I'd ignored it. Now I resigned myself to the inevitable. My own dumb fault to stay at a hotel old-fashioned enough to have a working landline.

"Lexie? You're still in New York?" I had a sudden, gut-wrenching hunger to hear Allie's husky-sweet voice, however impossible, but it was only Janet calling, of course, trying for casual and not quite making it. "Let me know when to meet the train again, okay?" She drew a shuddering breath. I dropped the receiver and burrowed under the pillow.

When I came up for air, last night's little distraction was holding the phone. I remembered nudging her out of bed, expecting her to take a stab at my wallet once I'd zonked out. Maybe, if I were lucky, a stab at me. She hadn't even picked up the bills on the dresser.

"Don't you wanna know what else she said?"

God, an emotional voyeur. My head pounded. When Allie and I were young, there was no such thing as too much wine. Too much anything. I curled into a ball of misery.

"If you don't get back today, she's gonna come find you. And then she said, 'Lexie, you promised!'"

"I didn't promise her!"

The musk of sex hung heavy in the air. I lurched into the bathroom, hoping she'd get the hell out.

No such luck. When I stumbled out of the shower she eyed me in obvious hope of earning an honest bonus.

"I didn't think you'd be so...well, I've never been with a silver butch before."

"Yeah? You want a reference?" A year ago, my hair had still been dark. Six weeks ago, for the memorial service, I'd let Janet crop it down to the new gray. The only touch I would accept from her.

"You must work out or something," she said.

"I split a lot of firewood. You don't get calluses like this at a health club."

A flush tinged her neck as she glanced at my hands, reminding me briefly of Janet. Inconsequentially, I wondered whether I'd left enough wood to get the house through a Vermont winter. Janet is strong enough, and willing, but a klutz with an ax.

"The good life." I said. "Right. Fresh air, organic veggies, exercise." I'd tilled gardens, shoveled snow, rousted bales and boxes, and all I had to show for it was the strength to carry Allison in my arms, when it came at last to that, and never stumble.

I had a right to stumble now.

"Get dressed. Nyx, is it?" Her body didn't particularly appeal to me. Fashionably bony, marginally perky. Perky leaves me cold. In Allison's bountiful joys, I could lose myself. But Allie was gone.

Diversion had been my goal last night, not pleasure. I couldn't remember what impulse had driven me toward Nyx, but the kid had done well enough. In reward, I'd impelled her to a mewling extremity that seemed to astonish her. By her look at my callused hands, she wanted more.

Then she astonished me. "You get into people's heads, don't you."

"What, because I knew how to push your buttons?" Kids never believe in experience.

"Besides that." Her neck reddened again. "I felt you at the trade show, checking me out."

She must have some rudimentary talent herself to be so certain.

"Yeah, well, reconnaissance never hurts," I said. "It wasn't a woman you were trolling for, but I had a feeling you might settle."

That was unfair. She'd been paid to make that fuck-me leather butt-sling with the gold zipper down the back look good to buyers for leather/fetish shops. I'd been the one trolling, checking out the pseudo-street-smart section of the trade show. None of that stuff is right for our...my... store. What tourists will buy in the Village or Soho isn't what they're after in Vermont. Always play to the customers' fantasies.

"My boss was pissed that you didn't place an order," she said.

"Did you tell him my card had my hotel room number on it?"

"He figured. He's not so dumb."

"So, are you still trying to sell me?" She had some hidden agenda, but I didn't think that was it.

"More trying to buy something. Like some help you could maybe give. But it could be dangerous, and I don't have much to pay with." If she'd planned to bargain with her body, she realized now that the bargaining power was on my side.

I started to yank on some clothes. "If it's dangerous enough, I just might bite." I felt her nudging at my mind and blocked her.

She picked up on my mood anyway. "What's the matter, you into suicide or something?"

Too perceptive. But Allison had made me promise.

"Just get on with it. What's your story?"

"I need to find somebody. I mean, I know where he is, sort of, but...he isn't really there."

I sprawled on the chair and covered my eyes. Was this going anywhere? If there was ever a time for a cigarette!

But I didn't have any, hadn't had any for fifteen years. Could ignoring the Surgeon General's warning be considered a suicide attempt?

"Tim is—was—my roommate, a real sweet kid from Kansas. We helped each other through some tough shit, had sort of a trust thing going. Not much sex because of his medication, which didn't matter to me—kinda like women better anyway—but there's more to love than that, isn't there?"

I grunted assent.

"It mattered to him, though. He stopped his meds and got so paranoid I couldn't get him on them again. Somebody told me about a doctor who treats that kind of stuff without pills, and I talked Tim into going, but after his second appointment he just...didn't come back."

"Did you check out the doctor?"

"Her office wouldn't give me the time of day. Neither would the police. Known crazies aren't high priority on the missing persons list."

"But you know where he is." I'd given up hope of anything useful, but it wouldn't hurt to let her vent.

She sat cross-legged on the bed clutching the spread around herself. "Yeah, but it's him and not him. A girl I know works at a health club near Washington Square. A couple of weeks ago, she saw him there, and when she checked the club register, he had a different name and an upscale address. I cruised that neighborhood till I saw him, but he really, really didn't know me. He brushed me off, hard, and the doorman wouldn't let me past. And then, when I was almost home, I felt somebody following me, and started to turn around, and a knife whipped right by my neck and into the door. Clipped my ear right here."

The scar might have been from a torn-out earring. I wasn't convinced. If anything, it had been only a warning. There are better, less dramatic tools than knives for getting rid of somebody. "Lucky move, huh? Anything else?"

"I didn't wait to find out. Been crashing since then at my brother's place in Jersey."

"Why didn't you stay there? And why the hell are you trusting me?"

"I've gotta know what's happening. Besides, the modeling gig was lined up already, and my sister-in-law doesn't feed me for free." She let the spread slide from her naked body and flopped back, legs splayed. "Anyway, you were pretty up front about what you wanted." She wriggled her skinny hips.

"So are you, but I'm not in the mood now. Look, I'd like to help, but what's the point? There's nothing illegal about multiple personalities."

"Tim had delusions, sure," she said, "but not that multiple stuff. And something else. When I looked real close to be sure it was him, I saw a humongous scar on the back of his neck going up under his hair."

Right. Maybe the guy's delusions were contagious. "Who told you about this doctor in the first place?"

"The bartender at a club in Chelsea. The Gay Cuntessa."

"No shit, they really call it that? We used to kid about using the name, but it was officially 'Marlene's' twenty years ago. Hey," as she gaped at me, "I haven't always lived in Vermont."

I hadn't looked anyplace like that for diversion for fear somebody would recognize me and ask about Allison. Sooner or later, I'd have to face it. If there had to be a later.

"Okay." I swung to my feet and waited for the pounding in my head to subside. "I'll pump the bartender and maybe go by the doctor's office. I'll take a stroll by your guy's place. But even if I get a chance to probe, I won't know whether he's himself, since I've never met him."

"I could come with you."

"Stay here. I'll call if I need you. Get some room service. If I'm not back in twenty-four hours—well, just tell Janet I was helping out a friend."

I could walk now, cease to exist, loose ends as tied-off as they'd ever be. Janet would get the house and store. She'd kept the business going when Allison got too sick for me to leave. She deserved more than I could ever give her.

I should have brought her along to learn the ropes of ordering at trade shows. When she'd cropped my silver hair a little shorter, and said I looked too hot to let loose in the city, we'd both pretended my ulterior motive was casual sex. But she'd known better. "Lexie, you promised..."

My motive now was more complex. Curiosity isn't much as emotions go, but it sure beats despair.

The Gay Cuntessa had been through some changes, but they hadn't messed too much with the ambiance. Downright old-fashioned by today's standards. There was still a wall of signed photos beside the small raised stage.

The bartender fit the description Nyx had given, solid, blunt-featured, shaved head—but so would plenty of others. It was early yet, only two thirty. I'd spent several hours observing the doctor's sleekly impersonal office and the upscale condo building on Washington Square.

Neither surveillance had turned up anything useful, and I found I was out of practice at blocking the city's frenetic mind-buzz. Eccentrics especially seem to emit a wavelength that penetrates my defenses. A shriveled bag lady near Washington Square Park, wrapped head to toe in black trash bags, had hit me with waves of non-thought blank and hard as walls, all the while scribbling with jerky motions in a notebook. Just thinking about her plastic shroud in the August heat made me sweat.

"Anything cold and dark on tap," I told the bartender.

"Sure thing." She plunked down a glass. I laid a fifty on the counter, keeping a grip on it.

"And some information. About a doctor with some rather, um, unorthodox treatments for special cases." Vague to the point of inanity, but I sensed a jolt of fear behind her tough facade.

"Can't help you with that."

"The hell you can't." I pinned her arm as she reached for the fifty. "I'll get what I want, through you or over you.

Somebody I care about needs help." Forgive me, Allison, for using you, I thought, and memory supplied at once her rich, lazy voice: *S'okay, Lexie, go for it.*

"Yeah? You're not some kind of cop?"

Dumb move, letting me see she had something to hide. I let go of her arm. "Check out the photo just to the left of the mirror, halfway up." I'd looked on the way in, twisting the knife in my own wound. "Does the name Allison Foyle ring a bell?"

"Sure, old folk singer, right? Hey, isn't this place named for one of her songs?"

"My lyrics, actually."

"You're Lexie?" Her tone gave the name mythic overtones. And a hint of undertone.

"You must hang out with a pretty over-the-hill crowd to have heard of me."

"Hey, I hang out with whoever plunks her ass down on a barstool. They tell some wild stories about you."

"Yeah, well, nostalgia is the opiate of the masses. Sorry to have inflicted 'The Gay Cuntessa' on you, anyway."

"What the hell, it brings in the tourists. So, what are you guys up to? Still together?"

The gray cloud descended over my already grief-filled mind. I lost interest in breathing, and gulped down the beer without tasting it. It was cold, at least, which helped me get a grip.

"Bringing in the tourists in Vermont. No," as she cocked a pierced eyebrow, "nothing that interesting. A book and music store, some gifts and clothing, local crafts, souvenirs." I plunged on toward the point. "About this doctor. What do you get for feeding him customers?" I fingered the fifty still on the bar.

"Her," she corrected. "I get nothing, yet. Building up credit. She lines up the customers, I just feed her crazy meat."

I'd only tuned in enough to catch any lies. I don't do mental invasion casually. Well, I did with Nyx, and look where that got me. But an image swirled from her brain into mine, tiny, blonde, Barbie-doll cutesy. Surely not the doctor? Her own little chew toy? None of my business. I concentrated on the implications of what she'd said.

"Crazies for spare parts?" Black-market organ transplants. Revulsion sparked a perverse exhilaration, almost like caring about something.

"Isn't that what you came for?"

This bitch's mouth was going to bite her in the ass.

"It's too late for that. The cancer spread so far..." The haze of despair closed in again and muffled her reply.

"Need more than just parts, huh? I dunno if she'll do another radical transfer yet. The first one seems to be working out okay, but it's not easy to find meat prime enough for a package deal. Bag ladies just don't cut it, and young schizos tend to stink of testosterone." Her tone was oddly wistful.

I stared blankly, the words drifting together into some kind of delayed coherence. Then I flashed on her image of the little blonde bimbo, and knew suddenly why she wanted "credit" with the doctor. The haze burned away in a hot blast of rage. If it was possible, and I hadn't known. Allison could have had my body! What good was it to me without her?

I had thought I would hold some part of Allie forever, all those times I cradled her essence, shielded her, bore what I could of her pain, until that final time, her own will driving me—*Go for it, Lexie, do it, love, now!*—when I pressed the pillow over her face and felt the life drain from her body, her spirit fading, fading, into an infinite distance where I couldn't go. Leaving me empty, and alone.

"Hey, you all right?" The bartender jostled my shoulder. "Looked like you died right in front of me."

"It's not that easy, believe me."

"Well, if you're gonna be okay... I can't tell you anything, but I'll take you to somebody who might." The glitter of excitement in her eyes as she scanned my photo beside Allison's on the wall would have warned me off if I'd had any interest in self-preservation. "The dishwasher can cover for me. It's dead enough this time of day."

She led me, no surprise, to Washington Square. As I paid the cab driver, I glanced across to the park and saw the black-wrapped bag lady huddled among her bundles, still scribbling under the blazing sun. I'd have expected the security patrols to have removed her by now, not allowing that particular type of local color in the theme park the Village had become.

What the hell, Vermont was pretty much a theme park now, too. But one without, I hoped, quite as stark a disconnect between the haves and have-nots.

"I'll be right back." I darted across to a vending cart and

bought a bottle of cold iced tea. A futile gesture—the bag lady, radiating empty thoughts and putrefaction, took no notice of my offering, so I set the drink down with a twenty-dollar bill tucked under it.

As I straightened, she tore the top sheet from her note-book and dropped it at my feet. The wrappings fell away from her outstretched arm. From wrist to elbow its inner surface was scarred in long, wide stripes, as though the skin had been surgically peeled away.

I fought a wave of dizziness as I bent to pick up the paper. The bartender's voice intruded. "Hey, what's up?"

The heap of black plastic seemed to shrink in on itself. I moved away. "Just a handout." Then, as she stared past me with a puzzled frown, I snapped, "Look, are we doing this or not?" and strode back across the street.

The doorman pushed a buzzer, gave my guide's name, and let us through. We rode in silence to the sixth floor. As we stepped off the elevator, I glanced again at the sheet of paper crumpled in my hand.

One word, over and over. *LexieLexieLexieLexie.*

Adrenaline swept away the gray curtain of despair.

The apartment door was ajar. Designer-scented shower steam drifted through the designer-sterile living room and out an open window.

"So, what's the big deal, Mickey?" The baritone voice was muffled by a towel as our host rubbed at his wet blonde hair. The rest of him was damp and plausibly buff, although his left foot dragged a little as he came down the hall.

The bartender, Mickey, ignored the question, her eyes intent on us. I wondered what the hell she expected. The naked male body so casually displayed held no interest for me, and he could have no idea who I was.

But I was wrong about that last part. His expression veered from mild annoyance to recognition. The towel dropped, and I tried to see the scar Nyx had mentioned, but he came at me with a look in his eyes that belonged to another time, another photo pinned up behind the bar's stage even before I'd met Allison. Another mind.

"Lexie!"

I blocked a damp hug. "What the hell?"

Mickey grabbed at my arm. I sent her sprawling. She hit the edge of the marble-framed fireplace and bobbed up again with no show of anger. "Is she all there?" she asked urgently. "Come on, I gotta know if she's really all there!"

"How about it, Renate, are you all there?" I asked. "Apart from your new toys?" I flicked a finger across her dangling cock, and she looked down proudly as it responded with a jerk.

"You have no idea, Lexie! It hasn't been easy," and she touched the base of her skull gingerly, "but I'm getting the hang of it. Especially the being hung part. Check it out!" She grabbed my hand and pulled it toward her crotch. If I hadn't been more or less dazed by the bizarre situation, she'd have lost her pride and joy right then. As it was I sent her staggering backward.

"Jesus, Ren, if I had any interest in that I'd never have fucked you in the first place. Can't remember now why I ever did."

"Bitch!" The sulky boy-face reddened. I evaded the telegraphed lunge. Renate wasn't as at home in her new body as she claimed. I speculated briefly on trying to make her mad enough to kill me, but there was no way I'd really let her do it.

"Wow, a testosterone moment!" I said. "Cool it, Ren, I don't begrudge you getting what you always wanted. It's just a shock."

But I did, in fact, begrudge how she got what she wanted, when I thought of my many good friends who'd taken the hard routes to transition, harming no one. An even greater shock was the sudden memory of the old bag lady and a belated sense of recognition. "What's become of your old...um...outfit, anyway? It did have its points, now I come to think about it."

"Deep-freeze," she said sullenly. "The contract says they have to preserve it intact, no harvesting parts. It wasn't in that great shape, anyway." She looked at me more closely. "How the hell do you manage to look so good? Clean living in Vermont, is it?" Then, as a grudging afterthought, "How's Allison?"

"Allie... It's bad. Cancer. That's why I'm here." All perfectly true.

"To see Dr. Zahl? Do you really think you can afford it? On top of all the other expenses, you'd have to go to Switzerland for the actual procedure."

That was Renate, all right. The supercilious curl of the lip almost got her pretty-boy face trashed.

"I'll manage. But do you really think a contract for something so grossly illegal is worth shit?" I moved to the open window and looked out. "Come over here for a minute."

A black figure, plastic flapping like tattered crow's feathers, stared up from the edge of the curb. Waves of empty thought battered at my mind. "There's what's left of you," I told Renate. "I don't know about internal organs, but there's certainly some skin missing, nice neat strips for grafting. You always took such good care of your skin." I lurched toward a chair. Once out of sight, the mental assault subsided. "I'm not sure who's still home in there, but something is trying its damnedest to get through to me."

I'd forgotten Mickey, but suddenly she was in my face, grabbing my shirt. I was too drained to shake her off. "So, there is something left behind? Come on, I gotta know, would I be all there?" The image of the blonde dolly hovered in the air between us like a hologram. Was that particular morsel of "crazy meat" already lined up? Maybe there was somebody left in this world I could save before I went.

"For all I know, it could be the previous occupant of Studly here. Except..." I pushed her away and pulled the crumpled paper from my pocket. "Except that he wouldn't have known my name."

Renate recovered first, and grabbed the phone. "You go get that...that scarecrow, and bring it up here," she barked at Mickey. Then, into the receiver, "Get Dr. Zahl to the phone! Yeah, this is Mr. Lindquist. Just get her!" A pause, then, "Right, I knew she was coming, just forgot the time."

She turned to me with a self-conscious downward glance at her prized possessions. "She's on her way already. You made me forget our...therapy session."

"Therapy, huh? You're right, I can't afford her."

Mickey smirked, and Renate took a swipe at her. "You get the hell outside, and if you meet the doctor, keep your fat mouth shut or I'll bend you in half till you can suck yourself!"

When we were alone, panic stared out of blue eyes she had no right to wear. "Lexie, please, check me out. Am I all here?"

She had never been so open, and I had never had less inclination to enter her mind. There was something beyond obscene about the whole situation. But that was why I was here. "Put on a robe or something, for God's sake." When she'd complied, I pressed her back onto a couch, kneeling over her in a ghastly travesty of times long past.

"Relax, dammit!" Advice more for myself than for her. I hadn't gone so far into anyone but Allie in twenty years. The only way I could do it now was to skip over everything that was Renate and search for what might not be. Since I had never known Nyx's friend, I couldn't tell anything for sure, but when I came up against the subconscious, there was a sense of pressure, of something trapped. I couldn't bring myself to go there.

"It's been so long. We've all changed. There's no way I can be sure." I released her wide shoulders and wiped my hands on my pants as I leaned back. I wouldn't have reassured her even if I'd been certain. "What difference does it make now, anyway? It can't be reversed, can it?" Renate had a history of getting what she wanted and then deciding she wanted something (or somebody) different. Any reputable sex change clinic would have turned her down.

"No." Tears welled in the blue eyes, and the long, masculine body began to shake. She reached up to touch me just as the door opened.

"Timothy?" The outraged voice rose to a shrill squeal. I stood slowly and looked the woman over. She might have been passable without the pinched expression, but I'd bet her research wouldn't be complete until she'd figured out how to work a transplant on herself.

"Edna, this is Lexie," Renate said in a strangled voice.

"An ex-lover," I said. "Decidedly 'ex,' however much Renate might want to have her cake and eat it, too."

"The one who reads minds?"

I could feel the doctor's thoughts struggling between calculation and apprehension. "Surely you don't believe in parlor tricks like that."

"I know too much about the complexities of the brain to dismiss anything so well documented. Was that what you were doing just now? Did you find anything of interest?" She tried to sound cool and detached, but her eyes were as avid for reassurance as Mickey's had been.

"You mean, 'Is she all there? Does it really work?' Jesus, Renate, do you realize how much of a guinea pig you are?"

"What? No! She's done others, no problems!"

"She lied," I said with certainty. "The same way she lied about that." I nodded toward the doorway.

An apparition out of a horror comic book huddled there, trailed by Mickey. The black wrappings had slipped so that much of the emaciated torso was revealed. Besides strips of scar tissue where skin had been peeled away, there were several poorly healed incisions, so many that I wondered how she had enough internal equipment left to function at all. From the aura of decay, it seemed impossible that she could still be upright.

"I don't know how it got away." Dr. Zahl was defensive. "There can't have been any autonomous function left."

"Yeah, right, escaped from the deep-freeze," Renate said bitterly. "You've had it on life support until you could mine everything worth selling. Why couldn't you just finish it off? That would have been better than...than this!"

I knew then that I wasn't going to be able to goad her into turning against the doctor. Maybe Mickey?

Mickey's wide face was ghastly, her eyes fixed on the pitiful shell before us.

"See?" I said. "It doesn't work. Something of her is still in there. And something of him," I jerked my head toward Renate's masculine body, "is in there." I didn't care whether it was true or not.

"But how much? Maybe..."

No go. I'd underestimated the power of their fantasies. No choice but to handle it myself, with no guarantee that anybody would take me out. I turned toward the fireplace.

The little gun was out of the doctor's purse when I swung back with the wrought iron poker. Relief flooded through me. It was just a matter of timing now—a final, deadly, simultaneous climax.

She waved back Renate, who had stepped toward us. "Just what is your agenda, anyway?"

"She's a customer, Edna, she can pay, or if she can't I'll make up the difference!"

"Thanks, Renate." I meant it. "But Allie's dead. Six weeks ago." A surge of grief transmuted into white-hot fury, and I slashed the poker down at the doctor's head the way I'd split a log. A searing pain split my own head...I raised my arms to strike again...and Allie's rich, honeyed voice, not lazy now at all, filled my consciousness.

Get a grip, Lexie! How often I'd heard that, when my temper threatened to spill over, or when she'd driven me to the edge of erotic combustion but still had more to give. I staggered backward.

A flurry of black tatters, a flash of Allie's brilliant smile and oak-russet hair only my eyes, my heart, could see. Then the scarecrow dragged the doctor to the open window. And then they were gone.

I leaned out into space, ready to follow, until one more message penetrated my unresisting mind. *I'll find you again, Love. Just don't block me out next time!*

My heart clung to "next time." My fingers clung to the sides of the window frame. I couldn't move, couldn't close my eyes to the broken, bloody bodies on the pavement far below. The commotion in the room behind me seemed more distant than the sounds from the street.

An arm went around me. A gentle hand tried to loosen my grip. "Lexie, Lexie." The hand became less gentle, the voice sharper. "Damnit, Lexie, let go! I've got you!"

Janet had come for me, sooner than she'd threatened. I slumped back into the room and let her practical fingers explore my scalp.

"Just creased, I think, but we should get you checked out." Her flat Yankee tone would have sounded unemotional to anybody who didn't know her.

"When we get home," I muttered, and felt a shuddering breath of relief go through her body.

"You sure she's all right?" Nyx's back was against the door, the doctor's gun in her hand. Renate and Mickey looked stunned.

"I'll make sure," Janet said, as I let her help me to my feet.

"I figured you were here," Nyx said to me. "But...is he..." She stared at Renate, slumped on the couch.

"He may be in there somewhere. It's up to you to figure it out." I'd done all I could by planting doubt in Renate's mind. "And you," I nudged the clumsy male foot with mine until I knew she was listening, "had better get on to your lawyer. The cops will arrive any minute, and what they find down there is going to bring on one hell of an investigation. You'll probably come out all right. Who'd believe the truth? I'll keep my mouth shut as long as I hear regularly from our friend Nyx here that you're treating her okay."

I didn't much care what became of Renate. In my mind a scent of decay clung to her now, in spite of designer cologne and robust body. But I did care about Nyx. Maybe they could work something out.

"Tell that snotty doorman to get a cab!" Janet snapped at Nyx. Her arm was still around me and she could feel me wavering. "I'm getting Lexie out before the police come."

"You sure scared the shit out of him," Nyx told Janet with grudging admiration as she picked up the phone. "When we heard the gun go off, I thought you were gonna claw a hole through his guts to get past!"

In the cab, I held Janet's handkerchief against my bleeding scalp and shivered as reaction set in. "It was Allie," I said unsteadily. "She was there, in that hulk, there was no Renate left inside, Allie did it all, even led me to Nyx." Janet was the one person in the world who could believe me. "I heard her, felt her."

Janet had worshipped Allie from the day we'd hired her to work in the store, and in a way, she'd lost almost as much as I had. She'd also, I knew, had a thing for me. And now she had saved me.

She lay a cold, tentative hand over mine. I let it stay, let some of her anguished need percolate into my mind, breathed in the clean scent of her wholeness. Allie's spirit was still with me. Life was still with me. I didn't think I could ever give Janet as much as she wanted, but there was no reason I couldn't at least keep her warm. And not just with firewood.

Gargoyle Lovers

"I'm siingin' in the raaiin..." But that was from the wrong Gene Kelly movie, and it wasn't quite raining, and I was only whistling. My speaking voice gets me by, but singing blows the whole presentation.

Hal glanced down, her face stern in that exaggerated way that makes me tingle in just the right places. I shoved my hands into my pockets, skipped a step or two, and knew she felt as good as I did. Hal's hardly the type to dance through the Paris streets like Gene Kelly, especially across square cobblestones, but there was a certain lilt to her gait.

Or maybe a swagger. "That pretty-boy waiter was all over you," I said slyly. "And giving me dirty looks every chance he got." A gay guy making a pass always sparks up her day.

"Lucky for you I'm not cruising for pretty boys, then. But don't give me too much lip or I might change my mind."

I couldn't quite manage penitence, but at least I knew better than to remind her that she already had a pretty boy, for better or worse. Still, some punishment games would be a fine end to the evening. Last night we'd been too jet-lagged to take proper advantage of the Parisian atmosphere.

"That maitre d' with a beak like a gargoyle was sure eyeing me, too, especially from behind." I gave another little skip.

Hal ignored the bait. "Thought you'd had your fill of gargoyles today."

A cathedral wouldn't have been her first choice for honeymoon sightseeing, but the mini-balcony of our rental apartment had a stupendous view of Notre-Dame de Paris. I'd oohed and ahhed about gargoyles over our croissants and café-au-lait, so she'd humored me and we'd taken the tour.

To tell the truth, being humored by Hal unnerved me a bit. I didn't want being married to make a difference in our relationship. The fact that she'd shooed me out of that sex toy shop in Montmartre while she made a purchase was reassuring, but just in case, I decided I could manage some genuine penitence after all.

I hung my head and peered up at her slantwise. "I know I was a real pain. I can't figure out what it is about gargoyles that just gets to me. They're sort of scary, but not really, and sort of sad, and some of them are beautiful in a weird kind of way." Just as Hal was, but I'd never say that. "I'm sorry I went on about them like that."

"What makes you think they're sad? Just because their butts are trapped in stone?" She was trying to suppress a grin. I felt better.

"Well, I'd sure hate that myself."

That got me the squeeze on my ass I'd been angling for. "I'd rather have these sweet cheeks accessible," she said. The squeeze got harder than I'd bargained for, startling me into a grimace.

She eased off with a slow stroke between my thighs. "You should've seen your face just now. Could be there's something like that going on with the gargoyles. Not rage, or fear, or pain at all—unless it's pain so good it makes them howl with lust."

I was awestruck. Hal was generally the blunt, taciturn type, but I loved it when her wicked imagination burst forth. Almost as much as I loved the vulnerability that once in a while gave an extra gruffness to her voice.

She was on a roll now, face alight like a gleeful demon. A lovable demon. "There's somebody hidden behind the stone, in another dimension, or time, or whatever, giving the gargoyle the fucking of its life. A reaming so fine, it's been going on for centuries."

"Yes!" I was very nearly speechless. To lean out high above Paris, in the sun, wind and rain of eons, my face forever twisted in a paroxysm of fierce joy while Hal's thrusts filled me eternally with surging pleasure...

A few drops of rain began to fall, but that wasn't what made us hurry faster across the Pont de Saint-Louis. The great ornate iron gates at our apartment building had given me fantasies that morning of being chained, spread-eagled, against them, but now I rushed across the cobblestoned courtyard and through the carved oak door, so turned on that the four flights of stairs inside scarcely slowed me down—which might also have been because Hal's big hand on my butt was hurrying me along.

At our apartment, though, she held me back while she opened the door. "Over-the-threshold time. It'll be more official when we get back home, but this will have to do for now."

So, I entered the room slung over Hal's shoulder, kicking a little for balance, until she dumped me amongst the red cushions brocaded in gold on the couch. They went tumbling off as I struggled to get my pants lowered.

"Not here," she mused. "Maybe up there?" There was a sturdy railing across the loft that held the king-sized bed.

"Out there! Please?" The balcony was really only a space where the French windows were set back into the wall about a foot, but there was an intricate iron fence along the edge, and with the windows wide open it had felt like balcony enough at breakfast time.

"Can you be quiet as a gargoyle?"

"You can gag me."

"No. I want to see your face." Hal pulled open the windows, grabbed the bag from the sex toy store, heaved me up, and the next minute, I was kneeling on the balcony and clutching the fence.

She moved aside a couple of pots of geraniums and tested the fence for strength and anchoring. "This would take even my weight," she muttered. In seconds, she'd fastened my wrists to the railing with brand new bonds that looked uncannily like chains of heavy iron links, even though they weren't as hard as metal and had just a hint of stretch to them. "Feel enough like a gargoyle?"

"Mm-hm." I was drifting into a space I'd never known before. Lights from the Quai D'Anjou below and the quais across the Seine were reflected on the dark river, flickering like ancient torches as the water rippled past. Even the lights of modern Paris on the far bank took on a mellow glow that could have fit into any century.

"Hold that thought." Hal backed away into the room. I scarcely heard the rustling of the shop bag or the running of water in the bathroom. Then she was back, soundless, a dark looming presence that might have been made of stone.

The night air drew me into its realm. I leaned out over the railing as far as my bonds would allow, my butt raised high. Then Hal had one arm around my waist, holding me steady, while her other hand probed into my inner spaces that she knew so well. Need swelled inside me, shuddered through my body, catching in my throat as strangled, guttural groans. My face twisted with the struggle not to make too much noise, my mouth gaped open, and my head flailed back and forth.

A whimper escaped when her hand withdrew, and so did a short, sharp bleat as something new replaced it— smooth, lubed, not quite familiar, not any of Hal's gear I'd felt before. I heard her heavy breathing, felt her thrusts, and lost all sense of anything beyond the moment, anything beyond our bodies. A scream started forcing its way up through my chest and throat.

Just in time, Hal snapped open the bonds on my wrists, lifted me from behind, and lurched with me across the plump back of the couch. With a rhythm accelerating like a Parisienne's motorbike she finished me off, then found her own slower, deep pace, and her own release. I could still barely breathe, but I managed to twist my neck enough to see her contorted face at that moment. Yes, magnificently beautiful in its own feral way.

In the aftermath we curled together, laughing when she showed me the new gargoyle-faced dildo slick with my juices. "Those French don't miss a trick when it comes to tourists," I said.

Hal grew quiet. I thought she was dozing, but after a while she cleared her throat. "Those French..." Her voice was unusually gruff. She tried again. "They claim to be tops in the lover department, too, I've heard. But I've got the best deal in the whole world with you. The best lover..." She stroked my still simmering pussy. "The prettiest boy..." She touched my cheek. "The best wife... And the wildest gargoyle in all of France."

I remembered her wild face just minutes ago, and knew that the last part wasn't true. Still, the wisest response seemed to be a kiss that moved eventually from her mouth along her throat, and lower, and lower, with more daring than I'd ever risked before. And eventual proof that the best lover part, at least, was absolutely certain.

Publication Credits

"Bull Rider" was originally published in *Best Lesbian Erotica 2003*, edited by Tristan Taormino (Cleis Press, 2003).

"Lipstick on Her Collar" was originally published in *Lipstick on Her Collar*, edited by Sacchi Green and Rakelle Valencia (Pretty Things Press, 2008).

"Jessebel" was originally published in *Women of the Bite: Lesbian Vampire Erotica*, edited by Cecilia Tan (Alyson Books, 2009).

"Spirit Horse Ranch" was originally published in *Haunted Hearths and Sapphic Shades: Lesbian Ghost Stories*, edited by Catherine Lundoff (Lethe Press, 2008).

"Carved in Stone" was originally published in *Desire Behind Bars*, edited by Salome Wilde and Talon Rihal (Hillside Press, 2015).

"Sgt. Rae" was originally published in *Duty and Desire: Military Erotic Romance*, edited by Kristina Wright (Cleis Press, 2012).

"The Pirate from the Sky" was originally published in *Like a Treasure Found*, edited by Joy Crelin (Circlet Press, Inc., 2011).

"The Dragon Descending" was originally published in *She Shifters: Lesbian Paranormal Erotica*, edited by Delilah Devlin (Cleis Press, 2012).

"Meltdown" was originally published in *Don't Be Shy* (Volume 1), edited by Astrid Ohletz (Ylva Publishing, 2015).

"Pulling" was originally published in *Lesbian Cowboys*, edited by Sacchi Green and Rakelle Valencia (Cleis Press, 2009).

"Finding Carla" has not been previously published.

"Flying the Prairie Lily" was originally published in *Best Women's Erotica 2005*, edited by Marcy Sheiner (Cleis Press, 2005).

"In the Flesh" has not been previously published.

"Gargoyle Lovers" was originally published in *XOXO: Sweet and Sexy Romance*, edited by Kristina Wright (Cleis Press, 2013).

About the Author

Sacchi Green lives in the five-college area of western Massachusetts, with occasional forays into the real world. She began her writing career with science fiction, fantasy, and historical fiction, but became seduced by the erotic side of the Force, writing scores of steamy stories and editing fifteen anthologies, most of them lesbian erotica, and two of them Lambda Literary Award winners. She still can't resist a good opportunity to return to fantasy or historical settings, and co-edited *Through the Hourglass: Lesbian Historical Romance* with Patty G. Henderson, winning a Golden Crown Literary Society Award. When a chance to write for *Learning Curve* came along, the theme was so appealing that she took a chance and used an historical setting and characters who had been on her mind for years.

Find her at:
facebook.com/sacchi.green or
sacchi-green.blogspot.com

Other Books by Sacchi Green

Edited as Sacchi Green

Rode Hard, Put Away Wet: Lesbian Cowboy Erotica, co-editor Rakelle Valencia. Suspect Thoughts Press.

Hard Road, Easy Riding: Lesbian Biker Erotica, co-editor Rakelle Valencia. Lethe Press.

Lipstick on Her Collar and Other Tales of Lesbian Lust, co-editor Rakelle Valencia. Pretty Things Press.

Girl Crazy: Coming Out Erotica. Cleis Press.

Lesbian Cowboys: Erotic Adventures, co-editor Rakelle Valencia. Cleis Press.

Lesbian Lust: Erotic Stories. Cleis Press.

Lesbian Cops: Erotic Investigations. Cleis Press.

Girl Fever: 69 Stories of Sudden Lust for Lesbians. Cleis Press.

Wild Girls, Wild Nights: True Lesbian Sex Stories. Cleis Press.

Me and My Boi: Queer Erotic Stories. Cleis Press.

Best Lesbian Erotica of the Year, 20th Anniversary Edition, Cleis Press.

Witches, Princesses and Women at Arms: Erotic Lesbian Fairy Tales. Cleis Press.

Best Lesbian Erotica of the Year Volume 2. Cleis Press.

Best Lesbian Erotica of the Year Volume 3. Cleis Press.

Thunder of War, Lightning of Desire: Lesbian Historical Military Erotica. Lethe Press.

Through the Hourglass: Lesbian Historical Romance, coedited with Patty G. Henderson. The Liz McMullen Show Publications.

Edited as Connie Wilkins:

Time Well Bent: Queer Alternative Histories. Lethe Press.

Heiresses of Russ 2012: the Year's Best Lesbian Speculative Fiction. Co-edited with Steve Berman. Lethe Press.

Collection of Sacchi Green's work:

A Ride to Remember and Other Erotic Tales. Lethe Press.

Coming Soon from Dirt Road Books

South Paw
Garoul Book 6
by Gill McKnight

As an introvert and a germaphobe, Elizabeth Wren is struggling in her new job, working for Martha Meeke, the flamboyant literary agent. Now their most famous client, bestselling Priscila Purloin, has gone AWOL, and Elizabeth is dispatched to South Paw, a skiing resort famous for its beautiful Christmas ambience, to track her down. Luckily, Elizabeth also suffers from OCD—obsessive Christmas disorder—so maybe South Paw will not be a washout after all. Naeva Garoul dreads snow season, when her tranquil mountain home becomes a Mecca for ski sport enthusiasts and Christmas-themed lunacy. Winter means family visits, too, and when your family consists of werewolves, it usually involves chaos. Werewolves want to hunt deer, run in the woods, and howl at the moon, while all Naeva wants to do is sit by the fire, write, and eat broccoli. It's hard being a vegetarian werewolf, never mind a romance novelist who wants to be alone.

Rise and Shine
by Jove Belle

For best friends Emily and Sarah, a zombie outbreak seems like a pretty good reason to skip third period. And to skip town, for that matter. The girls pack up and start out on a 400-mile road trip to a bunker Emily's survivalist dad built. With a little luck, they'll survive long enough to make it to safety, and maybe fall in love along the way.

Queen of the Glens
by Gill McKnight

Alecka Kruche's brother, Howie, has gone AWOL in Ireland. AWOL is not an unusual state for Howie, and his level-headed sister is dispatched to collar him and return him home. Again.

But this time, it's different. Howie has fallen in love. As Alecka tries to extract him from the village of Inish Og in the beautiful Glens of Antrim on the north Irish coast, she instead finds herself drawn in. The folklore, culture, and sheer magic of the Glens begin to break down her reserve. She's charmed—and entirely unsure what to do about it— by the villagers and by Johneen, a headstrong woman who isn't nearly as charmed by Alecka.

A Matter of Blood

Far Seek Chronicles 2 (Second Ed.)
by Andi Marquette

Outlaw Torri Rendego can't shake her past, which most often involves Kai Tinsdale, her former Academy bunkmate and now commander in the hated Coalition forces. Torri's convinced that the Coalition is up to no good on Kai's family holdings and decides to investigate. Problem is, the Coalition is definitely up to something, and Torri and the crew of the Far Seek have to pursue an outrageous plan to gather information and pass it along to Kai somehow.

But even the best-laid plans can go dangerously awry, especially where Kai's concerned. Risking herself, her crew, and a tenuous tie to a shared history, Torri goes deep into Coalition territory to uncover a secret with far-reaching consequences for a distant and ancient culture. The stakes of this venture may prove way too high, even for a gambler like Torri.

Borage

Book 1 in Sisters of the 13th Moon Series
by Gill McKnight

Astral is the last of the Projector witches on a special mission to find an evil critter that is damaging her coven. Her search brings her to Black & Blacker, a company run by the enigmatic Abby Black. But who is bewitching who?

Hollister Investigations: The Shell Game
by Jove Belle

Since coming to work for Laila at Hollister Investigations, Trinity finds herself in a rut. She misses the excitement of being a hacktivist, and the tedium of investigating unfaithful spouses does nothing to stimulate her brain. But the inexplicable and undeniable pull of Laila Hollister keeps Trinity in her orbit, and she can't leave until she figures out what that means.

Laila is happy. Or as close to happy as she can get. Her company is solid and growing, her employees are elite at what they do, and adding Trinity to the roster only increased their earnings. But she makes Laila crazy, in ways that Laila can't understand. When rumors that Trinity might regret working there reach Laila, she lets Trinity work a case pro bono, just to make Trinity happy. Together they uncover layers of corrupt employees, identity theft, and bank fraud, and work to protect the vulnerable patients at the care facility where Trinity's Alzheimer's-affected mom lives.

Sweet and Sour

Book 1 in The Culinary School Series
by R.G. Emanuelle

Giovanna (Jo) Rossini is graduating from culinary school, but just as she's about to realize her dream of opening up a restaurant, her six-year relationship with Brenda starts to fall apart. Afraid that Brenda is resentful of the financial burden that's been placed on her, Jo begins to suspect that she's having an affair.

Sofia Gibb is dubious when the owner of the lesbian bar she manages wants to turn it into an eatery. Reluctantly, she goes to several restaurants to review sample menus, including the one where Jo is interning. There's an instant spark, but Jo is in a relationship and too preoccupied with her plans to deal with her feelings.

In the whirlwind of a restaurant opening, a fracturing relationship, and an attraction that she can't do anything about, Jo tries to keep her business afloat and herself together. In this prequel to the novella *Add Spice to Taste*, we visit with Jo again and join her on the journey that leads her to The New York Culinary Institute.

Also from Dirt Road Books

Learning Curve:
Stories of Lessons Learned
An Anthology
Various Authors

Building a house, rebuilding a relationship, finding your purpose, learning archery, relearning the piano, discovering your family lineage, going on a journey, learning to face tragedy, teaching a kid to play ball, uncovering a truth in your heart, paying your dues on a ski slope. These are all themes that can be found in Learning Curve, and they are all lessons of one kind or another. The characters in these stories learn skills, life lessons, and how to open up to love and friendship.

This anthology of short stories brings together some of your favorite authors, as well as new writers who we're sure you'll enjoy. Our contributors include: Lori Lake, Sacchi Green, KD Williamson, Jessie Chandler, Stefani Deoul, Catherine Lane, Anna Burke, Michelle Teichman, Jove Belle, Andi Marquette, and R.G. Emanuelle.

Dirt Road Books is proud to donate all proceeds from this anthology to One Girl, an organization dedicated to educating and advancing the lives of girls around the world.

The Potion
by R.G. Emanuelle

A secret formula. A mysterious blue potion. A woman determined to perfect an experiment that will change everything for women in an era when women are not free to choose. In the tradition of mad scientists, Vera Kennedy will stop at nothing to create the elixir that will give women the power to live according to their own desires. But when Georgette Harris comes to her with a plea for help in finding the key that could rescue her from destitution, Vera is pleasantly distracted. Together, they will unravel a mystery that includes ghostly elements and unscrupulous men.

Little Dip
Garoul Book 5
by Gill McKnight

It's 1977, and Connie Fortune has an easy, freewheeling life as a wildlife illustrator. A contract with a periodical brings her to Little Dip, but a clash with Marie Garoul ruins the deal. Next year, Connie tries again—but Marie is waiting for her.

Friends in High Places
Far Seek Chronicles 1 (Second Ed.)
by Andi Marquette

Outlaw Torri Rendego and her crew are working to fulfill a black market contract on Old Earth, but they have to contend with hated Coalition forces. Kai Tinsdale, a part of Torri's past she never expected to see again, shows up, and Torri's survival depends on their ability to trust one another.

Bitterroot Queen
by Jove Belle

Sam Marconi and her teenage daughter move to Bitterroot, Idaho, to open a motel, but they find it in a derelict state. Sam posts an ad in town for someone to help her with renovations. Olly Jones, another newcomer to the area, is the only one who shows up for the job, even though her first meeting with Sam went badly. Sam hires her regardless, and eventually realizes that Olly is exactly what she needs to save the Bitterroot Queen. Will they find a way to build the life they've both been searching for? Or will they cling to the ties holding them to the past?

CPSIA information can be obtained
at www.ICGtesting.com
Printed in the USA
FFHW010201200919
55067784-60792FF

9 781947 253346